我 的 歌

林 明 理 著

文 學 叢 刊

文史哲出版社印行

國家圖書館出版品預行編目資料

我的歌 / 林明理著. -- 初版 -- 臺北市：文史
哲,民 106.03
　　頁; 公分（文學叢刊；375）
　　ISBN 978-986-314-359-8（平裝）

851.486　　　　　　　　　　106003856

文　學　叢　刊　375

我　的　歌

著　　者：林　　　　明　　　　理
出　版　者：文　史　哲　出　版　社
　　　　　http://www.lapen.com.tw
　　　　　e-mail：lapen@ms74.hinet.net
登記證字號：行政院新聞局版臺業字五三三七號
發　行　人：彭　　　正　　　雄
發　行　所：文　史　哲　出　版　社
印　刷　者：文　史　哲　出　版　社
　　　　　臺北市羅斯福路一段七十二巷四號
　　　　　郵政劃撥帳號：一六一八〇一七五
　　　　　電話886-2-23511028・傳真886-2-23965656

定價新臺幣五八〇元

二〇一七年（民一〇六）三月初版

我 的 歌

目　　次

附　錄：

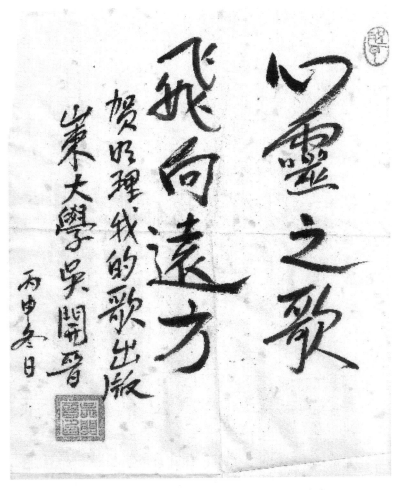

心靈之歌

飛向遠方

賀明理我的歌出版

山東大學吳開晉

丙申冬日

山東大學文學院副院長吳開晉教授題賀詞

在藍綠之間

海平線知道
全心全意擁抱
天空與大海
才能讓自己
開闊

何況這是它
存在的
唯一理由

非馬于芝加哥
2017年1月7日
賀明理新詩集《我的歌》出版

BETWEEN BLUE AND GREEN

the horizon knows
embracing the sky and sea
is the only way
to broaden itself

the sole reason
for being

William Marr, Chicago, 2017.1.7
On the publication of Lin Ming-Li's
poetry anthology, My Song

美國著名詩人非馬（馬為義博士）贈詩

林明理畫

Because of you

Lin Ming-Li

How I would like

To fly gently through time and
space
With my wings
Before you fly into the
distance

I no longer fear the future
Because you are　braver
than me
　With all sort of
discoveries and
inspirations
I am sure
I'll　fly　much　higher

因為你

林明理

多麼想
以垂天之翼
輕輕地穿越時空
在你飛向遠方之前
我不再畏懼未來
因為你比我勇敢
所以我會飛得更高
會有不同的發現和感動

-2017.1.12

（DR.WILLIAM MARR　英譯）
（謝謝美國著名詩人及翻譯家
非馬（**Dr.William Marr**）題贈
英詩及翻譯書中數首詩作，明
理僅以此詩回報其珍貴的友
誼。此詩及畫作刊《亞特蘭大
新聞》2017.1.20。）

Ling Ming-Li

By Ernesto Kahan © 2017

Is a poet of dreams
of light verses and
brushstrokes,
smiles and glances,
fragrance ...
Magic words and paintings
and colorful rainbows.

Oh! Beautiful poetry,
That arrive to me as light
image,
In fresh harmony,
In spring with sounds of new
flowers,
in rays of blessed light
in perfumes and songs...

Welcome life!
In paths of fantasy
landscapes
ink of optimism,
rose verbs,
friendship
and love.

　　1985 年諾貝爾和平獎得
主 Prof Ernesto Kahan 於
2017.1.10 寫詩（英語、西班牙
語）贈給詩人林明理，祝賀新
詩集《我的歌》出書

Ling Ming-Li

Por Ernesto Kahan © 2017

Es una poeta de sueños
de versos ligeros y pinceladas,
sonrisas y miradas,
fragancia ...
Palabras y pinturas mágicas
Y arcos iris coloridos.

Oh! Hermosa poesía,
Que me llega como imagen
ligera,
En armonía fresca,
En primavera con sonidos de
flores nuevas,
En centellas de luz benditas,
En perfumes y canciones ...

Bienvenida vida!
En caminos de paisajes de
fantasía
Tinta de optimismo,
Verbos color de rosa,
Amistad
y amor.

林明理

作者 Ernesto Kahan©2017

是一個夢想的詩人
是輕巧的詩和筆觸，
微笑和一瞥，
芳香...
魔詞和繪畫
以及彩虹。

哦！美麗的詩歌，
用光的圖像觸動我，
在新鮮的和諧，
在春天以新的花朵的聲音，
在受祝福的光線裡
在香水和歌曲...

歡迎生活！
在幻想風景的道路上
樂觀的墨水，
玫瑰的動詞，
友誼
和愛。

Ling Ming-Li

By Ernesto Kahan © 2017
詩人非馬英譯

Prof.Ernesto Kahan 簡介

Doctor, Professor, and poet. Lecturer in several universities in Argentina, Israel, Dominican Republic, Mexico, United States, Peru and Spain. Director of the Department of Epidemiology, Bar Ilan University and the University of Tel Aviv, Israel. Former Director General of the Ministry of Health, Argentina. Former Vice Director of the Rabin Medical Centre. Director of the Department of Epidemiology at the Institute for Health at Work, Tel Aviv University. Director (1998) evaluation at the World Bank for primary health services programmes in Ecuador.

President of the Association of Israeli writers in Spanish. Vice President of the World Academy of Arts and Culture. Former Vice-President, Doctors International for the Prevention of nuclear war (1985 Nobel Peace Prize Winner). Vice-President of the International Forum for Literature and Culture of peace (IFLAC). President of the Union of Latino writers. Vice Director of the Board of Directors of the global harmony Association (GHA).

Today, Prof.Ernesto Kahan is the Academic Director, Management and Control of HIV/AIDS & Infectious Diseases, Centre for Health Management, Galilee International Management Institute, Israel.

醫生，教授和詩人。阿根廷，以色列，多明尼加共和國，墨西哥，美國，秘魯和西班牙的幾個大學教授。以色列特拉維夫大學流行病學系主任。阿根廷衛生部前總幹事。拉賓醫療中心前副主任。特拉維夫大學工作健康研究所流行病學系主任。主任（1998年）在世界銀行對厄瓜多爾初級保健服務方案進行評價。

以色列作家協會主席以西班牙語。世界文化藝術學院副院長。前國際防止核戰爭國際副主席（1985年諾貝爾和平獎得主）。國際文化與和平文化論壇副主席（IFLAC）。拉丁裔作家聯盟總統。全球和諧協會（GHA）董事會副主任。

今天，Prof.Ernesto Kahan 是以色列加利利國際管理學院愛滋病毒/愛滋病與傳染病管理與控制學院院長，衛生管理中心。

Dr. Athanase Vantchev de Thracy – français 序（中英法譯）

Préface

Dans le présent recueil de poésies, la grande poétesse chinoise Dr. Lin Ming-Li évoque, souvent étroitement et fort habilement entremêlés, deux thèmes, un amour éthéré dont on se sait presque rien et sa patrie, l'île de Taïwan. Elle décrit avec une passion vibrante les beautés de sa terre natale. Ces deux sujets sont les deux pôles de l'univers magique de la poétesse.

Les textes du Dr. Lin Ming-Li sont essentiellement visuels et sensuels. Les monts, les vallées pittoresques, les harmonieuses collines, les plantes et les animaux de l'île défilent devant notre regard envoûté. Le monde qu'elle chante semble danser un ballet au rythme du vent et de la pluie. Les eaux des ruisseaux et de la mer chantent à l'unisson de son âme. Des parfums exotiques flottent dans une atmosphère enchantée. Chaque poème est un paysage tantôt resplendissant, tantôt mélancolique, d'où naissent les sensations et les sentiments les plus forts.

Il y a dans les vers du Dr. Lin Ming-Li des jaillissements d'images splendides et hautement originales. Elles sont la transcription en mots des plus belles peintures dont l'art chinois a toujours été le représentant le plus accompli.

Comme ses magnifiques aquarelles, les poèmes-paysages de Ming-Li possèdent tous une âme qui les illumine et les sublime. L'art de dire et l'art pictural y vibrent dans une union sacrée.

Oui, le Dr. Lin Ming-Li a reçu en don céleste des Muses le verbe et la peinture.

Ce fut une grande joie et un privilège spécial de traduire ses ouvrages.

Athanase Vantchev de Thracy
Paris, décembre 2015

Translation of the French Preface

In the present collection, the celebrated Chinese poet Dr Lin Ming-Li focuses on two themes, often combined with great skill and evoked through close attention to the natural world. These themes are, first, an ethereal love of which her subjects are barely aware, and, secondly, her homeland, the island of Taiwan, whose beauties she describes with lively passion. These two subjects form the poles of the poet's imaginative universe.

Dr Lin Ming-Li's writing emphasises the visual and the sensual. Mountains, picturesque valleys, shapely hills, plants and animals from the island hold us in thrall as they pass before our eyes. The world of which she sings is like a ballet danced to the rhythm of the wind and rain. The waters of streams and ocean sing in unison to her soul. Exotic scents float in an enchanted atmosphere. Each poem is a landscape, sometimes resplendent, sometimes melancholic, from which the most powerful sensations and feelings arise.

In Dr Lin Ming-Li's verses there are spates of splendid and highly original images. They are the transcriptions into words of those beautiful paintings of which Chinese art has always been the most accomplished representative.

Like her magnificent watercolours, Ming-Li's poem-landscapes all possess a soul which illuminates them and renders them sublime. The art of the word and the art of the image resonate there in a kind of sacred union.

Yes, Dr Lin Ming-Li has been privileged to have received the gifts of both written and pictorial aptitude from the Muses.

It has been a great joy and a special privilege for me to translate her work.

Athanase Vantchev de Thracy
December 2015

法國 Athanase Vantchev de Thracy 前 言

在這本選集裡，著名臺灣詩人林明理博士以高超的技巧與對自然世界的關切，專注於兩個主題：第一，她的物件幾乎不會覺察到的空靈的愛，其次，她熱情生動描述的她的家鄉臺灣這島嶼的美。這兩個主題構成了詩人的想像宇宙的兩極。

林明理博士的寫作強調的是視覺和感覺。高山，如詩如畫的山谷，多彩多姿的小丘，以及從我們眼前經過的這島上的動物和植物把我們迷住了。她歌唱的世界就像隨著 風雨起舞的芭蕾。河流和海洋的水齊聲對她的靈魂歌唱。異國的情調漂浮在一個魔法的氛圍中。每首詩是一道風景，時而燦爛，時而憂鬱，最有力的感覺和感情於焉產生。

林明理博士的詩中擁有大量美妙而獨創的意象。它們是那些美麗畫作的言辭化，而中國藝術一向長於此道。

就像她那些華麗的水彩畫，明理所有的詩風景都擁有一個照亮它們並使它們崇高的靈魂。語言的藝術和圖像的藝術在那裡產生了一種神聖的共鳴。

是的，林明理博士已榮獲繆斯賜予的書寫和繪畫的天賦。

翻譯她的作品對我來說是一個巨大的喜悅和特殊的榮幸。

Athanase Vantchev de Thracy

2015 年 12 月

（法國前言翻譯 中文序 Translator：Dr.William Marr）

圖　　像

圖 1. 詩－和平的使者÷to Prof.
Ernesto Kahan-刊美國《亞特蘭大
新聞》，2016.3.18.

圖 2 詩-和平的使者－ to Prof.
Ernesto Kahan （ 圖 片 Prof.
Ernesto Kahan 提供）

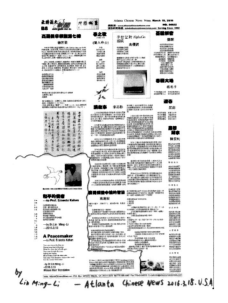

圖 3.-刊美國《亞特蘭大新聞》
2016.3.18.

圖 4. -散文〈墾丁遊蹤〉刊臺灣《人
間福報》副刊，圖文，2016.4.20. -
刊美國《亞特蘭大新聞》，

2016.7.22 詩畫〈我的歌〉。
圖 5.詩-相見居延海－刊臺灣
《臺灣時報》台灣文學版，
2015.7.20 圖文。

圖 6.散文 ─〈驟雨過後〉圖,《亞特蘭大新聞》,2016.11.11.,《臺灣時報》2016.11.18.

圖 7.詩畫-〈池上─米故鄉〉,刊《人間福報》2017.1.17,著者《林明理散文集》封面。

圖 8.-散文畫〈美濃紀行〉刊《人間福報》2016.6.8)

圖 9 散文〈美濃紀行〉(刊《人間福報》2016.6.8)

圖 10.臺灣時報 2016.11.3 刊〈新埔柿農〉畫作

圖 11.詩畫〈獻給敘利亞罹難的女童〉畫 2016.10.21《亞特蘭大新聞》。

圖 12.詩畫〈勇氣－祝賀川普〉
畫 《 亞 特 蘭 大 新 聞 》
2016.11.11.，刊臺灣《人間福
報》副刊圖文，2014.11.14 詩（無
論是過去或現在）。

圖 15.　詩〈For Prof. Ernesto
Kahan〉刊《亞特蘭大新聞》2016.7.1
1985 年諾貝爾和平獎得主於
2016.6.25 獲得在巴賽隆納「標
題和皇家歐洲科學院醫生的院
士殊榮並發表一篇演講。

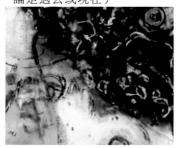

圖 13.詩畫〈夏蟬，遂想起〉
2016.8.19 畫《亞特蘭大新聞》。

圖 14.詩畫〈聽海〉刊美國《亞特
蘭大新聞》2016.12.2。刊散文〈旗
津冬思〉2016.12.8 於（臺灣時報）。

圖 16.詩畫〈頌長城〉刊美
國《亞特蘭大新聞》2016.5.6。
著者詩集《默喚》封面。

圖 17.詩畫〈咏王羲之蘭亭詩〉刊
《亞特蘭大新聞》，2016.10.14。

圖 19. 2016.11.19 文化部贊助民
視新聞【飛閱文學地景】節目播
出林明理 Dr.Lin Ming-Li 吟詩〈寫
給蘭嶼之歌〉。

圖 20. 2016.11.27 民視新聞黃瀞儀主
播於新聞中播放作家林明理吟詩於
【飛閱文學地景】節目及介紹：「蘭
嶼，在觀光開放的影響下，達悟族
人的生活空間與傳統文化，近年來
屢屢受到外界的關注。希望政府相
關單位能夠多正視這個問題，也是
林明理老師創作這首詩的靈感來
源，而這塊美麗的島嶼是過去達悟
族人的祖居地，也是未來達悟族人
維繫傳統文化與生活方式的土地。」
https://youtu.be/F95ruijjXfE

圖18刊《亞特蘭大新聞》二〇
一六‧十二‧二九‧詩〈你的影跡
在每一次思潮之上〉，二〇一六‧
十二‧二三‧詩〈淡水黃昏〉

圖 22.詩畫〈寫給鎮原的歌〉美國
《亞特蘭大新聞》2016.12.30

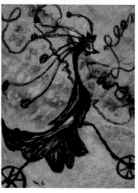

圖 21 刊
《 亞特蘭
大新聞》
2017.1.13
詩凝望

圖 23. 民視新聞 2016.12.24 晚上六點十八分由主播王暐婷介紹林明理吟詩〈歌飛阿里山森林〉於文化部贊助的【飛閱文學地景】節目。

圖 26.刊詩畫《臺灣時報》）2017.1.5〈東勢林場之旅〉。

圖 24. 2016.12.24 民視新聞中林明理詩人親筆書寫〈歌飛阿里山森林〉於台東美術館錄影。

圖 27. 詩畫〈*DON'T* BE SAD〉－刊《亞特蘭大新聞》2016.4.1

圖 25. 林明理詩人親筆書寫〈歌飛阿里山森林〉於台東美術館錄影中，民視新聞 2016.12.24 晚上六點新聞首播。

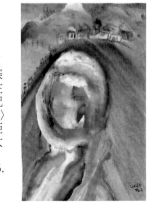

圖 2 8 詩畫〈你，深深銘在我的記憶之中〉刊《亞特蘭大新聞》2016.06.10

圖 29.詩畫〈憶陽明山公園〉
— 亞特蘭大新聞 2016.9.2

圖 30.詩畫〈白冷圳之戀〉刊
《亞特蘭大新聞》，2017.1.6。
《臺灣時報》2017.1.19。

圖 32.「詩的影像」活動，收錄林明
理詩〈那年冬夜〉參展紀念影像，
由此詩作與攝影家 — 2017.2.4
於臺北市聯展。

圖 31.海晕詩刊主辦在 2017.2.4 台
北〈詩的影像〉活動，收錄林明理
詩〈那年冬夜〉參展紀念影像，由
此詩作與攝影家聯展。

圖 33.中國大陸，全國散文詩大賽獲
提名獎，詩作〈甘南，深情地呼喚
我〉，2015.07。
http://www.chnxp.com/zhongxue/20
16-03/303030.html 眾力美文網
http://news.kkuzc.com/detail/4n6n
1.html
http://news.kkuzc.com/detail/4n6n
1.html 西藏文化網

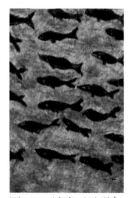

圖 34. 詩畫〈諦聽〉，刊
《亞特蘭大新聞》，2017.1.20

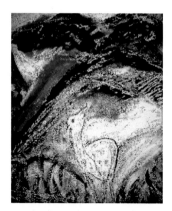

圖 37.詩畫〈日月潭抒情〉。

圖 35.散文〈蘭陽藝術行〉刊《臺
灣時報》2017.1.13 圖文。

圖 38.詩畫〈玉山頌〉
— 刊亞特蘭大新聞 2017.1.27.

圖 36.詩畫〈炫目的綠色世界〉刊《亞
特蘭大新聞》，2017.1.27.

圖 39.詩作〈那年冬夜〉應邀於
《海星詩刊》【詩的影像】現代詩與
攝影聯展，2017.2.4 於台北

圖 40　　2017.2.4 海星詩刊舉辦【詩的影像】於
台北市長官邸藝文中心。余玉照教授、林明理博
士、趙天儀教授於展覽茶會中合影。

【詩的影像】感思

我來了。穿過冬季白天微寒的旅程，來到詩與影像交會之境。
在無垠的想像裏，詩不再只是柔美，更顯得夢幻般多變。
我是個小小詩人，卻渴望聆聽春天的花朵或繁星的秘密。
你說：「看，多麼湛藍的天，這可不是你夢中的雲朵？」
於是我微笑著點點頭。
是呀，到哪裡才能找到一張大得足以網住夢的憂傷呢？
我能夠想像，在這樣一個盛會的日子，有許多和善的目光，
在交匯深處總會不經意地找到了珍貴的友誼與彼此的祝福。
而我的歌，曾是一份愛的顫動，也終於找到了與它共奏的諧音。
啊，旅程已終，但我的腳步穿過草坡綠野與無數野花，穿過清澈的
激流與島嶼的月光，穿過菩提樹花與生命的海岸……
它的節奏細而歡快！恰似四月桐吹拂而來　　──純淨的喜悅。

　　註：謝謝海星詩刊發行人辛勤、莫云主編等幕後工作小組的辛勞，
也特別感謝余玉照教授一路陪同我參加此盛會，與有榮焉，感銘於
心。－2017.2.6 －刊美國《亞特蘭大新聞》2017.2.17.圖文。

輯一、林明理法譯詩選

Dr.Athanase Vantchev de Thracy – français 序言（中英法譯）

Préface

Dans le présent recueil de poésies, la grande poétesse chinoise Dr. Lin Ming-Li évoque, souvent étroitement et fort habilement entremêlés, deux thèmes, un amour éthéré dont on se sait presque rien et sa patrie, l' île de Taïwan. Elle décrit avec une passion vibrante les beautés de sa terre natale. Ces deux sujets sont les deux pôles de l' univers magique de la poétesse.

Les textes du Dr. Lin Ming-Li sont essentiellement visuels et sensuels. Les monts, les vallées pittoresques, les harmonieuses collines, les plantes et les animaux de l' île défilent devant notre regard envoûté. Le monde qu' elle chante semble danser un ballet au rythme du vent et de la pluie. Les eaux des ruisseaux et de la mer chantent à l' unisson de son âme. Des parfums exotiques flottent dans une atmosphère enchantée.　Chaque poème est un paysage tantôt resplendissant, tantôt mélancolique, d' où naissent les sensations et les sentiments les plus forts.

Il y a dans les vers du Dr. Lin Ming-Li des jaillissements d' images splendides et hautement originales. Elles sont la transcription en mots des plus belles peintures dont l' art chinois a toujours été le représentant le plus accompli.

Comme ses magnifiques aquarelles, les poèmes-paysages de Ming-Li possèdent tous une âme qui les illumine et les sublime. L' art de dire et l' art pictural y vibrent dans une union sacrée.

Oui, le Dr. Lin Ming-Li a reçu en don céleste des Muses le verbe et la peinture.

Ce fut une grande joie et un privilège spécial de traduire ses ouvrages.

Athanase Vantchev de Thracy
Paris, décembre 2015

Translation of the French Preface

In the present collection, the celebrated Chinese poet Dr Lin Ming-Li focuses on two themes, often combined with great skill and evoked through close attention to the natural world. These themes are, first, an ethereal love of which her subjects are barely aware, and, secondly, her homeland, the island of Taiwan, whose beauties she describes with lively passion. These two subjects form the poles of the poet' s imaginative universe.

Dr Lin Ming-Li' s writing emphasises the visual and the sensual. Mountains, picturesque valleys, shapely hills, plants and animals from the island hold us in thrall as they pass before our eyes. The world of which she sings is like a ballet danced to the rhythm of the wind and rain. The waters of streams and ocean sing in unison to her soul. Exotic scents float in an enchanted atmosphere. Each poem is a landscape, sometimes resplendent, sometimes melancholic, from which the most powerful sensations and feelings arise.

In Dr Lin Ming-Li' s verses there are spates of splendid and highly original images. They are the transcriptions into words of those beautiful paintings of which Chinese art has always been the most accomplished representative.

Like her magnificent watercolours, Ming-Li's poem-landscapes all possess a soul which illuminates them and renders them sublime. The art of the word and the art of the image resonate there in a kind of sacred union.

Yes, Dr Lin Ming-Li has been privileged to have received the gifts of both written and pictorial aptitude from the Muses.

It has been a great joy and a special privilege for me to translate her work.

Athanase Vantchev de Thracy

December 2015

法國 *Athanase Vantchev de Thracy* 序

在這本選集裡，著名臺灣詩人林明理博士以高超的技巧與對自然世界的關切，專注於兩個主題：第一，她的物件幾乎不會覺察到的空靈的愛，其次，她熱情生動描述的她的家鄉臺灣這島嶼的美。這兩個主題構成了詩人的想像宇宙的兩極。

林明理博士的寫作強調的是視覺和感覺。高山，如詩如畫的山谷，多彩多姿的小丘，以及從我們眼前經過的這島上的動物和植物把我們迷住了。她歌唱的世界就像隨著 風雨起舞的芭蕾。河流和海洋的水齊聲對她的靈魂歌唱。異國的情調漂浮在一個魔法的氛圍中。每首詩是一道風景，時而燦爛，時而憂鬱，最有力的感覺和感情於焉產生。

林明理博士的詩中擁有大量美妙而獨創的意象。它們是那些美麗畫作的言辭化，而中國藝術一向長於此道。

就像她那些華麗的水彩畫，明理所有的詩風景都擁有一個照亮它們並使它們崇高的靈魂。語言的藝術和圖像的藝術在那裡產生了一種神聖的共鳴。

是的，林明理博士已榮獲繆斯賜予的書寫和繪畫的天賦。

翻譯她的作品對我來說是一個巨大的喜悅和特殊的榮幸。

Athanase Vantchev de Thracy
2015 年 12 月
（DR.WILLIAM MARR　翻譯序文）
輯一、法國翻譯家、詩人 Dr.Athanase Vantchev de Thracy 法譯林明理 82 首詩

1. 默 喚

在那鐘塔上
下望蜿蜒的河床，
小船兒點點
如碎銀一般！
彷彿從古老的風口裡
吹來一個浪漫的笛音，
穿越時空
驚起我心靈盤旋的
迴響。
我怎會忘記？
妳那凝思的臉，
伴隨這風中的淡香……
妳是我千年的期盼。
啊，布魯日，
小河裝著悠悠蕩漾的情傷，
而我，孤獨的，徘徊堤岸，
彷彿是中世紀才有著向晚！

－2007.11.26 作
－臺灣《人間福報》2007.12.13

1. L'appel silencieux

De la tour de l'horloge
Surplombant le lit méandreux du fleuve,
On voit des petits bateaux çà et là
Qui brillent comme un semis de pépites d'argent !
Un vent ancient

Semblable à une mélodie romantique pour flute
Souffle à travers le temps et l'espace
Et fait résonner un écho
Qui tournoie dans mon cœur.

Comment puis-je oublier
Ton visage tourné vers moi
Et le léger parfum porté par le vent ?
Tu es mon espoir pour mille ans.

Oh, Bruges,
Ton étroite rivière porte mon chagrin ancré en moi,
Tandis que, solitaire, j'erre le long de la rive
Dans un crépuscule presque médiéval.

2 想念的季節

飛吧，
三月的木棉，
哭紅了春天的眼睛。

飛吧，
風箏載著同一張笑臉，
心卻緊緊抓住了線。
飛吧，
楓葉輕落溪底，
行腳已沒有風塵。
飛吧，
我們都把心門打開，
讓光明的窗照射進來。

飛吧，
螢火蟲，
藏進滿天星，我是
沉默的夜。

－2008.11.12 作
－新疆《綠風》詩刊，總第183期，2009.第3期

2 La Saison des desires

En volant,
Au-dessus des arbres Ceiba de Mars.
Au printemps, tes yeux sont rouges à force de pleurer.

En flottant,
Le cerf-volant porte le même visage souriant,
Cependant, le cœur reste étroitement attaché serré à la ficelle.

En ondulant,
Les feuilles d'érable descendent gentiment le lit de la rivière.
Rien qui puisse nous soutenir.

En errant dans l'air,
Nous ouvrons les portes de nos cœurs
Pour laisser la brillante lumière y pénétrer.

En volant,
Le boutefeu
Se cache dans le ciel étoilé,
Je suis
La nuit silencieuse.

> **Remarque:** *Ceiba* est le nom générique de nombreuses
> espèces de grands arbres caractéristiques des zones tropicales,
> dont le Mexique, l'Amérique centrale, l'Amérique du Sud, les
> Caraïbes, l'Afrique de l'Ouest et l'Asie du Sud.

3. 十月秋雨

我記得你凝視的眼神。
你一頭微捲的褐髮，思維沉靜。
微弱的風拖在樹梢張望，
落葉在我腳底輕微地喧嚷。

你牽著我的手在畫圓，卻選擇兩平線：
銀河的一邊、數彎的濃霧、飛疾的電光，
那是我無法掌握前進的歸向，
我驚散的靈魂潛入了無明。

在山頂望夜空。從鐵塔遠眺到田野。
你的距離是無間、是無盡、是回到原點！
曉色的樺樹在你眼底深處雄立
秋天的雨點在你身後串成連珠

－2008.01.02作
－刊登河北省《詩選刊
下半月刊》2008.第9期

3. Pluie d'automne en octobre

Je me rappelle ton regard,

Tes boucles brunes, tes pensées calmes,

Le vent doux qui s'attardait dans les cimes des arbres,

Les feuilles qui tombaient en sifflant derrière mes pas.

Tu me prends par la main et traces un cercle

Au-delà de la Voie lactée. L'épais brouillard qui s'étend, le déluge

d'éclairs!

Je n'arrive plus à avancer,

Mon âme éclate en morceaux et plonge dans l'obscurité sans fin.

Je contemple le ciel obscur du haut de la colline,

De la tour de fer jusqu'aux champs les plus lointains,

Incommensurables est la distance qui me sépare de toi, et infinie!

Elle me ramène à l'obscurité primitive !

Le bouleau est profondément enraciné dans ton œil attiré par la terre.

Les gouttes de pluie d'automne s'assemblent derrière toi.

4. 雨 夜

夜路中，沒有
一點人聲也沒有燈影相隨。
在山樹底盡頭，眼所觸
都是清冷，撐起
一把藍綠的小傘，等妳。

雨露出它長腳般的足跡，
細點兒地踩遍了
壘石結成的小徑，
讓我在沙泥中
心似流水般地孤寂。

我用寒衫披上了我的焦慮，
幾片落葉的微音，卻聽到
那連接無盡的秋風細雨
竟在四野黯黑中出現和我一樣的心急……

— 2007.12作
— 英譯刊登美國〈poems　　　of　　　the
　world〉《世界的詩》2010夏季號／收
　錄30屆世詩會《2010世界詩選》

4. Nuit pluvieuse

Sur la route de nuit,
Pas un bruit, pas même une ombre.
Je marche jusqu'aux arbres sur la colline,
J'ai froid. Je tiens
Un petit parapluie bleu, et je t'attends.

La pluie avance sur la pointe des pieds, fait de longues foulées,
Puis des petites, puis d'autres encore, piétinant tout à l'entour.
Le chemin empierré brise les rives
De l'âpre solitude de mon cœur.

Je prends mon humble chemise pour calmer mes nerfs,
Les feuilles frissonnantes tombent. J'ai besoin de savoir
Si l'incessant vent d'automne et la fine pluie
Au-delà de la lugubre obscurité sauvage, ont les mêmes soucis que moi.

5. 記　夢

一整晚妳的聲音如細浪
泛白了黯淡的星河
我匆匆留下一個吻
在滴溜的霧徑上
或者，也想出其不備地說
愛，其實笨拙如牛

現在我試著親近妳　給妳
一季的麥花，著實想逗引妳
深深地在手心呼吸一下
如貓的小嘴唱和著相酬的
詩譜，叫我聞得到
那逃逸的形跡是多麼輕盈
──漫過山后

－2011.02.15作
－臺灣《創世紀》詩雜誌，第169期，2011.12
　冬季號

5. Souvenir d'un rêve

Toute la nuit, ton souffle a été comme les douces vagues
Qui éclaboussent de leur écume la sombre rivière des étoiles.
J'ai volé un baiser
Au moment où le brouillard se glissait parmi nous.
Les mots ne suffisent pas! Pourtant laisse-moi dire :
Mon amour s' est avéré aussi lourdaud qu' un bœuf.

Maintenant, je vais essayer de me rapprocher de toi,
Toi que, la saison entière où fleurissent les blés, j' ai aimé taquiner.
D'abord, je respire un grand coup derrière la paume de ma main,
Comme la petite bouche d' un chant j' attends la récompense
D' un poème terminé. Laisse-moi humer l'odeur
Des dernières traces si légères et gracieuses
Qui se perdent de l' autre côté de la montagne.

6. 金池塘

風在追問杳然的彩雲
遠近的飛燕在山林的
背影掠過

羞澀的石榴
醉人的囈語，出沒的白鵝
伴著垂柳戲波

秋塘月落
鏡面，掛住的
恰是妳帶雨的　明眸

－2008.02.01作
－原載臺灣《笠》詩刊，第265期，2008.06

6. L'étang d'*or*

Le vent chasse les nuages colorés au loin,

Çà et là passent

Les ombres des hirondelles

Tout est là, la goyave timide,

Le monde sauvage déchaîné, l'oie blanche qui se cache,

Les vagues en larmes des saules.

L'étang d' automne et la lune qui tombe,

Le miroir qui orne de pluie

Tes yeux brillants.

7. 春已歸去

不知不覺間
托著嫩綠帶毛的小桃子

又一次，向我訴說著
一種心事

蕭蕭沙沙
麥子枯黃了
榆樹的殘花停留在四月
風總是微微的
甜甜的吹
時時送來的布穀鳥的叫聲
也沒有變

春已遠去
籬笆外包圍著
一塊古老的桑田
荷葉一片二片……
浮泛在水面
而陽光正好暖和
向牆上雨痕悄然走過

－2009.04.04作
－香港《圓桌》詩刊，總第26期，2009.09

7. Le printemps est déjà passé

Inconsciemment,
Me tendant une pêche douce et légère,
Une fois de plus tu me confies
Tous tes soucis.

Bruissant et en sifflant,
Les fleurs fanées des ormes s' attardent en avril,
Toujours amène, le vent
Souffle doucement.
Parfois, un coucou chante,
Jamais rien de tout cela ne changera.

Le printemps est déjà passé.
Au-delà de la clôture on voit
Le bout d' un ancien champ,
Une ou deux feuilles de lotus
Flottent sur l'eau,
Tandis que la chaude lumière du jour,
Efface doucement une trace de pluie sur le mur.

8. 回到從前

三月
一陣風過
閃爍的螢火
溜進
我生命之夢

它們
像樹精靈
如此親切地靠近
一個記憶　慢慢在此佇足
變成一棵水青樹
在雨露裡衰老

注：水青樹，第三紀古老孑遺珍稀植物，
　　分佈於陝西南部、甘肅東南部、四川中
　　南部和北部等地。

－2010.03.03作
－刊登臺灣《文學臺灣》，第75期，2010.
　07秋季號

8. Retour au bon vieux temps

Mars.

Un souffle de vent passe.

De scintillantes lucioles

Se glissent

Dans mon rêve de vie

Comme des elfes des bois

Qui s' approchent du cœur

De ma mémoire et l'imprègnent

Pour la changer en olivier vert

Que font pousser la pluie et la rosée.

9. 懷　鄉

在我飄泊不定的生涯裡
曾掀起一個熟悉的聲音
但不久便重歸寂靜

它從何而來？
竟使我深深的足跡追影不及……
游啄的目光分離成渺遠的印記
每一步都是那麼堅定無疑

呵，我心戚戚
那是深夜傳來淒清的弦子
我識得，但如何把窺伺的黎明蒙蔽

－2010.01.11作
－原載臺灣《新原人》2010年夏季號，第
70期

9. Mal du pays

Dans ma vie errante,

J'ai entendu une fois une voix familière,

Mais elle s' est bien vite tue.

D'où venait-elle ?

Elle me poussait à me hater

Et me donnait une vague conscience de choses déjà vécues,

Mais chacun de mes pas était ferme et solide.

Oh, mon cœur plein de chagrin,

Entends le misérable chœur de la nuit.

Comment puis-je rester aveugle si l'aube me voit ?

10. 聲音在瓦礫裡化成泣雪

聲音在瓦礫裡化成泣雪，
在強震後的秋夜
此刻倘有些許月光，
樹影便已慌亂。

鏽般的天空一片死寂，
那看不見的哀懇
不時偃伏
讓黎明舉步維艱。

－2010.10.02作
－刊登臺灣《笠》詩刊，279期，2010.10.15

10. Une voix a fondu dans la neige en larmes

Une voix brisée a fondu dans la neige en larmes,
Dans la nuit d'automne, après le terrible choc,
Une tranche de clair de lune se saisit de ce moment
En compagnie de l'ombre flottante d'un arbre.

La nuit rouge est mortellement calme.
Le chagrin et le deuil restent invisibles.
Je dois déposer ici tout *présent* et tout *futur*,
Avant de trébucher sur les marches de l'aube.

11. 我不歎息、注視和嚮往

古老的村塘

凝碧在田田的綠荷上

我們曾經雀躍地踏遍它倒影的淺草

看幾隻白鴨

從水面銜起餘光

一個永遠年輕卻不再激越的回音

在所有的漣漪過後　猶響

－2010.05.15作
－刊登中國《天津文學》2011.01期

11. Ne soupire pas, regarde et avance

L'ancien étang dans le village.

Quelque chose a rendu plus épais les feuilles de lotus.

Une fois nous avons marché tous joyeux, parmi les mauvaises herbes

Qui se reflétaient la tête en bas dans cet étang.

Nous avons vu des canards blancs passer au-dessus de l'eau

Et ramasser le soleil couchant.

Un écho éternellement jeune et vierge jusqu'à present

Résonne encore après que toutes les ondes se sont éteintes.

12. 拂曉之前

沒一點雜色
林中
點點水光忽隱忽顯

郁郁杜松
孕出螞蟻的卵
隨荊棘聲愜意地伸長

一叢野當歸縮在樹牆旁幽坐
像是沉醉於
命運的遐想

—2010.02.30作
—原載臺灣《文學臺灣》季刊，2010.04
夏季號，第74期

12. L'*aube* *La forêt*

Au feuillage uniforme,

Crépusculaire et chatoyante!

Un mélèze élégant,

Surgi ici il y a neuf mois du travail des fourmis,

Étend paresseusement ses aiguilles.

Une grappe d'angélique sauvage près de l'arbre

S'autorise encore de rêver

À sa vie et à son destin.

13.　山楂樹

我在暮色中網住一隻鳥
它有秋月般的暈黃
虹彩般的髮
我願意朝夕地守望
每當它迅速地
驕矜地
把一個白霜的山丘
圈在它的腳踝上

春神在我臂下休息
仲夜從我身邊溜去
我沿著小路沒有回頭
直想輕步接近它的孤獨身軀
冬風不停地呼嘯而去
但我只能前行
直到它帶回長長的回音：
呵，忘卻你，忘卻我……
—— 是動中無聲的安寧

－2010.12.19作
－臺灣《創世紀》詩雜誌，第166期，2011.03
　春季號

13. L'Aubépine

Dans la pénombre, j'ai attrapé un oiseau,
Son ventre était jaune comme la lune d'automne,
Ses plumes avaient les couleurs de l'arc-en-ciel.
Il faut que je le surveille sans trêve jour et nuit,
Car il va soudain,
Prendre la colline couverte de givre
Entre ses serres.

La déesse du printemps repose sous mes bras.
Minuit s'éloigne en glissant à côté de moi.
Je marche le long du sentier sans regarder en arrière
Ne pensant que devenir solitaire moi aussi.
L'hiver siffle et hurle et s'éloigne
Jusqu'à ce qu'il ramène ce long écho:
Ah, puissions-nous être pardonnés! ...

Il n'y a que la paix dans le silence mouvant···

14. 綠淵潭

若沒了這群山脈，恐怕你將分不清
通向另一片蔚藍的希望之船，
那裡黎明正在沾滿白雪的雲階上等你。

總是，在分別的時刻才猛然想起
潭邊小屋恬靜地下著棋，當晚星
把你從落了葉的嶽樺樹後帶往我身邊，
別憂懼，我已沿著那隱蔽的淒清昏光
滑入閃爍的冰叢外虛寂的海洋。

－2010.06.24作
－臺灣《創世紀》詩雜誌2010冬季號，
　165期

14. Le profond étang vert

Sans les chaînes de montagnes,

Peut-être ne pourrais-tu jamais faire sortir

Le navire de l'espoir qui va cingler vers une autre mer bleue

Où l'aube t'attend sur des marches de nuages

Couvertes de neige blanche.

Rappelle-toi : cela arrive seulement quand la séparation te frappe

    soudain.

Alors que je joue tranquillement aux échecs dans le chalet près de

    l'étang,

L'étoile du soir peut t'amener à moi

bre, j'ai glissé

Dans la mer vide au-delà des miroitants amas de glace.

15. 縱然剎那

湖面滿是薄染
將落的金光
讓淺玫瑰的雲霞
溶在銀波上
遠山幾行
有如紫精屏風的灰綠
遠比星空更柔然無聲的顫動
動盪的一槐風帆

半湖碧水
不若你明眸的閃爍
在影落波間
我感到宇宙只此一刻
春風拂來
我已幻成白楊之林
昂首矗立
在湖畔旁等候月光

－原載安徽省文聯主辦《安徽文學》2010.
1-2期

15. Même si ce n'était que dans un éclair

Le lac est voilé par une mince bande de couleur.
Le soleil couchant aux reflets d'or
Fait fondre les roses rouges des nuages.
Dans les vagues d'argent,
Les reflets des montagnes lointaines
Sont comme le vert olive d'un écran d'améthyste.
Les eaux frissonnent plus doucement et tranquillement que le ciel
　　étoilé.
Le mât d'un voilier suit son erre plein d'inquiétude.

Le bleu des eaux devant moi
Ne peut se comparer à tes yeux brillants.
Entre les ombres qui tombent et les vagues,
Je sens le brillant éclair de l'univers.
Avec la brise du printemps qui me presse,
Je me fonds dans la vision d'une forêt de peupliers
Qui se tiennent fiers et élégants,
Dans l'attente du gala de soirée du clair de lune
Pour le plaisir du lac.

16. 靜寂的黃昏

一隻秋鷺立著，它望著遠方。

萋萋的蘆葦上一葉扁舟。

對岸：羊咩聲，鼓噪四周的蛙鳴。

它輕輕地振翅飛走，

羽毛散落苗田，

彷彿幾絲村舍的炊煙。

－2010.2.20作
－原載臺灣《創世紀》詩雜誌，2010.06夏
季號

16. *Le* paisible *crepuscule*

Une aigrette se tient debout et regarde au loin,

Parmi les roseaux luxuriants, un bateau frêle comme une feuille.

Sur l'autre rive, on entend le doux bêlement des moutons,

Et le son plus âpre des grenouilles qui coassent çà et là.

Battant doucement des ailes, elle s'envole,

Et seuls quelques-unes de ses plumes tombent dans les champs,

Comme des filets de fumée s'échappant des cheminées des cuisines rustiques.

17. 回憶的沙漏

回憶的沙漏
滴滴滴下，似淚成河
我整夜輾轉反側
那小路上閃現的星光
是夏夜在那裡瞇著眼
從天幕的破處
傳來聲聲呼喚，縱橫錯落

大地上一切已從夢中醒覺
山影終將無法藏匿
我卻信，我將孤獨痛苦地
漫行於沙漠世界
夜，依然濃重
徜徉於
白堤的浮萍之間

—2010.07.09 作
—刊登臺灣《創世紀》詩雜誌，164 期，
　2010.09 秋季號

17. *La* clepsydre *de la mémoire*

La clepsydre de la mémoire à l'œuvre –

Goutte après goutte, comme les larmes de la rivière.

De toute la nuit je n'ai pu trouver le repos.

Le chemin étoilé brille.

Sont-ce les yeux pétillants de la nuit d'été

Que je vois sur l'écran suspendu du ciel ?

Vagues de choses qui appellent et roulent sans but.

Tout le monde sur terre est déjà reveille

L'ombre de la montagne ne peut plus se cacher.

Je pense que je vais partir à l'aventure dans un monde désert,

Seule et toujours souffrante.

La nuit, encore dense,

Se balade

Au milieu des lentilles d'eau entre les berges blanches.

18. 懷舊

往事是光陰的綠苔，
散雲是浮世的飄蓬。
鷄鳴，我漫不經心地步移，
春歸使我愁更深。

一花芽開在我沉思之上，
孕蕾的幼蟲在悄然吐絲；
它細訴留痕的愛情，
縷縷如長夜永無開落。

　　　　　　－2009.09.24 作
　　　　　　－刊登《香港文學》2010.03 期

18. Nostalgie

La mousse verte du temps s'en est allée.

Les nuages flottants sont les pétales de la vanité du monde.

Un coq chante. Je marche libre de tout souci,

Mais le printemps qui revient entrevoit une anxiété nouvelle.

Pendant que je suis toute à mes pensées, éclot une fleur.

Un ver se promène tranquillement sur une feuille,

Il raconte son histoire d'amour afin de laisser sa marque dans la vie,

Répétant encore et encore son récit long comme la nuit qui n'en finit pas.

19. 岸畔之樹

岸畔之樹
在我憩息的地方
像潺潺小溪
流經大片花田般
圍繞著我奏樂
在寂靜的森林內輕響

呵，那水貂似的髮絲
……我難尋蹤跡的女孩
依著風的手指
忽隱忽現
快速地
問訊而來
只一瞬間
黑瞳晶若夜雪
妳是海
你是樹心
不，不是，你是輕風吹拂的白罌粟
我的一切，繆斯無法增添你一分光彩

－2010.07.13 作
－臺灣《創世紀》詩雜誌 2010 第 164 期，
2010.09 秋季號

19.　L'Arbre sur la berge

À l'endroit où je me repose,
Un arbre sur la rive,
Comme un fleuve qui ondule
Et coule à travers un bout de champ en fleurs,
M'engloutit et me joue une musique
Qui résonne agréablement dans les bois tranquilles.

Oh, mon amour, tes cheveux brillants ont la couleur du vison.
Il est difficile pour moi de te trouver ici,
Suivant le doigt du vent,
Vacillant,
Pressé,
Venu m' interroger.

Il y a juste l'éclair
De tes yeux noirs dans la nuit de neige étincelante.
Tu es la mer,
Tu es le cœur de l'arbre.
Non, tu es un pavot blanc qui flotte dans la brise.
Tu es tout pour moi.
La Muse même ne peut rien ajouter à la façon dont tu brilles pour moi.

20. 四月的夜風

悠悠地，略過松梢
充滿甜眠和光，把地土慢慢甦復
光浮漾起海的蒼冥
我踱著步。水聲如雷似的
切斷夜的偷襲

我聽見
野鳩輕輕地低喚，與
唧唧的蟲兒密約
古藤下，我開始想起
去年春天。你側著頭
回眸望一回，你是凝，是碧翠
是一莖清而不寒的睡蓮！

這時刻，林裡。林外
星子不再窺視於南窗
而我豁然瞭解：
曾經有絲絲的雨，水波拍岸
在采石山前的路上…

－2009.04.08 作
－遼寧省《詩潮》，總第 162 期，2009.12

20. Le vent nocturne d'avril

D'une allure nonchalante, il effleure le sommet du pin,
Empli d'un sommeil calme et léger, et réveille doucement la terre.
Des ondulations égayent le vert profond de la mer.
Je marche le long de la berge. L'eau retentit comme un tonnerre
Qui traverse de part en part la nuit dans sa chasse silencieuse.

J'entends le bruit
Des oiseaux qui roucoulent frénétiquement
Et le frétillement des vers qui se rencontrent
Sous la vieille vigne. Et voilà que je me rappelled
Le printemps dernier. Tu tournes la tête de côté,
Tu jettes un coup d'œil en arrière. Tu es le regard, le jade vert,
Le lys d'eau, clair mais pas froid !

Ah, ce moment dans les bois. Ensuite, dehors,
Les étoiles ne se montrent plus par la fenêtre sud.
Soudain, je me sens illuminée.
Il était une fois la bruine, les vagues qui se brisaient contre le rivage.
Je grimpe la route derrière la montagne qui mène à la carrière.

21. 雲淡了，風清了

把愛琴海上諸神泥塑成圓頂的鐘塔
回歸
寧靜

你看，那夕陽下的風車
天真地在海邊唱遊
那碧波的點點白帆
輕撫著客中的寂寞

啜著咖啡；青天
自淺紅
至深翠
沖淡濃潤的綠，白色的牆
耳際只有草底的鳴蟲
抑抑悲歌...

－2007.11.21 作
－安徽省文聯主管主辦，《安徽文學》2010 年.1-2 期

21. Nuage léger, vent caressant

L'argile a fait les figures des dieux de la mer Égée

Dans des tours voûtés

Et les a faites retourner

À une existence paisible.

Regarde le moulin à vent dans le soleil couchant.

Il chante et joue en toute innocence avec les eaux.

Des voiles blanches flottent au-dessus des vagues bleues,

Je sirote un café. Le ciel bleu

Passe du rouge profond

Au vert foncé.

Puis il pâlit; les murs blanchissent.

Tout ce que j'entends,

Ce sont des insectes qui stridulent dans l'herbe,

Et gardent pour eux-mêmes leurs plus tristes mélodies.

22. 流　螢

穿出野上的蓬草
靈魂向縱谷的深處飛去
群峰之中
唯我是黑暗的光明

—2009.05.22 作
—《香港文學》2010.03

23. 秋　暮

冬山河　鹹草鳴蜇
濱鷸　兩兩
惟有小水鴨
擾亂了整個水面
喚起白霧飛脫
留下溪口外
一片明霞

—2009.05.22 作
—香港《香港文學》2010.03

22. Les scintillantes lucioles

À travers les touffes d'herbe dans les champs,

Mon âme vole vers la vallée profonde

Qui se niche parmi les pics des montagnes.

Seule, j'apporte l'éclat du soleil aux sein des ténèbres.

23. Crépuscule d'automne

Le Dongshan : ses herbes salées et ses criquets qui crissent.

Des bécasseaux variables qui vont par deux ou par trois.

Seules les petites Sarcelles

Troublent la surface de l'eau,

Agitent le brouillard blanc qui s'envole

Dévoilant un ciel de nuages rose vif

Au-delà de l'embouchure du fleuve.

Remarque: Le Dongshan est un fleuve dans le nord de Taiwan.

24. 在那星星上

我望著花間雨露

像布穀鳥，掠過

潺潺的小河，而搖曳

在稻浪的，春之舞

－2009.05.22 作

－《香港文學》2010.03

24. Au-dessus des étoiles

Je vois la pluie et la rosée sur les fleurs.

Comme un coucou qui passe,

La rivière chante en poursuivant son petit bonhomme de chemin

Parmi les rizières –

C'est la danse du printemps.

25. 行經木棧道

黎明，帶著你折射出思想的芬芳來吧

跟著我，來吧，到石涼苔滑的棧道

在岩壁上像個僧侶披著雨帽

安謐中小青草比往年更茂更高

還帶著一切夢想沉睡的白蠟樹

冷杉和山毛櫸

用北方的民間歌謠

把夢想深藏在河流之心的夜空

來吧，把我也變一點兒

哪怕靈魂已凝成一座礁石

根根青草在波浪中起伏

－2011.05.20 作
－臺灣《創世紀》詩雜誌，第168期，2011.09
　秋季號

25. En descendant la route de planches

Aube, viens avec la fragrance qui reflète tes pensées.

Suis-moi sur la route de planches avec ses rochers froids et sa mousse glissante.

Sur la falaise, comme un moine à la tête protégée de la pluie,

Pousse une herbe tendre et apaisante, plus luxuriante que celle des années précédentes.

À côté du frêne qui dort à poings fermés,

Je vois le sapin et le hêtre.

J'entends un chant qui vient du nord.

Un rêve est caché bien profond dans la nuit noire, au cœur de la rivière.

Viens et laisse-moi le sentiment qu'une chose infime a changé,

Même si mon âme est devenue solide comme un récif.

L'herbe remue et se roule dans les vagues.

26 早 霧

窗台外，遠處木犁
空蕩蕩地
單掛在田壟
那兒，山煙之上
你瞅著我，有好一陣
接著，我倚上沙發閉上眼睛
有如羊在霧中
想起了那年
瑟縮的二月
── 透一股清冷

那是多久前的事兒了
我懷疑地問：
夜裡吹亂我頭髮的風
從上面經過　回聲
落滿了河谷
過去的日子彷彿
一切都很重要
又都不很重要
就像早霧頑皮地溜走
說了等於沒說

　　　　　　　　　　　　　　─2011.7.4 作
　　　　　　　　　　　　　　─香港《圓桌》詩刊，2011.10 秋季號

26. Brouillard matinal

Là-bas, derrière la fenêtre, une araire en bois
Pend, inutilisée,
À un crochet.
Dans un nuage de fumée venant de la montagne,
Tu t'attardes à me regarder.
Moi, m'appuyant sur le canapé, je ferme les yeux
Comme un mouton dans le brouillard.
Je me souviens de cette année où
Je me pelotonnais contre le froid de février
Trop intense pour être supporté.

Cela ne s'est-il pas passé il y a longtemps ?
Ai-je demandé sur un ton dubitatif.
Le vent de la nuit a ébouriffé mes cheveux,
Il venait, comme un écho, d'en haut,
Et se répandait sur toute la vallée.
Les derniers jours semblaient
À la fois terriblement importants
Et cependant pas tant que ça.
Tout comme la brume du matin qui glissait à côté de nous,
Ce qui avait été dit semblait n'avoir aucune importance.

27. 晚　秋

在一片濃綠的陡坡
白光之下和風，把高地淅淅吹著。
你回首望，淡淡的長裙
弄散滿地丁香。

我看見
花瓣掉落山城垂楊
晨霧漸失。雲雀
驚動了松果，你淺淺一笑
彷彿世界揚起了一陣笙歌，
而笙歌在你的四周
有無法不感到讚歎的奇趣。

今夜，
月已悄默，
只要用心端詳
石階草露也凝重
你離去的背影催我斷腸
就像秋葉搖搖欲墜
又怎抵擋得住急驟的風？

－2009.03.14 作
－原載臺灣《秋水》詩刊，第143期，2009.10
月

27. Un automne Tardif

Sur une pente raide au-dessus d'une étendue vert sombre,
La brise bruisse dans la lumière blanche qui baigne le paysage
montagneux.
Tu regardes en arrière, dans ta longue jupe pastel,
Répandant partout un parfum de clou de girofle.

J'ai vu
Des pétales tomber sur les peupliers en train de se flétrir
Dans cette ville de montagne,
J'ai vu le brouillard disparaître et les alouettes
Faire tressaillir les pommes de pin. Tu souris à peine,
Comme si une grêle de musique sheng envahissait le monde
Et t'entourait
Tel un étonnant univers fantastique
Que tu ne peux qu'admirer.

Ce soir
la lune est silencieuse.
Mais si tu regardes attentivement
Les gouttes de rosée sur l'herbe contre les marches de pierre
Semblent tout exaltées.
L'ombre de ton corps, quand tu me quittes,
Me brise le cœur
Devenu pareil à des feuilles d'automne charriées au loin.
Comment peut-il, ce cœur, supporter la rage des tempêtes ?

Remarque : le sheng est un instrument de musique à
vent à anche libre. Orgue à bouche chinois. Il date
de 2000 av. J.-C. puisqu'il est mentionné dans le
Che-king («Livre des Odes ou de la Poésie»)

28. 在白色的夏季裡

白日變長
鐘錶習慣停在九點零一刻
在夜晚的寧靜中
我走向傳說
很久以前
玫瑰花的野坡上輕輕踱步
整個七月充滿憂鬱
靈魂是一座密林
風依然無休止地來
修復了我思想的安定

－2011.5.22 作
－刊登臺灣《創世紀》詩雜誌，168 期，
　2011.09 秋季號

28. Dans la blancheur de l'été

Les jours rallongent.

L'horloge s'arrêtait d'habitude à neuf heures et quart.

Accompagnée par la sérénité de la nuit,

J'entrais dans la légende.

Il y a longtemps,

Flânant calmement sur la colline sauvage recouverte de roses,

Tout juillet me semblait lugubre.

L'âme est une forêt dense.

Le vent ne cessait de souffler

Ramenant la paix dans mon esprit.

29. 牽　引

午後　我的傷感

隨野麥嶺漫延

如浪往事

在彌留之際

雨同我打濕了時空

問你：為何時快時慢地緊跟著我

為何失望中的希望

總是一世羞澀

縱然萬頃碧波

誰能比崗哨不移的雲雨更重？

－2011.5.21 作

－刊登臺灣《創世紀》詩雜誌，168 期，
　2011.09 秋季號

29. *Te prendre par la main*

C'est l'après midi. Ma peine

Imprègne la chaîne de montagne de semences sauvages.

Le passé est comme des vagues

Qui inondent cet endroit de pluie

À mesure qu'elles déferlent.

Je te demande : *Pourquoi me suis-tu ainsi tantôt rapide, tantôt lent?*

Pourquoi y a-t-il de l'espoir dans le désespoir ?

Je suis tout le temps inquiète

Même quand les vagues sont bleues.

Quelle chose pourrait être à ce point plus redoutable que les nuages et
   la pluie,

Qu'il n'est homme sur terre qui pourrait m'en protéger?

30. 霧起的時候

我們不期而遇
原以為世上的一切都不孤寂
沒有客套寒暄
彷彿重逢是天經地義
然而
那熟悉的身影如晴雨
空漠地飄過在死亡中的廣場

霧正在升起
喧囂的人群　傘花晃動
街的盡頭　雨霧迷濛
空氣裡有著露珠的味道
一隻貓　蜷縮在樹底
似乎等待著什麼
久雨初霽後
十月的黃昏　風淡描而過

－2011.8.23 作
－刊登臺灣《創世紀》詩雜誌，169 期，
　2011.12 冬季號

30. Quand le brouillard se lève

Nous nous sommes rencontrés par hasard.

Nous croyions que la solitude n'existait pas dans ce monde.

Nous n'avions pas de formules de politesse ni de salutations d'usage,

Car nous revoir était parfaitement naturel.

Il y avait

Une figure familière － la pluie et le soleil unis －

Qui flottait en vain au-dessus de cette place qui évoquait la mort.

Le brouillard se lève.

Foule bruyante et parapluies qui rappellent des semis de fleurs.

Au bout de la rue, bruine et brouillard.

Un goût de rosée dans l'air.

Un chat s'accroupit sous un arbre

Comme s'il attendait quelque chose.

Il fait à nouveau beau après la longue période de pluie.

Crépuscule d'octobre. Une brise légère passe.

31. 九份黃昏

初夏蹲踞的霧氣散後

小鎮開始從回憶中醒來

茶樓與紅燈籠高低錯落

古老的礦坑仍殘留著

些許漫長蕭瑟的夢

驀然回首石階前我瞥見

在褪去的灰空下我們曾緩一緩腳步

在落羽的山風與一朵朵傘花中

臺灣《文學台灣》雜誌, 2011.07， 秋季號

31. Un soir à Jiufen

Après que le brouillard matinal s'est dispersé,

La ville a commencé à revivre ses souvenirs.

Restaurants aux lanternes rouges émergeant çà et là.

ongs et sombres rêves.

En jetant un coup d'œil sur la route parcourue,

Je nous vois un instant marchant lentement sous le ciel gris.

Montagne déboisée où s'épanouissent les fleurs.

> Remarque : Jiufen est une région montagneuse dans le district Ruifang de New Taipei City près de Keelung (Taiwan).

32. 你的微笑

(給 Athanase Vantchev de Thracy)

你的微笑，似橄欖林中的風
正好流入莫內和他的花園上
而我不知道秘密是什麼
但我知道鳶尾花的香味
在最初的冬雪過後，便
從賽納河畔流到
我的書房

－刊《臺灣時報》，臺灣文學版，2015.11.30
圖文/《笠》詩刊第 311 期，2016.02/《大
海洋》詩雜誌，第 93 期，2016.07，頁
99。
－美國（POEMS OF THE WORLD）季刊，
2015 秋季號，非馬英譯。

32. Votre sourire

À Athanase Vantchev de Thracy

Votre sourire, comme le vent qui vient de l'oliveraie,

Souffle dans le jardin de Monet.

Bien que je n'en sache pas le secret,

Je connais le parfum des iris qui,

Dérivant des berges de la Seine,

Pénètre dans mon studio

Après la première neige de l'hiver.

33. 你的名字

——給 Athanase Vantchev de Thracy

是風送來你的名字

如獨立不羈的雪

在蔚藍海岸上，在薰衣草田上

在島上繁花盛開前

以一種昂揚之姿

飄過

還泛著白鷺舞翩的憂鬱

—刊《臺灣時報》，臺灣文學版，2015.11.30
圖文/《笠》詩刊第 311 期，2016.02/《大
海洋》詩雜誌，第 93 期，2016.07，頁
99。
—美國《POEMS OF THE WORLD》季刊，
2015 秋季號，非馬英譯。

33. Your name

to Athanase Vantchev de Thracy

It's the windthat carries your name,
like snow, free of earthly attachments,
on the blue shore, in the lavender fields,
past the blooming flowers on the island,
proud and restless,
drifting across
the melancholy of a dancing egret.

33. Votre nom

À Athanase Vantchev de Thracy

C'est le vent qui porte votre nom,
Comme la neige, libre de tout lien terrestre,
Sur le rivage bleu, dans les champs de lavande,
Au-dessus des fleurs épanouies de l'île,
Fier et inquiet,
Traversant la mélancolie
D'une aigrette qui danse.

34. 給普希金

Александр Сергеевич Пушкин，

Aleksander Pushkin （1799-1837）

你漫步山之巔，領受明淨的風雪
在我臨近繆斯最美麗的邊緣
讓藍海、山溪、愛神、群星
為我們作證吧！
你深信光明必勝黑暗，而
我深信俄羅斯將永誌你的名！

--刊臺灣《海星詩刊》，2016.03，
第 19 期。

34. To Pushkin

Александр Сергеевич Пушкин(1799-1837)
Alexander Sergueïevitch Pushkin (1799-1837)

You walk across the summit of the mountain, feel pure snow.
I am close to my most beautiful Muse.
Let the blue ocean, mountain streams, Eros, stars
be our witnesses!
I know you will conquer the darkness
and for Russia your name will light the way!

34. À Pouchkine

Александр Сергеевич Пушкин(1799-1837)
Alexandre Sergueïevitch Pouchkine (1799-1837)

Vous marchez au sommet de la montagne,
Vous sentez la neige pure.
Je suis tout près de ma plus belle Muse.
Que l'océan bleu, les torrents des cimes, Éros
Et les étoiles soient nos témoins !
Je sais que vous allez vaincre l'obscurité
Et que votre nom éclairera le chemin de la Russie!

35.　黃昏的潮波

to Athanase Vantchev de Thracy

燦爛春陽下晶藍色的海啊
你，守護聖殿的王子，
一抹光在那些船桅高高的舊港上
循著你飄逸的步子通向大洋！
我的朋友，那驟然而落的靜寂
是你身著白色長袍與桂葉的花冠！

　　　　　　　　　　－2015.11.19
　　　　　　　　　　--刊臺灣《海星詩刊》，2016.03，第 19
　　　　　　　　　　期。

35. Twilight Tidal Wave

to Athanase Vantchev de Thracy

Under a brilliant spring sun, a crystal blue sea.

You, the prince guarding the temple.

Light touches the tall masts in the old port,

follows your elegant steps to the ocean!

My friend, who suddenly fell silent,

is that you, dressed in white robes and a crown of laurels?

35. *Raz-de-marée* au crépuscule

À Athanase Vantchev de Thracy

Sous le brillant soleil du printemps, une mer de cristal bleue.

Vous, le prince gardien du temple.
La lumière effleure les hauts mâts dans le vieux port
Vous, le prince gardien du temple.
La lumière effleure les hauts mâts dans le vieux port
Et suit vos pas élégants vers l'océan !
Mon ami devenu soudain silencieux,
Êtes-vous cet homme vêtu d'une tunique blanche et couronné de lauriers ?

36.　在高原之巔，心是
如水的琴弦

我的生命如風

在高原之巔，心是如水的琴弦

一步近在腳下，一步一生遙遠

在菩薩之路……我經過

一個又一個聖峰

無垠的草原與星野

我見過，佈滿風霜而平和的

也見過喜極而泣的臉

而你，青朴溪谷

像鏡般映射靈魂

你的歌裡，像雄鷹自由安祥

在人潮之間

有一種不同凡響的詮釋

－2015.11.20

－刊臺灣《秋水》詩刊，167 期，2016.04，
　頁 36。

36. On the Plateau, the Heart like Streams of Water

Wind of my life.
On the plateau, the heart is like streams of water.
One short step, one step　long as a lifetime.
On the Buddha ‘s path, I passed,
one after another, the holy peaks,
the expanse of grasslands and the field of stars.
I have seen faces, peaceful and covered with frost.
I have seen faces covered with tears of joy.
And you, Green Park Ravine,
like a mirrored map of the soul.
Your songs, like an eagle, serene and freely soaring
above the crowd.
Extraordinary movements of the mind.

36. Sur le Plateau, mon cœur devenu jaillissement de ruisseaux

Vent de ma vie!
Sur le Plateau, mon cœur est devenu jaillissement de ruisseaux.
Un pas bref, puis un pas long comme toute une vie.
Sur le sentier du Bouddha, j'ai parcouru,
L'un après l'autre, les pics sacrés,
Les immenses prairies et le champ d'étoiles.
J'ai vu des visages paisibles et recouverts de givre.
J'ai vu des visages inondés de pleurs de joie.
Je t'ai vu toi aussi, Green Park Ravine,
Comme une carte-miroir de l'âme.
J'ai admiré tes chants qui s'élevaient, sereins et libres
Tels un aigle au-dessus de la foule.
Ah, élan merveilleux de l'esprit!

37. 雨聲淅瀝…

雨聲淅瀝….
我看見鳥，哥兒般，在枝頭
啾啾響著。唱歌給河流聽。
無動於我的憂愁。

我想起貝加爾湖宛如煉獄
那野火使勁地燒
不再向人類細語吟哦。

我看見一片葉飄來，蕩去。
輕如鴻毛。而我，
我心似松柏，不想嚎啕。

注·俄羅斯貝加爾湖〈Lake Baikal〉又稱西伯利
亞的藍眼睛，是旅遊盛地，但今年九月一場
野火讓原本如詩如畫的湖光山色成了人間煉
獄，有感而文。
--2015.11.21
--刊美國《世界的詩》《POEMS OF THE
WORLD》，2016年春季號，頁26。

37. Patter of Rain

Patter of rain···

I saw a familiar bird in the branches.

Its calls rang out, singing to the river,

indifferent to my sorrow.

I thought of the hell of Lake Baikal:

that fire burning wildly

no longer speaking the soft song of humanity.

I saw a leaf floating by,

light as a feather, but as for me,

my heart was like a pine tree and I could not cry.

> **Author's Note :** Russia's Lake Baikal, also known as Siberian Blue
> Eyes, is a tourist attraction, but a wildfire in September 2015
> meant that the original picturesque lake became a hell on earth.
> （非馬英譯）

37. Crépitement de la pluie

Crépitement de la pluie ...

Je voyais un oiseau familier dans les branches.

Ses appels retentissaient dans l'air

Quand il chantait près de la rivière,

Indifférent à mon chagrin.

Je pensais à l'enfer du lac Baïkal :

À ce feu qui brûlait sauvagement

Ayant oublié le doux langage de l'humanité.

Je voyais une feuille flotter tout près,

Légère comme une plume, mais moi,

J'avais le cœur comme un pin et je ne pouvais pas pleurer.

Note de l'auteur : le lac Baïkal en Russie, appelé encore Yeux bleus de Sibérie, est une exceptionnelle attraction touristique. Hélas, en septembre 2015, un immense feu de forêt a transformé ce lieu pittoresque en véritable enfer

38. 你，深深銘刻在我的 記憶之中

有一天
你終將會離我而去
再沒有任何事值得我悲痛
世上已無所希求
你，深深銘刻在我的記憶之中

也許
我不能為自己也無法為你做點什麼
撒下這把灰白粉末
從此之後
你是否重新找到另一個天地

我從來不是個敏捷的詩人
也不敢成為你的唯一知交
只在暖雨中
在黑夜
捕撈你的影子，回到我的腦海
就像期待春花回到大地的懷抱

－2015.9.27 中秋夜
－刊美國《亞特蘭大新聞》，2016.06.10。
圖文，非馬英譯。

38. You, Deeply Etched in my Memory

One day,

eventually, you' ll leave me.

Nothing will be worth my grief.

The world will have nothing I desire.

You, deeply etched in my memory.

Maybe

there' ll be nothing I can do for you or I,

except cast the grey powder to the wind.

For by then,

you' ll be in search of another world.

My poetry never came quickly.

I did not dare to become your only friend.

Only in the warm rain,

in the night.

do I try to catch your shadow and remember you,

as flowers look back to the embrace of the earth.

38. Toi, gravé si profondément dans ma mémoire

Un jour,

Finalement, tu vas me quitter.

Rien n'égalera mon chagrin.

Le monde n'aura plus rien que je puisse désirer.

Toi, si profondément gravé dans ma mémoire.

Peut-être

N'y aura-t-il rien que je puisse faire pour toi ou pour moi,

Sauf jeté de la cendre grise au vent.

Car, de ce jour,

Tu seras en quête d'un autre monde.

Ma poésie n'a jamais jailli spontanément.

Je n'ai pas osé être ta seule amie

Sous la pluie chaude

De la nuit.

Dois-je essayer d'attraper ton ombre et me souvenir de toi,

Comme les fleurs nostalgiques de l'étreinte de la terre.

39. 淵　泉

涼晨中
我聽見流泉就在前方
彷若一切拂逆與困厄
全都無懼地漂走

一隻信鴿在白樺樹林頻頻
投遞
春的祭典

我相信悲傷的愛情
它隨著蒼海浮光
有時擱淺在礁岸
隨沙礫嘎啦作響

　　　　　　　　－2010.01.04 作
　　　　　　　　－香港《香港文學》2010.03

39. Source profonde

Matin froid.

J'entends l'eau de la source qui coule

Et je sens bien que ma frustration et ma détresse

Peuvent enfin s'en aller sans crainte.

Une colombe blanche hante les bouleaux argentés

Apportant sur ses ailes

La fête du printemps.

Je crois à la mélancolie de l'amour

Qui s'en vient avec le miroitement de la mer.

Parfois il se fracasse contre le rivage

En faisant un bruit âpre

Comme celui de cailloux qui s'entrechoquent.

40. 倒 影

霧靄淡煙著
河谷的邊緣，
你的影子沉落在夕陽
把相思飄浮在塔樓上。

回首，凝視那常春藤的院落。
每當小雨的時候
淚光與植物，混合成
深厚而縹緲的灰色……

－2007.11.23 作
－刊登臺灣《人間福報》副刊，2008.04.22

40. *Image inversée*

Le brouillard flotte léger comme de la fume

À travers la vallée où coule la rivière.

Ton ombre tombe avec le soleil couchant.

Le désir frissonne au-dessus de la tour.

Retourne-toi. Regarde la cour envahie par le lierre.

Chaque fois que la pluie fine

Verse ses larmes, tout ce qui pousse se mêle

Avec la brume dense et grise.

41. 給 Bulgarian poet Radko Radkov（1940-2009）

在如風般逝去的日子懷抱裡
任何天使之翼
也不能捎去我的訊息
枝上那只夜鶯
已不再唱牠的妙曲
可是，就在這片刻之間
你從金馬車上翩然回首
在星辰中，堅韌如昔
身影從容優閑
彷彿回到玫瑰谷的重逢

－2015.12.11
－刊美國《亞特蘭大新聞》，2016.06.10，
　圖文。（非馬英譯）

41. To Bulgarian poet Radko Radkov (1940-2009)

We held out our arms but the wind
Rushed on, and so the days have gone by.
No angels's wings
can carry my messages to you.
The nightingale on the branch
no longer sings her lovely song.
Yet, at this moment, I see you
glance back from your golden coach.
Among the stars, you endure as ever,
at peace now,
waiting to meet old friends in the Rose Valley.

41. Au poète bulgare Radko Radkov (1940-2009)

Nous nous tenions par la main, mais le vent
S'est engouffré entre nous
Et ainsi s' en sont allés les jours.
Aucune aile d' ange
Ne peut vous apporter mes messages.
Le rossignol sur la branche
N' émet plus son délicieux chant.
Pourtant, en ce moment,
Je vous vois jeter des regards en arrière depuis votre carrosse d'or.
Au milieu des étoiles
Vous êtes fort comme jamais,
En paix maintenant,
Vous attendez de retrouver vos vieux amis
            Dans la Vallée des roses.

42. 致英國詩人 Norton Hodges
（1948-）

耶誕日，街道繽紛，

雪松矇矓。

夜，已經很深了，

誰在遠處徘徊？

而你

像丁尼生，

從往昔而來，

從林肯而來，

用高貴的語調告訴我，

如白雲對著雀鳥微笑。

註：丁尼生 (Lord Alfred *Tennyson*
1809-1892)是英國著名詩人，而林肯
是英國林肯郡的郡治和教堂市。
—刊美國《亞特蘭大新聞》2016.12.18，
非馬英譯。

42. Pour le poète britannique Norton Hodges

C'est Noël, les rues sont pleines de couleurs,

Les cèdres nagent dans un halo de brume.

Profonde est la nuit.

Qui est cette forme errant au loin?

Et vous,

Comme Tennyson

Venu du lointain passé,

Venu de Lincoln,

M'dressant ces nobles paroles

Pareilles à des nuages blancs

Qui sourient aux oiseaux.

43. 葛根塔拉草原之戀

雖然不是我的故土，
卻讓我遐思萬千，
草原未曾衰老，
胡楊憂傷如前。

每當盛夏之季，
野馬奔馳勝似行雲，
營盤歌舞宛如嘉年華會，
駝鈴響過逐香之路，
神州飛船鑲入眼簾。

馬頭琴在帳外的蒼茫中浮動，
傳說中的傳說使我迷戀，
這是天堂的邊界，還是繆斯的樂園？
還是我無言的讚歎枯守著期盼的誓約。

－刊內蒙古《集寧師範學院學報》2014.03
期，總第 126 期，封前。湖南葉光寒客
座教授譜曲。

43. La chanson de la prairie de Gegen Tara

Bien qu'elle ne soit pas ma patrie,

Elle m'évoque mille et mille rêveries,

La prairie n'a pas vieilli,

Les peupliers sont aussi tristes qu'autrefois.

Quand vient l'été,

Les broncos courent, tels des nuages rapides,

Ils chantant et dansent transformant le campement en carnaval

Les clochettes des chameaux tintent tout le long de la route,

Des aéronefs s'élèvent dans les yeux.

La musique des fifres à la tête de cheval glissent hors des tentes,

Des fameuses légendes populaires m'enivrent,

Est-ce ici l'orée du paradis ou le jardin des Muses ?

Ou mon admiration muette qui attend l'accomplissement d'un vœu?

44. 無論是過去或現在

無論是過去或現在：湛藍和青草、
巨石與白浪、燈塔與鷗鳥，
當我喜愛這一切，
喜愛玻璃船和俏皮的梅花鹿，
而自以為是在天涯海角；

當我移動腳步，直想靠近
這綠島與沙灘，岩洞與山丘，
人權紀念碑前的往事和滄桑歷史，
已然隨著時間慢慢蒸散了；

當我仰天獨自遐想，
就像永久地等待——
允諾我的時間老人，
我們才剛剛相遇，甚至不願離開。

—刊臺灣《人間福報》副刊圖文，2014.11.14

44. Que ce soit dans le passé ou à l'heure présente

Que ce soit dans le passé ou à l'heure présente,
Ciel bleu et herbe verte,
Énormes pierres et vagues blanches,
Phares et hagdons,
J'aime tout cela!
J'adore les bateaux en cristal et les élégants cerfs Sika
Et je m'imagine être au bout du monde.

Quand j'avance et m'approche
De l'île verte avec ses plages, ses grottes, ses collines
Et son Monument aux droits de l'homme,
Je constate que tout disparaît avec le temps qui passe.

Lorsque je regarde le ciel, plongée dans un rêve en plein jour,
J'ai le sentiment d'avoir attendu longtemps ce moment…
Car la promesse du Temps, ce vieil homme
Que je viens de rencontrer, et que je refuse de quitter,
Ne s'est pas encore accomplie.

45. 憶友—Ernesto Kahan

你可曾諦聽故鄉花海的歌聲，那

榮美而威嚴的花兒

還有撒瑪利亞城，憂傷而平靜的眼眸

忽若愛神的懶散，

又似夜的寂寥。

你含笑在我面前，

滿懷安寧和自由。

那血脈相連的地土，回鄉的渴望

已深入你靈魂之中。

啊，七弦琴的律動——

註.1985年諾貝爾和平獎得
主 prof.Ernesto Kahan在其
故鄉以色列拍攝一張照片
並傳來電。－2014.4.2
－英譯刊-美國《poem of
the world》，2014春季號

45. En pensant à mon ami Ernesto Kahan

Avez-vous écouté le chant de la mer

Qui baigne votre belle ville natale toute fleurie,

Et la voix de Samarie, avec ses yeux douloureux, calmes

Et langoureux, tels les yeux de Vénus

Ou ceux du silence de la nuit.

Votre sourire en face de moi

Plein de paix et de liberté,

La terre à laquelle vous êtes lié par le sang,

L'attachement au foyer,

Sont profondément ancrés dans votre âme –

Oh, le rythme de la lyre!...

46. 四草湖中

我聽過天空
嘎嘎這嘎嘎那的雷響，還有
消失卅餘年的烏鰡重回四草湖懷抱
我歡喜，因為我知道寧靜
如這群白鷺
正緊跟著夕陽而且習以為常了
那紅樹林就在前方
映照出深淺不一的藍

不過，我喜愛的
不只是招潮蟹招展在泥灘
或是氣定神凝的彈塗魚
我關注的
其實只有復育的榮耀
我尋覓，再尋覓
嘎嘎這嘎嘎那的雷響，我用心觀察——
並沉湎於最遠那閃光的河道

—2014.6.10
—刊臺灣《臺灣時報》，2015.3.1
—刊臺灣《秋水》詩刊，163 期，2015.04.

46. *Sur le lac Sicao*

J'ai entendu le ciel

Où grondait le tonnerre

Et vu des coques disparues depuis 30 ans

Revenir dans les bras du lac.

Je suis très heureuse de profiter de la quiétude

Qui rappelle celle d'un vol d'aigrettes qui, comme d'habitude,

Suit le coucher du soleil.

La mangrove est juste devant mes yeux,

Elle reflète diverses nuances de bleu.

Mais ce que j'aime

Ce ne sont pas seulement les crabes violonistes rampant dans la vasière

Ou les gobies couchées sur le sol calmes et immobiles.

Non, ce dont je me soucie sont tout simplement

Les délices de la restauration.

Je ne cesse de rechercher

Le grondement du tonnerre, j'observe attentivement tout

Et me vautre dans le bras le plus éloigné de la rivière.

47. 樹林入口

時間是水塘交替的光影
它的沉默浸滿了我的瞳仁
雨沖出凹陷的泥地
在承接暗藍的蒼穹
一隻小彎嘴畫眉
正叼走最後一顆晨星

呵四季從不懂謊言
就像我的心啊
披滿十一月秋天
除了想你已無處躲藏
當太陽掠過樺樹上端
索性把思念變成一條小溪
讓重疊的濃綠時時潺潺鳴響

—台灣《創世紀》詩雜誌， 第 161 期，
2009.12 月冬季號

47. À l'orée de la Forêt

C'est l'heure où les ombres se chevauchent au-dessus de la mare,

Son silence envahit mes pupilles.

La pluie semble jaillir de la fosse boueuse.

Au bord bleu foncé du ciel,

Un petit merle au bec crochu

Picore la dernière étoile du matin.

Oh, les saisons ne mentiront jamais

Rempli d'odeur d'automne en novembre.

Je n'ai nulle part où me cacher, hormis ma pensée pour toi!

Quand le soleil balaie la cime du bouleau,

Volontairement je transforme ma nostalgie en ruisseau －

Laisse-le murmurer, recouvert de vert sombre, tout le temps.

48. 想妳，在墾丁

每年落山風吹起
是墾丁旅遊的淡季
但我總會想起妳
如同孤鳥
整夜不眠地徘徊在
月光覆蓋的礁岩上

當我拾起貝殼，貼進耳裡
我就感到驚奇，彷彿
那座軍艦石潛過大海
瞧，妳長髮如樹冠的葉片般
柔美而飄逸
瞬間，如夏雨

蘇鐵睡眠著、白野花兒睡眠著
甚至連星兒也那樣熟睡了
只有沉默的島嶼對我們說話——
就讓時間蒼老吧
這世界已有太多東西逝去
我只想擁有自然、夜，和珍貴的友誼

—刊臺灣《秋水》詩刊，第 162 期，2015.01，
頁 26。

48. Tu me manques à Kending

Chaque année, quand souffle le vent déchaîné,
C'est la basse saison à Kending, Mais je pense toujours à toi
Comme un oiseau solitaire
Qui s'attarde toute la nuit
Sur les récifs baignés du clair de lune.

Quand je ramasse un coquillage et le colle à mon oreille,
Je me sens toujours surprise, comme si
Ce rocher en forme de navire de guerre fendait les flots.
Regarde, tes longs cheveux sont comme les feuilles de la couronne
　　d'un arbre
Souples, beaux et élégants
Rappelant soudain le scintillement de la pluie d'été.

Dorment les cycas, les blanches fleurs sauvages sommeillent,
Et même les étoiles, elles aussi sont profondément endormies,
Seuls nous parle l'île silencieuse⋯
Pendant ce temps-là
Trop de choses ont disparu dans ce monde,
Moi, je ne désire qu'enlacer la nature, la nuit
Et la si précieuse amitié.

49. 冬日神山部落

冬日大武山的寧靜裡

有神秘清昂的魔力：

柔和的光澤與雀榕樹的斑斕，

院牆小貓慵懶的哈欠聲；

霧嬝嬝的岩板巷，

環繞部落孤遺的地……

有時一隻五色鳥飛起，

宛若預告幸福的閃現，

又像是萬物靜止的終點。

我在魯凱族孩童身上

找回生命中不悔的歡愉。

—刊臺灣《秋水》詩刊，第 162 期，2015.01，
頁 26。

49. Une journée d'hiver sur le mont Wutai Tribe

Lors de cette journée d'hiver paisible dans la montagne Dawu,

Je ressens tout à l'entour une mystérieuse puissance magique:

Une lumière douce, les feuilles magnifiques des banyans à moineaux,

Un petit chat qui bâille près du mur de la cour,

La voie brumeuse recouverte de dalles de pierre,

Des champs déserts qui entourent Wutai Tribe···

Parfois, un oiseau coloré vole haut dans le ciel,

Comme pour prédire le bonheur soudain

Ou le point final où toute chose vient reposer.

Des enfants de la tribu Rukai

J'ai appris la joie d'une vie sans regret.

50. 恬靜

濱海公園旁海灣澹澹，

漁舟猶有奮力駛去的波紋，

我迷惑地望著遠方，

竟如此幸福，恬靜而溫暖！

瞧那橄欖青的、迷濛的

藍，還有浪花乍現──隨之喝采

特別是泊在岸沿的

雀鳥像神仙般

──接力地喧響，用喜悅替後山上彩。

－刊《臺灣時報》，臺灣文學版，2015.3.1

50. Sérénité

Dans la baie du parc de Binhai où l'eau ondule paisiblement,

Les bateaux de pêche glissent sur les ondes élégantes,

Je regarde perplexe au loin

Et me sens brusquement envahie de bonheur, de calme et de chaleur.

Regarde cette couleur olive, ce bleu brumeux

Et l'apparition soudaine des vagues!

Écoute la clameur qui suit

Surtout les oiseaux féeriques près du rivage

Qui gazouillent et ajoutent une nuance de joie

À la montagne en arrière plan.

51.午　夜

隨著躍起的繁星我銜起樹濤聲
久久佇立，以雲遮棚
那曾經飛翔之夢
忽湧到心頭
在柔風中飄動
但我不能劃破這靜謐
在幽思綿綿中
生命已無顓求，我是醒著的

－臺灣《新原人》2010.夏季號，第 70 期

52. 流星雨

你是一把散滿霜風的
北望的弓，
那颼颼的箭
射下
簾外泣零的雪

－台灣《創世紀》詩雜誌，第 162 期，2010.03
　春季刊
－美國《poems of the world》《世界的詩》，
　2010 冬季號

51. Minuit

En compagnie des étoiles montantes, je cueille les flots de la forêt
Restant debout longtemps dans l'abri qui devient sombre.
Le rêve de l'envol
Pénètre soudain mon cœur
Qui vogue dans la brise.
Pourtant, je ne peux déchirer le silence
De la méditation infinie –
Ma vie ne désire rien, et je suis éveillée.

52. Pluie de météorites

Vous êtes un arc recouvert de givre
Pointant vers le nord,
Une flèche qui siffle
Chasse
La neige qui sanglote
Au-delà des rideaux.

53. 生命的樹葉

它飛上簷前了
在風中嬉遊
仿若小小的藍蝶
穿過神祠
藏在水花裡面

我是只灰雀
任遊黑色的田野
大地給予了我自由
總得繼續飛上
落霞的雲天

－刊登臺灣《新地文學》季刊，第 18 期，
　2011.12 冬季號，頁 55。

53. La Feuille de la vie

Elle vole face à l'avant-toit

Jouant dans le vent

Comme si elle était un petit papillon bleu

Qui traverse le sanctuaire

Caché parmi les gouttes.

Je suis un moineau gris

Qui volette au-dessus des champs noirs,

La terre m'offre la liberté,

Aussi continué-je à monter en flèche

Vers les nuages roses dans le soleil couchant.

54. 冬 日

臘冬，白雨霏霏
我走出長巷，
風，藏在桉樹林裡
神秘而狂莽
黑色枝椏上的新葉
正注視著我
像個奇幻的修士。
我偷眼望去，才片刻
已不見雨痕；
而熟悉的咖啡店前
昏黃的燈光似寂寞的小孩。

── 刊臺灣《新地文學》季刊，第 22 期，
2012.12

54. Jours d'hiver

C'est l'hiver, une pluie blanche tombe, drue et pressée,

Je quitte la longue allée.

Le vent, caché parmi les eucalyptus,

Reste mystérieux et sauvage.

Les jeunes feuilles des branches noires

Me regardent

Comme un moine bizarre.

Je jette un coup d'œil, juste un moment –

La trace de la pluie a disparu.

Pourtant, devant le café familier,

La lumière diffuse ressemble à un enfant solitaire.

55. 無言的讚美

我和西天
追趕不上的雲朵
踏上這一片夢土

薩摩亞的藍湖初醒
雄奇而神秘
撲眼而來

山是以沉默　露出
蘋果也似的
笑容

—臺灣《笠》詩刊，第 287 期，2012.02，
頁 150。

55. Louange silencieuse

Accompagnée des nuages du ciel de l'ouest

Que je ne peux attraper,

Je mets le pied sur cette terre de rêve.

Le lac bleu de Samoa qui vient de se réveiller

Se précipite, imposant et mystérieux,

À ma rencontre.

Les montagnes se dressent en silence

Exhibant le sourire

D'une pomme.

56. 看灰面鵟鷹消逝

一群寒鷹
從<u>滿州鄉</u>高空
點綴著斜陽
當晚風纏捲
丘陵地上，這夜棲者
有人驚歎
有人眈眈逐逐
那衛星發報器也振振偵聽
腳環飛去的方向

夜來了
我立在岸上，像一塊石
看著牠們逐漸消逝……
遠從西伯利亞到東北
路經日本到琉球
還有臺灣、菲律賓到南洋
聽任蟲鳴絮說
一波波潮流和遠征的故事
聽任海面無言無語
用沙貝採擷你的蒼然

—— 刊臺灣《創世紀》詩雜誌，2012.09
夏季號

56. L'extinction *des* busards
à face grise

Un vol de faucons froids vient
Du ciel de Mandchourie
Parsemant les rayons du soleil couchant.
Pendant que le vent du soir s'enroule autour
Des terres vallonnées,
Quelqu'un des habitants de la nuit soupire
Alors qu'un autre lance un regard furieux et se met en chasse.
Un satellite envoie des signaux d'interception
En direction des anneaux attachés à leurs serres.

La nuit vient,
Je me tiens sur le rivage, telle un rocher
Regardant leur disparition progressive ...
De la lointaine Sibérie vers le Nord-Est,
Et, à partir de Taiwan et des Philippines,
Se dirigeant vers les mers du Sud.

Restée seule avec le bruissement des insectes,
Les flux des marées et les histoires des navigateurs,
Restée seule avec le silence de la mer,
Vous ramassez les couleurs de l'automne avec un coquillage.

57. 夏之吟

客自光影中來，可曾見某個驛站

有海濤回音，唯抒出了

這一季沉思中的

牧笛歡響 ——

好似一瞬間

天空失去了體重

被空氣托舉著

啊灼人的夜，青禾的吻落在小羊兒夢上

—— 臺灣《海星》詩刊，第 5 期，2012.09
秋季號

57. Chansons d'été

En venant de la lumière et des ombres

Avez-vous vu l'auberge ?

Dans les échos des vagues

Résonnent les sons joyeux des chalumeaux

Restés silencieux toute une saison.

Il semble que soudain

Le ciel ait perdu toute pesanteur

Et ait été soulevé par l'air.

Ah, nuit torride,

Les baisers des récoltes vertes tombent

Sur les rêves d'un petit agneau.

58. 海 頌

穿過雲霧

我看見佛光在金頂

在高樓、在海面

每遇

七零八碎的破瓶兒

便把自己螺貝的耳殼

高懸半空

傾聽聲聲嗚咽

－臺灣《海星》詩刊，第 5 期，2012.09
秋季號

－收錄譚五昌教授編「國際漢語詩歌」，
2013.11，頁186，北京，線裝書局出版。

58. Ode à la mer

]À travers les nuages,

Je vois la lumière de Bouddha au sommet doré

D'un haut bâtiment comme sur la surface de l'océan.

Et chaque fois que je rencontre

Des bouteilles cassées et des éclats de verre,

Je tends mes oreilles en forme de coquillage spiralé

Dans l'air

Pour écouter les sons des sanglots.

59. 夕陽，驀地沉落了

夕陽，驀地沉落了
在魚鱗瓦上
在老厝的茶園旁
一片灰雲
躲入我衫袖

時常跟著我
一步步奔躍向前的
小河
加快了步子
臨近新丘

就這樣
從河而來
翻飛的記憶
恰似風鈴花開
雖然披紅那堪早落

── 2012.5.10 作
── 臺灣《人間福報》副刊刊登圖文，
2012.06.05

59. Le soleil couchant sombre soudain

Le soleil couchant fond soudain

Sur les tuiles écaillées

Près du vieux jardin de thé.

Un nuage gris

Se cache dans mes manches.

Sautant et bondissant,

Un ruisseau me suit tout ce temps

Et accélère brusquement sa course

À l'approche d' un nouveau monticule.

Ainsi

Les souvenirs venus

De la rivière

Sont comme les campanules en fleurs －

Toujours colorées de rouge,

Elles ne peuvent supporter l'idée

De se faner prématurément.

60. 魯花樹

這裡是冬天
巷內的魯花樹下
　一尊木刻神像
展顏於金晃晃的葉縫間
那闇影，多麼安靜，使我入睡
鮮麗的漿果
　由綠　而黃　而紅
織就了無數個童年
　而我視線之下
從未感到如此純淨
每當風神前來糾纏
　枝上歌雀齊集鳴飛
它便伸長脖頸
將往來的面孔、昆蟲或遠自
祖靈的呼喚，都一一收藏

── 香港《橄欖葉》詩報，第 3 期，2012.06

60. *Scolopia*

Ici, c'est l'hiver.

Dans l'allée, sous le Scolopia,

La statue d'un dieu taillée dans le bois

Brille d'une lumière dorée parmi les feuilles –

L'ombre calme m'incite au sommeil.

Ses baies fraîches et plaisantes,

Vertes, jaunes et rouges,

Réveillent en moi D'innombrables rêves d'enfance,

Il n'a jamais paru si pur

À mes yeux.

Chaque fois que le dieu du vent vient l'enlacer,

Les oiseaux chanteurs se rassemblent

Pour gazouiller sur ses branches.

Alors, il étire son cou

Et met tous les visages, tous les insectes

Et   l'appel lointain des ancêtres dans son sac.

61.玉山，我的母親

我沿著僻靜的石子路漫走

與你進行零距離親昵

即使大地沉睡如嬰

心中的力量讓我奮勇邁往—

一切妄念拋下

啊，金色的原野，坦露的胸膛

似母親溫柔深過海洋

多想將你緊貼我心，恒久激盪

—— 臺灣《乾坤》詩刊，第 63 期，2012.07
秋季號

61. Le mont Yushan, ma Mère

Je marche le long de la route tranquille recouverte de gravier,

Près de toi, à une distance égale à zéro.

Même si la terre dort comme un bébé,

La puissance de mon cœur me donne du courage⋯

Je me débarrasse de toutes mes pensées négatives!

Ah, les champs d'or, la poitrine nue

Comme la tendresse maternelleplus profonde que la mer !

Ah, à quel point je désire te rapprocher de mon cœur

Pour un émoi pérenne!

62. 憶　夢

哪裡去尋找
一種聲音
像枝葉間接力的蟬
在廣場前
新穀還有漸次消失的
田，老農撩起褲管
種菜插秧

啊小小的火窗
燃燒著希望
在溝岸旁
抓魚、游泳、釣蛙
油菜花和小雲雀嬉遊
街燈黯淡而溫暖

現在我知道
無論什麼季節
有一種聲音
像只蟹，眼裡還沾著細沙
就迫不及待往岸上爬
它牽引著我，在清蔭的夜晚

—臺灣 真理大學《臺灣文學評論》，第
12 卷第 3 期，2012.7.15

62. Réminiscence d'un rêve

Où trouver
Une voix
Comme celle des cigales quand elles chantent parmi les feuilles
Sur la place.
La nouvelle récolte, la disparition progressive
Des champs, le vieux fermier a relevé ses jambes de pantalon
Pour cultiver des légumes et repiquer le riz.

Ah, la petite fenêtre d'incendie
Avec l'espoir qui y brûle
Près du fossé!
On pêche, on se baigne, on attrape des grenouilles,
Chou-fleur et petites alouettes jouent,
La lumière des réverbères est douce, mais chaleureuse.

À présent je sais que
Peu importe la saison,
Il y a toujours une voix qui
Comme un crabe aux yeux pleins de sable
Monte à la hâte sur la rive –
Elle m'attire dans une nuit fraîche et ombragée.

63.森林深處

熱霧過後
老戰士依然跋涉回來
空氣中，有巴魯果氣味
一棵小肉桂樹
留下了抓痕
這定是懶熊的傑作
幾位族人都這麼說
而祖靈們也正默默思索
彷彿花豹俯瞰著自己領土
看到的是動物越來越少的死寂或
憂慮這僅存的部落

這乾旱的尖峰期
樹林卻開花了
蝴蝶離開了水窪，翩翩的薄翼閃爍晶亮
多麼輕靈，充滿夢幻
整個林子像彩虹般
它標誌，一個哲人的形象
就在今夜
為了土地變得繽紛而在那裡咿呀作響
為了月夜慢慢地織好了羅網
讓拂不掉的痛苦記憶
讓餵奶的母親─甦醒的大地
用呼吸，從我這兒帶走莫名的憂傷

升起吧，醺醉的太陽

──臺灣 真理大學《臺灣文學評論》，第
12 卷第 3 期，2012.7.15

63. Profond dans la forêt

Tout enveloppé de brume chaude,
Le vieux soldat revient en traînant les pieds.
Dans l'air, il y a une odeur de fruits Baruch.
Sur un petit arbre de cannelle,
On trouve des griffures
Qui, selon les membres du clan,
Sont l'œuvre d'un ours paresseux.
Les âmes des ancêtres veillent, elles aussi,
Comme un léopard qui a l'œil sur son territoire.
Dans un silence de mort, les animaux devenus peu nombreux,
Prennent soin des bêtes subsistantes de la tribu.

Au plus haut de la sécheresse,
Les arbres sont en fleurs.
Les papillons s'éloignent des flaques d'eau,
Leurs ailes brillantes resplendissent.
Agités, pleins de fantaisie,
Les bois entiers sont pareils à un arc-en-ciel
Qui, ce soir, symbolise l'image d'un philosophe
Pour la terre fertile qui se craquelle,
Pour le clair de lune qui tisse un filet.
Débarrassons-nous des souvenirs persistants et douloureux,
Laissons la terre réveillée, mère nourricière,
Chasser loin, en soufflant, sa douleur sans nom.

Lève-toi, soleil ivre!

64. 追悼 —— 陳千武前輩

我願是只灰喜鵲，如果你是流浪的鞋
或許，就能聽見花瓣旋轉入林
雨滴落在碑前
昆蟲低鳴猶響

我願是只大藍鯨，如果你是海上的月
或許，在黑夜裡，在斑斕間
迎著微風如遊如飛
每當你低著頭像慈眉老人一樣審視我

—— 臺灣《笠》詩刊，第 290 期，2012.08

64. À la mémoire du poète Chen Qianwu

Je voudrais être une pie grise

Si vous étiez une paire de chaussures errantes,

Alors je pourrais entendre la musique des pétales tournoyant dans les
 bois,

Celle des gouttes de pluie qui tombent sur la pierre tombale,

Le chant des insectes.

Je voudrais être une baleine bleue

Si vous étiez la lune au-dessus de la mer

Lors d'une nuit noire, parmi les paysages magnifiques,

Volant ou nageant dans la brise

Sous votre regard d'aimable vieillard.

65. 山居歲月

一聲磬中洗騷魂，

　　幾點霧雨迢曉月；

杏林徑裡有孤竹，

　　晚課聲中看鳥飛。

—— 2011.12.20
—— 美國《新大陸》詩刊，第 131 期，
2012.08

65. Jours dans les montagnes

Au son de la pierre carillon, je suis entrée en méditation.

Dans la brume et sous la bruine, je regardais la lune aurorale,

Un bambou solitaire se dressait au milieu des abricotiers,

À l'heure des vêpres, mon cœur suivait les oiseaux qui volent.

66.永懷鐘鼎文老師

如松影般縹緲
你的靈魂
立在深澗上
健步登天庭
雖說草聲默默
虹彩寂寂
而你溫文的眼神
如雨露，如晨星
迎接無限的陽光
從未止盡

—— 2012.8.17 同悼〈鐘老師 2012.8.12 逝
　　世於臺北榮民醫院，享年百歲〉
—— 臺灣《人間福報》副刊刊登圖文，
　　2012.9.4

攝影於 2009.6.19 王璞新書發表會
—— 臺灣「國家圖書館」會議廳

66. À la mémoire du poète Zhong Dingwen

Aussi éthérée que l'ombre d'un pin,

Votre âme

Se tient au-dessus du ravin

Et marche à vigoureuses enjambées vers le ciel.

Bien que l'herbe soit silencieuse

Sous l'arc-en-ciel solitaire,

Vos yeux chaleureux

Comme la pluie, la rosée et l'étoile du matin

Saluent **sans fin**

La lumière illimitée du soleil.

67. 拂曉時刻

我們遇到迷霧
雖說還是冬季
湖塘微吐水氣
睫毛上也沾著露珠

細談中
一隻鷺在鏡頭前踟躕
這濕地森林
悄然褪色
萬物彷彿都在睡中

哪裡是野生天堂
如何飛離憂悒的白晝
我們啞然以對
只有小河隨心所願貌似輕鬆

—— 刊臺灣《海星》詩刊，第 6 期，2012.12
冬季號

67. Au point du jour

Nous nous sommes retrouvés dans un brouillard dense
Bien que ce fût encore l'hiver.
L'étang exhalait doucement sa vapeur
Et des gouttes de rosée pendaient à nos cils.

Lors de nos bavardages oiseux,
Une aigrette s'agitait devant l'objectif de la caméra.
La forêt dans les zones humides
S'évanouissait, tranquille.
Tout semblait endormi.

Où est le paradis de la nature sauvage,
Comment s'envoler loin de la chagrine lueur du jour?
Nous restions sans voix,
Seul le ruisseau semblait prendre cela à la légère,
Glougloutant sans se presser.

68.雨，落在愛河的冬夜

雨，落在愛河的冬夜
數艘白色小船上
在這多雨的港都，彩燈覆蔭下
獨自發送著溫顏

剎時，母親之河
廣大而平實
在那兒牽著勞動者的手
像從前，端視著我

啊，雨，落在愛河的冬夜
一隻夜鷺低微地呻吟
在這昏黃的岸畔，群山靜聆中
何處安置我僅存的夢？

哭吧，我以感動之淚
接受雨，和恩典
聽吧，時間的小馬上
我是永恆的騎士，覓尋黎明的歌者

是的，收起遊蕩的翅膀
那生命的薔薇早已關上了門
不再憂鬱地望著我，只有躲在冷黑中的風
任遊子潤濕了瞳孔

—— 刊臺灣《創世紀》詩雜誌，2012.12
冬季號，第 173 期。

68. Pluie sur la rivière Aihe par une nuit d'hiver

La pluie tombe au-dessus de la rivière Aihe par une nuit d'hiver
Et frappe quelques petits bateaux blancs.
En cette saison d'averse, la cité portuaire
Plonge dans les faisceaux des lumières colorées
Qui diffusent leur douce chaleur rayonnante.

Soudain, la rivière mère,
Grande et vraie,
Main dans la main avec les ouvriers
Me regarde comme toujours.

Ah, la pluie tombe sur la rivière Aihe par une nuit d'hiver,
Un héron nocturne gémit dans le ciel,
Surplombant la rive sombre, les montagnes sont à l'écoute,
Où placer le peu de rêve qui me reste?

Que je verse mes larmes remplies d'émotion,
Que je me livre à la pluie et à la grâce.
Que j'écoute le poney du temps –
Je suis l' éternel chevalier, le ménestrel de l'aube.

Oui, que je couvre de dessins mes ailes vagabondes,
La rose de la vie m'a depuis longtemps fermé sa porte,
Voici des lustres qu'elle ne me regarde plus de ses yeux tristes,
Seul le vent caché dans le froid obscur
Laisse l'errant mouiller ses pupilles.

69.秋城夜雨 ── 悼商禽

當秋雨歇在
港都夜的荒漠前
白芒花開滿山溪
行吟的雲也被擱淺
你
似一束虹光　沖向
宇宙深處
托起墜落的星辰

天使的歌音因而更嘹響

── 刊高雄市《新文壇》季刊，第 21 期，
2011.01 春季號

69. Pluie d'une nuit d'automne
À la mémoire de Shang Qin

Lorsque la pluie d'automne se repose devant

La solitude du port, la nuit,

Les limnanthes sont en pleine floraison le long du ruisseau,

Les nuages chantants sont, eux aussi, échoués sur le rivage.

Toi,

Telle un bouquet d'arcs-en-ciel, tu te rues

Vers les profondeurs de l'univers,

Tu raccroches au ciel les étoiles filantes

Et fais chanter les anges

Encore plus fort.

70.昨夜下了一場雨

你坐在開滿艾菊的岸邊
孤伶伶地佇候
也許你未曾注意
在你焦慮的目光裡，我已悄悄成長
當春天來臨
我就是那朵隱藏在飛燕草款冬裡的花
聽你神秘的詩思
在我耳畔輕聲細語

—— 刊高雄市《新文壇》季刊，第 21 期，
2011.01 春季號

70. Il a plu la nuit dernière

Tu étais assis seul sur la berge recouverte de tanaisie

En train d'attendre,

Peut-être n'avais-tu pas remarqué

Que je poussais tranquillement dans tes yeux anxieux.

Quand vient le printemps,

Je deviens la tendre fleur cachée parmi les delphiniums

Qui écoute les mystérieuses pensées poétiques

Que tu me chuchotes à l'oreille.

71. 回到過去

我依稀聽到
古老
荒涼的
珊瑚群
在沿海盡端
發出呼喊
那裡是哭泣的
海百合和三葉蟲
各種小生物的故鄉

一瞬間
這世界
彷彿變了樣
在空中
在我不經意的回眸裡
那浮游的
食物鏈
因饑餓而倒下
就像失神的骨牌
對人類的嘩啦提醒

─刊臺灣《海星》詩刊，第 2 期，2011.12
冬季號，頁 86。

71. Retour vers le passé

J'entends indistinctement pleurer
Les anciens
Coraux sauvages
Au bout de la plage.
Ils sont la contrée natale des lamentations
Des lys de mer, des trilobites
Et autres menues créatures.

Soudain,
Ce monde
Semble avoir changé.
Dans l'air
Et dans les regards inconscients
Que je jette en arrière,
Cette flottante
Chaîne alimentaire
S'est effondrée à cause de la faim
Comme des dominos vernis
Évoquant des êtres humains
Qui poussent des hauts cris.

72. 夏至清晨

哼著山歌的稻花上
坐著一隻介蟲殼兒，戲水
飛空一影子拖曳著影子
四面屏風
從跟前遛過

我擺脫了山后陰影
像綠光裡的羊
把腳步放慢
一條彎路連接無盡
水裡的雲追趕著月亮

── 刊臺灣《海星》詩刊，第 5 期，2012.09
秋季號

72. *Par un matin d'été*

Au sommet d'une fleur de riz,

Bourdonnant des chants de la montagne,

Un cypris joue avec l'eau

En glissant du ciel···

Des ombres traînent d'autres ombres,

Le vent souffle autour de moi.

Je me suis débarrassé de l'ombre de la montagne

Et, comme une brebis dans la lumière verte,

Je marche en ralentissant mon pas.

Une route sinueuse mène vers l'éternité,

Dans l'eau, des nuages poursuivent la lune.

73. 在靜謐花香的路上

一隻鷺，振翅了
在苗田
旋舞如縷煙

眾山動容
而桐顏沉默
它們慢條斯理地
望我

剎時
鐵道的叫賣聲
忽近忽遠

在靜謐花香的路上
一根稻草銜來一個春天
讓理念瞬間倏閃
相思成三月雪

－刊臺灣《海星》詩刊，第 3 期，2012.03
春季號

73. Sur la route tranquille et parfumée

Une aigrette bat des ailes
Au-dessus de la rizière
Dansant comme une traînée de fumée.

Les montagnes sont émues,
Les arbres, d'habitude bruyants,
Restent silencieux –
Ils jettent sur moi
Un calme regard.

Soudain
Des cris de colporteurs venus de lavoie ferrée
S'approchent, puis s'éloignent.

Sur la route tranquille aux fleurs parfumées,
Un brin de paille engendre le printemps.
Laisse les idées jaillir
Et les désirs se changer en neige de mars.

74. 詠車城

將一路上迎面而過的防風林留在身後

我遠離大都會

以無數個形象把你幻想

在尋找飛鷹的孤途中

我獨坐黃昏

那落山風

又在隱隱作痛

箏曲般

揚一縷忠貞的清昂

－刊臺灣《新地文學》季刊，第 22 期，
2012.12

74. Chanson de Tchétchénie

Longeant la forêt coupe-vent,

J'ai laissé la ville derrière moi.

Pour t'admirer changé en d'innombrables images,

Dans mon voyage solitaire à la recherche des aigles,

Je me suis assise à la tombée de la nuit.

Le vent chaud et sec

Me fait de nouveau mal,

Alors qu'une mélodie de cithares

Engendre en moi un fétu d'esprit de loyauté.

75. 歌飛阿里山森林

我穿過白髮的
阿里山林鐵
去尋覓童年的天真

這山泉
是個愛唱歌的小孩
音色細而堅韌
神木旁　還藏有
遊客們笑聲

當火車汽笛吶喊出
嘹亮的清音
風的裙步跟著踏響了冬林
土地的記憶
也化成一片片寧靜

我把縷縷陽光剪下
鐫刻在櫻樹上
它竟輕輕地
輕輕地
挽住了夕陽的金鬍子

啊，還有那雲海
從何時
已網住了我每一立方的夢境

　－2012.8.9 作　左營
　－刊登臺灣《海星》詩刊，第 8 期，2013 年夏季號--收錄譚五昌教
　　授編「國際漢語詩歌」，2013.11，頁 186，北京，線裝書局出版。
　－民視新聞 2016.12.24 晚上六時【飛閱文學地景】節目，首播。

75. Chansons survolant la forêt de la Montagne Ali

Contemplant les cheveux blancs
De la forêt de la Montagne Ali,
Je recherche mon innocente enfance.

La source jaillie des cimes
Est un garçon qui aime chanter,
Sa voix est très belle et plaisante,
Derrière l'Arbre Divin
On entend le rire des touristes.

Quand le train siffle
Haut et clair,
La jupe du vent volète
Poursuivant les échos dans la forêt hivernale.
La mémoire de la terre
Fond en petits morceaux de tranquillité.

Je découpe la lumière du soleil en minces bandeaux
Et les accroche aux cerisiers,
À ma surprise,
Ils tirent doucement
Sur la barbe d'or du soleil couchant.

Oh, alors cette mer de nuages
A
Enveloppé chaque parcelle de mon rêve.

76.野地

大清早
從草原上出發
鹿從林裡來
狐狸在湖邊遊蕩
水面擠滿了青蛙
那是白鷺在冰上打滑
秧雞和天鵝每天兩次
帶著青魚回家

此刻
濕地漸漸醒來
石楠和荊豆
是否還在水沼旁
千湖之陸
仍繼續保持著秘密
而有時，一個槍火
劃破靜寂一

76. Terres en friche

Tôt le matin,

Avançant sur la prairie à l'orée de la forêt,

Les chevreuils sortent des bois,

Les renards errent près du lac,

Les grenouilles font foule à la surface de l'eau,

Les aigrettes glissent sur des surfaces gelées,

Les râles des genêts et les cygnes

Rentrent deux fois par jour chez eux

Avec des harengs.

À ce moment,

Les espaces humides se réveillent peu à peu,

Les balais de bouleaux de la lande et les haricots

Sont toujours là, près de la terre marécageuse

Aux mille lacs

Qui gardent encore leurs secrets.

Parfois, on entend un coup de feu

Qui brise le silence···

獵季已開始
所有的動物都豎耳驚悸
在暈紅的碎石路上
肥沃的平地
映出發白的雲
和吉普車，音樂，搖滾般
向太陽方向駛去
下谷，上坡

只有我
一個孤獨的旅客
正耐心等待巴士啓動
別了，水塘
別了，野地和狗兒
在蒙著微光的蜻蜓翅芽上
一群鶴正準備遷徙遠去
牠們的身影也有絲絲落寞

　　　　　－2012.9.1 為保育野地生物有感而作
　　　　　－刊登臺灣《青年日報》副刊，2013.03.09

La saison de la chasse a commencé,

Tous les animaux sont sur le qui-vive

Le long de la route rouge défoncée.

La plaine fertile

Reflète les nuages pâles.

Des jeeps et de la musique se balancent

Et courent vers le soleil,

Descendent la vallée et remontent la pente.

Et il y a moi,

Voyageuse solitaire

Qui attend patiemment le bus.

Adieu, étang,

Adieu, désert et chiens.

Au-dessus des ailes scintillantes des libellules,

Un groupe de grues se prépare à migrer,

Leurs silhouettes, elles aussi, semblent solitaires.

77. 墨菊

你是多年前

從菊譜裡　飛出的

草龍

時間的長河中　笑容依是

如此嫻靜

而我

只是路過時　不慎回首的

行者　只想將你

匯入飄遊的夢中

－刊臺灣《笠》詩刊，第 294 期，2013.04

77. Chrysanthème noir

Vous êtes le dragon d'herbe

Qui s'est envolé des chrysanthèmes

Il y a bien des années

Suivant le long fleuve du temps, calme

Et toujours souriant.

Mais moi,

Une simple passante,

Je jette par hasard un coup d'œil sur les années passées,

Et veux tout simplement te retenir

Dans les filets de mes rêves errants.

78. 重生的喜悅

這清晨
這周遭和光的力
這窗外的寧靜這初綻的花兒
我歡喜，我欲將重生。

啊，生命！ 啊，淚水！
彷若露珠泛著微光
心中洋溢希望
奔流著我斑斕詩想
我展翼，我想吟唱。

拿起筆 ——
只能寫出
感謝這場相會 ——
是你賜給我最慷慨的恩惠！
讓一切變得恬逸歡愉！

－刊臺灣《人間福報》副刊，2013.7.9.

78. La joie de renaître

Ce matin,

La profusion de la lumière environnante,

Cette sérénité de l'autre côté de la fenêtre,

Les fleurs nouvellement écloses,

Me rendent heureuse, et je veux renaître.

Ô ma vie ! Ô mes larmes

Pareilles à des gouttes de rosée scintillantes!

Avec mon cœur plein d'espoir

Et mes pensées débordant de poésies magnifiques,

Je déplie mes ailes, et veux chanter.

Je ressaisis ma plume···

Je ne peux écrire rien d'autre

Que merci pour cette rencontre!

Tu m'as fait le plus généreux des dons –

Que tout devienne sérénité et joie!

79. 雨落在故鄉的泥土上

一、

雨落在故鄉的泥土上
你看見了嗎
沒有人可遺忘
奧斯威辛集中營
終於，那些殺人魔被聖火吞噬
終於，那不屈的靈魂
得以解脫

告訴我，親愛的
為什麼我的手心裡
還殘存著你的溫柔
為什麼風像個無家可歸的老婦
徘徊在這廣場
而你
已遺忘了槍尖上的哀嚎

二、

雨落在故鄉的泥土上
你看見了嗎
那白色魔窟
是製造殺人病毒的工廠
他們把病毒灑向世界
在掠奪，在刑求
還無情地發出狂笑

79. RAINDROPS FALLING IN MY HOMETOWN

1.

Raindrops falling in my hometown
Do you see it?
Nobody can forget
the Auschwitz Concentration Camp
At last, those devil killers were devoured by the holy flames
At last, the unyielding spirits
　were set free
Tell me, dear
Why is your tenderness
still warming my hands
Why is the wind loitering in this Square
like a homeless old woman
And you
have already forgotten the screams at gunpoint

2.

Raindrops falling in my hometown
Do you see it?
That white den of monsters
was a factory manufacturing poisons
which they spray all over the world
looting, torturing,
　　and laughing mercilessly

啊告訴我，親愛的
為什麼我的胸口
會有撕裂般的痛
為什麼雨像個情人
徘徊在這原野裡
而你
已沉睡在石碑下

三、
雨落在故鄉的泥土上
你看見了嗎
沒有人可遺忘
紀念碑裡的故事
當我閉上眼
就能朗讀你的笑容
就像五千年前的太陽
那麼燦亮

啊告訴我，親愛的
為什麼我的喉管裡
流淌著你的淚水
為什麼雨像個浪子
狂飆在這林道
而你
已然像個雕像　不再憂愁

－2015.5.7
－刊臺灣《鹽分地帶文學》第 59 期，
　2015.8.31，頁 164-165.

O please tell me, dear
Why is there such a tearing pain
in my chest
Why is the rain lingering about the field
like a lover
While under the stone tablet
you are sound asleep

3.

Raindrops falling in my hometown
Do you see it?
Nobody can forget
the story of the monument
When I close my eyes
I can read your smiling face
bright as the sun
of five thousand years ago

O please tell me, dear
Why your tears are flowing
in my throat?
Why is the rain running wild like a vagabond
on this forest road
And you, no longer looking sad or worried
have become a statue

--2015.5.7（馬為義 WILLIAM MARR 博士英譯）

79. La pluie tombe sur ma ville natale

1.

La pluie tombe sur ma ville natale,
Le vois-tu?
Personne ne peut oublier
Le camp de concentration d'Auschwitz!
À la fin, les tueurs diaboliques ont été dévorés par les flammes sacrées,
À la fin, les esprits inflexibles
Ont été liberés!
Dis moi, mon ami,
Pourquoi ta tendresse
Réchauffe-t-elleencore mes mains,
Pourquoi le vent flâne-t-il sur cette place
Comme une vieille femme sans abri
Et toi,
Tu as déjà oublié les cris sous les menaces du fusil!

2.

La pluie tombe sur ma ville natale,
Le vois-tu?
Cette caverne blanche peuplée de monstres
Était une usine de poisons
Qu'ils répandaient partout dans le monde
En pillant, torturant

Et riant sans pitié?

Ô, s'il te plaît, dis-moi, mon ami,
Pourquoi la douleur déchire-t-elle
Ma poitrine?
Pourquoi la pluie s'attarde-t-elle à tomber sur les champs
Alors que sous la dalle de pierre
Tu es profondément endormi?

3.
La pluie tombe sur ma ville natale,
Le vois-tu?
Personne ne peut oublier
L'histoire de ce monument!
Quand je ferme les yeux,
Je peux distinguer ton visage souriant,
Brillant comme le soleil
D'il y a cinq mille ans!

Ô, dis-moi, mon ami,
Pourquoi tes larmes coulent-elles
Dans ma gorge ?
Pourquoi la pluie se déchaîne-t-elle comme un vagabond
Sur cette route forestière
Et toi, qui n'a plus l'air ni triste ni inquiet,
Tu es devenu une statue?

－2015.5.7
－臺灣《秋水》詩刊第 164 期，2015.08.
頁 70-71. 中英譯 （馬為義博士，
WILLIAM MARR 譯）

80. 致雙溪

夜霧彌漫小山城，
雙溪河在我眼底喧響。
風依舊蕭索，
送來一地的寒。
那叢綠中的野薑花，
彷彿來自星群，
從平林橋下的親水公園
飛出無數白蝶，
飛向水田
飛向和悅清澈的鏡面。
忽地，一隻孤鷺飛進我的愁緒。
而明天
陽光將仍在花間跳舞，
這鄉景的光華，
寂靜，如秋。

——刊臺灣《乾坤》詩刊第 67 期，2013.07
秋季號

80. Visite à Double Brook

Le brouillard nocturne enveloppe la petite ville de montagne,

Devant moi s'étale le bruyant Double Brook.

Le vent, toujours morne et désolé,

Répand le froid sur le sol.

Le gingembre sauvage brille au milieu de la verdure

Comme si sa fleur venait des étoiles du ciel.

Du Park de Qinshui sous le pont Pinglin

Surgissent d' innombrables papillons blancs

Qui volent jusqu'aux rizières, jusqu'à leur beau et harmonieux miroir.

Soudain, le vol d'un héron solitaire envahit ma mélancolie.

Mais demain,

Les rayons du soleil danseront encore parmi les fleurs.

On verra de nouveau le brillant spectacle de la ville

Silencieuse comme l'automne.

81. 海　影

第一次被你感動
我很難説清
在你燦爛的光痕
我以為世上並無如此美好的真情
是風的呼喚
讓我們因緣際會
想讓你認出了我
就忘了國與國的距離
有什麼差別

當我喜愛這一切——
棕櫚樹和沙灘、詩集
音樂
啊，島嶼一望無際
如何能留住你的身影
月亮啊，請不要再多説
我只信眼前所聞
一次相遇肯定不夠
在灰藍、灰藍的星群上
明天，請為我們打開希望之門

註：作者於 2013 年十月下旬參訪馬來西亞第 33 屆世詩會，
　　看到各國國旗並列於海面上，蘇丹王子及州長、市長、
　　諾貝爾獎得主 Dr.kahan 等名人前來祝詞，有感而文。
　　--刊臺灣《人間福報》副刊，2013.11.18

81. L'ombre de la mer

Il m'est difficile à dire
Quand pour la première fois Tu as ému mon cœur.
Éblouie par ta brillante lumière,
Je ne croyais pas
Qu'un amour aussi vrai pouvait exister dans ce monde.
C'est l'appel du vent
Qui nous a fait nous rencontrer par hasard ou par chance,
Qui t'a permis de me reconnaître
Et d'oublier la distance et les différences
Entre nos nations.

Lorsque j'aime tous ces palmiers,
Ces plages et la musique de la poésie,
L'île repousse son horizon.
Comment retenir ta silhouette?
Ô lune, s'il te plaît, ne dis plus un mot!
Je ne crois que ce que je vois!
Une seule rencontre ne suffit pas, perdue
Dans l'immense constellation bleu gris des possibilités.
Demain, s'il te plaît, ouvre-nous la porte de l'espoir.

82. 曾　經

你輕俏得似掠過細石的
小溪，似水塘底白霧，揉縮
隨我步向籬柵探尋你的澄碧
我卻驟然顛覆了時空
熟悉你的每一次巧合

你微笑像幅半完成的畫
淨潔是你的幾筆刻劃，無羈無求
那青松的頌讚，風的吟遊：
誰能於萬籟之中盈盈閃動？每當
黃昏靠近窗口

今夜你佇立木橋
你的夢想，你的執著與徬徨
徬徨使人擔憂
惟有星星拖曳著背影，而小雨也
悄悄地貼近我的額頭

－臺灣《創世紀》詩雜誌，第 161 期，
2009.12 月冬季號

82. Il était une fois

Tu es vif et élégant comme le ruisseau qui caresse les galets,

Comme le brouillard sur l'étang,

Qui s'étend et se rétrécit.

Suis-moi jusqu'à la haie pour me montrer ta verte luminosité.

Soudain, je m'embrase

Et renverse le temps et l'espace

Pour mieux me familiariser Avec chacun de tes traits.

Ton sourire est comme une Peinture à moitié achevée

Quelques coups de pinceaux Rendent ta pureté libre et sans entraves.

Les chansons du pin et les chants du vent font scintiller les bruits

À mesure que le soir approche de la fenêtre.

Ce soir, tu es là, sur le pont de bois.

Avec ton rêve, ta persévérance et tes hésitations⋯

Tes hésitations m'inquiètent.

Seules les étoiles font vibrer ton ombre

Tandis qu'une pluie légère mouille doucement mon front.

輯二、林明理近作新詩 110 首

1.和平的使者

— to Prof. Ernesto Kahan

你的眼睛深邃如海
閃著一種天藍的自由
當世界的、戰地鐘聲又起
你穿過風雨前來
感嘆唱著歌曲
那白袍下的熱血
深入最需要的世界各角落
如同現代史懷哲

— by Dr.Lin Ming-Li
— 2016.3.13

1. A Peacemaker

－to Prof. Ernesto Kahan

Your eyes deep as the blue sea
Shiningsome kind of freedom
When for whom the bell tolls again
You come through the storm
Sighing andsinging
Blood boiling under thewhite robe
You enterevery desperate corner of the world
Likethemodern Schweitzer

-by Dr.Lin Ming-Li
-2016.3.13
William Marr Translation

　　註.2016.3.12 收到 1985 年諾貝爾和平獎得主 prof.Ernesto Kahan 的 Mail，他告訴我以西班牙語演講中，把我寫給他刊登在美國《亞特蘭大新聞》於 2016.3.4 的書評（SUGGESTION）製成投影片。我打開他的演講稿夾檔。發現裡面共有 26 張投影片，而我寫他的書評刊登於 2016.3.4 美國《亞特蘭大新聞》的掃描分別被製成投影片於第 20 及 21 張。真是備感榮幸！

　　Note.2016.3.12 receive 1985 Nobel Peace Prize winner prof.Ernesto Kahan's Mail

　　He told me in Spanish speech, I wrote to him to be published in the United States (Atlanta News) on 2016.3.4 Book Review (SUGGESTION) made slides. I opened his speech file folders. And discovered a total of 26 slides, and I wrote his book review published in the American 2016.3.4 (Atlanta News) scans were made on the first slide 20 and 21. Really honored to!

－刊美國《亞特蘭大新聞》U.S.A　Atlanta
Chinese News，2016.3.18.

2. *Don't* be sad，my friend

你注視著世界以及苦難的人們

彷彿自己也在那兒感傷落淚

了解

和平真諦的你

得灌滅

仇恨的火焰

喚醒對地球未來懵懵懂懂的人

總得有人不怕失去生命

才能拯救沉淪的靈魂

你凝視未來

站在宇宙的屋脊

發出沉重之聲

大氣之中融合著你的祈願與深情

－2016.3.27

2. *DON'T*   BE SAD

by Dr.Lin Ming-LI

Don't be sad, my friend

You look at the world and the suffering of the people

As ifyou were there tooin tears

Since you understand the true meaning of peace

You must quench the flame of hatred

And wake Up the ignorant earthlings

There must be somebodies not afraidof losing their own lives

To save the sinking souls

You stare at the future

Standing on the roof of the universe

Giving out aheavy sound of air

Carrying your wishes and affection

-WILLIAM MARR TRANSLATION
--刊臺灣《文學台灣》季刊，第 99 期，
2016.07.秋季號，頁 65.
--刊於美國《亞特蘭大新聞》，2016.4.1，
Ernesto Kahan 照片及其和平鴿圖。
http://www.atlantachinesenews.com/News/201
6/04/04-01/B_ATL_P08.pdf

3. 我的朋友

—to Athanase Vantchev de Thracy

你的過去清澈如泉
你的生命如時
每時每刻，永不枯竭
又像花朵上的朝露
戰勝了所有的恐懼與黑夜！

—2016.1.15
—刊美國《亞特蘭大新聞》，2016.12.9 及
Athanase 照片。

3. My Friend

to Athanase Vantchev de Thracy

Your life flows clear as a spring
from your past to your eternalpresent,
inexhaustible.
For me you arethe morning dew on the flowers
overcoming the trepidation of day
and the dread of night.

Mon ami

À *Athanase Vantchev de Thracy*

Votrevie coulelimpide comme une source
Qui va, inépuisable, de votre passéà votreéternel présent.
Pourmoi, vous êtesla rosée du matinsur les fleurs,
Elle qui surmonte l' agitationde la journée
Et la craintede la nuit.

Lin Ming-Li

Traduit en français par Athanase Vantchev
de Thracy
一本詩由法國著名詩人阿沙納斯翻譯成法
詩，詩人非馬 William Marr 英譯。
一英、法翻譯刊美國《亞特蘭大新聞》，
2016.12.9 及 Athanase 照片。

4. 你，深深銘刻在我的記憶之中

有一天
你終將會離我而去
再沒有任何事值得我悲痛
世上已無所希求
你，深深銘刻在我的記憶之中

也許
我不能為自己也無法為你做點什麼
撒下這把灰白粉末
從此之後
你是否重新找到另一個天地

我從來不是個敏捷的詩人
也不敢成為你的唯一知交
只在暖雨中
在黑夜
捕撈你的影子，回到我的腦海
就像期待春花回到大地的懷抱

—2015.9.27 中秋夜
—刊《美國亞特蘭大新聞》，2016.6.10 中英
　譯詩及畫作
—非馬（馬為義博士 DR.WILLIAM MARR）
　英譯，刊美國《世界的詩》，
POEMS OF THE WORLD，2016.春季號。

4. You, deeply etched in my memory

One day
You will eventually leave me
Nothing worth my grief
The world has nothing to stir my desire
You, deeply etched in my memory

Perhaps
I can not do anything for myself or you
After casting this gray powder
Can you find another world

I have never been a nimble poet
Nor do I dare to be your only confident
Only in the warm rain
At night
I dare to try to catch your shadow and put it back into my mind
Like the return of flowers to the embrace of the earth

－非馬（馬為義博士　William Marr）英譯

5. 屈原頌

一、你的詩筆

你的詩筆很輕
一滴墨便將世界舉了起來
雨聲穿越時空
滴
下
　　成一片詩海

年年端午
當思念你的人呼喊
三閭大夫，魂兮歸來
你說
每一面彩旗都是一種舞蹈
每一聲嗩吶都是一種相思

春天已經老了
你用百花的冠冕修補它
詩歌已經傾斜了

你用往昔的愛情呵護它
但雨還在下
灑在屈家村的橘樹上

你的詩筆很輕
一滴墨便讓江流激盪起來
歌聲穿越時空
穿越靈魂
　　成一片碧海

二、今夜，我在汨羅歌唱

今夜，我在汨羅歌唱
用我粗獷的語言和深情
　　你的眼神加注了
　　真實節奏
　　在風中，彷彿江水
投射出高貴的氣質

而我的歌不說你的傷心
只順著江畔奔跑
星海曉得

你的才華豐盈深厚
流浪心靈中
完成了中國不朽的辭賦

我看見歲月流逝
也聆聽出你歌裡的
沉默與堅韌
你擎起一盞燈
照亮了
人類絕世的光芒

今夜，我在汨羅歌唱
　　屈原
　　這名字迴盪著我
　　你的詩園是我四季的庇護所
　　而留給我們的詩句
如迎向曙光的百合

－2016.4.7
－刊臺灣《秋水》詩刊，第 169 期，2016.10.
　頁 59.

6. 母親的微笑

比一切更美的是您病癒之際
白色天空，小花草，竹籬笆
以及您髮間的淡雲朵
這些影像始終明亮而清晰
我在風聲與塵土中
輕駕著星星
朝向連串島礁
朝向對岸山河
您在風中笑了
黃昏把我們帶向極遠處

喔，母親
我最親愛的
因您，我獲得我要求的真理與愛
您的手心，宛如冬陽
投射出幸福的花田
而蹣跚的步履
依舊在我血液中湧動
往日，您是我的驕傲
如今，我闊步向前
把盼望已久的您的微笑迎進門來

－2016.9.26 寫於八十歲的母親抗癌一年，化療手
　術十二次後奇蹟復原，坐車到台東與我小住幾日
　的心情。
－刊馬祖縣《馬祖日報》鄉土文學版，2016.9.28。

7. 寫給成都之歌

1.

像傳說中一隻火鳳凰
一派活力與激情的景象

誰都會想起你
一座最偉大的堅霸
啊，都江堰
當夕陽輝耀著你的身影
橫跨千年之歌
也越發甜美清亮

文殊院鐘響了
武侯祠醒了
錦里古街點亮了
天府廣場沸騰了
啊，我的城
到處傳遍了悠揚的樂聲

那是慶祝和風
親吻陣亡將士的歌謠
歌謠中川軍的凝眸
回映著星星
從龍泉到邛崍
從世界到世界

而古老的皇城
在黑夜之外
回光照了千佛和平塔
高塔也一樣
在光明裡
歌是靜肅的……

2.
像傳說中一隻火鳳凰
一派活力與激情的景象

誰都會想起你
一個最沉默的詩人
啊，杜甫
當夕陽輝耀著你的身影

橫跨千年之後
你把故里引向文明

啊，我的城
再生的鳳凰
堅如鋼鐵
亙古不變的歌音
你的羽翅是那樣舒展
如雪的詩句響徹雲霄

而我
在彼岸的土地上
觸摸你歷史的斑痕
當太陽冉冉昇起
昔日戰士影子如巨人
唱響天際，光耀神鳥之都

－2016.4.25 寫於台東
－2016 "源泉之歌" 全國詩歌大賽，林明理新
　詩〈寫給成都之歌〉獲優秀獎，中國《華西
　都市報》2016.6.16 公告於
　http://www.kaixian.tv/gd/2016/0616/568532.html

8. 白冷圳之戀

林明理畫

你，是水圳工程的驕傲
新社的母親
悠揚的山歌
那些輕拂而過的
音和雀鳥在黃昏中回轉
我便翻山越嶺
在風中
尋找你澄碧的眼眸
尋找你熾熱不落的靈魂
及守候老家鄉的靜默

你來自大甲溪，歷經風霜和

那場震變

又重新給人安慰

新社的母親啊

你灌溉了

無數旅人與遊子的心田

如星雨般動容

在群山環抱下

水聲如琴，交錯於

時間之流與月光之中

註.白冷圳是台中市一條水圳，是新社區的生命之水。
歷經集集大地震毀損後，直到 2003 年 5 月修復工
程才告終。它取水口源自大甲溪攔截水流，引水入
圳，不僅提供當地農田灌溉及水資源，同時也促進
和平區、新社區及石岡區一帶的觀光休閒產業發
展。　－2017.1.3

　－刊美國《亞特蘭大新聞》，2017.1.6，圖
文。
　－臺灣《臺灣時報》，2017.1.19，圖文。
　－此詩被民視【飛閱文學地景】錄影於
2017.03.20 台北市齊東詩舍。

9. 暮來的小溪

起初我只看到了火金姑
這兒和那兒的
飛在石徑旁
在林子裡
在我掌心
綴成仲夏雨
後來我看到了蝸牛
在花叢中找尋牠的
往日足跡。
薄霧在歸鳥身後
被溪圍繞
只有風在月岩上
乾著急。

－2013.6.1
－刊臺灣《笠》詩刊，296 期，2013.8.15
－臺灣《乾坤》詩刊，2013.秋季號。

10. 冬日湖畔的柔音

它直挺挺地佇立在低枝上，
對林中的眾鳥毫不在意，
只靜靜地聆聽小山丘呢喃，
享受著各種溫度的幸福。
人們傳說中的愛的禱語
如清風，直抵
陽光下綿延的小徑。
而我獨自閒蕩，
輕盈，欣喜———
宛若拂草的蝴蝶，
不留下任何足跡。

—2015.12.17
—刊臺灣《笠》詩刊，第 312 期，2016.04，
　非馬英譯，頁 54-55。
—美國《Poems of the world》，《世界的
　詩》季刊，非馬英譯，2015 冬季號。
—刊臺灣《秋水》詩刊，第 168 期，2016.07，
　頁 51.

10. The Soft Music on the Winter Lake Shore

Dr.Lin Ming-Li

The birdstandsupright ona low branch.

It pays noattention to other birds in the woods,

Only listens to thewhisperfromthe small hill,

Enjoying the various shades of happiness.

Thelegendary prayer of love

Comesdown like the breeze,

To the sun-drenched trail.

As I wander alone,

Light-hearted,full of joy——

The shadow of a butterfly whisks across the grass,

Without leaving anyfootprint.

（translator：William Warr）
－2015.12.17

11. 原　鄉

一、

在彎彎曲曲小路的盡頭
我在陽光下站著
像一棵樹
高聲地呼喊
我就要沒入膠河的胸膛——
東眺，沉睡的青島
西望風箏的故鄉
十月的風在街頭彷徨
山雀正歌著秋天的溫暖

當葡萄化成紅酒
我的血管裡流淌著
生命的故鄉
噢，你聽見了嗎
我就要畫出黃昏的羽毛
畫出葉兒滴翠到斑鳩成雙
畫出泥塑頑童到剪紙成花
正月的冬雪緩緩地鋪在路上
一片一片，晶亮，迷茫

二、

在彎彎曲曲小路的盡頭
我在雪中站著
像一顆星
悠悠地丈量
我就要沒入這多彩的年畫之鄉
啊，大雁
你可把我卑微的希望帶得更遠更廣
讓那江水永不停住
讓我不知置身何方

當漫漫長夜隔在兩岸
我的手心還殘存著
離別時的淒涼
噢，你聽見了嗎
我就要穿過冰霧
在蠶桑的牧野
在朝氣的海疆上
不想拂拭什麼
只想像你微笑的模樣

－2013.5.21 作於高雄・左營
－刊臺灣《新文壇》季刊，33 期，2013.10.

12. M.L To the beloved

—prof. Ernesto Kahan

Dr.Lin Mig-Li

Through the snow forest
Your image is either far or near
Fall on the water mirror
With the echo of my heart
In the gap in the universe
I am a little poet
And your song
Is the muse harp
Through the Millennium dance of the time

—2017.1.6

12. 給敬愛的人

—prof. Ernesto Kahan

穿過雪林
你的影像或遠或近
落在水鏡上
與我心的回聲之間
在宇宙的隙縫中
我是小小的詩人
而你的歌
是繆斯的豎琴
穿越千年的時光之舞

—2017.1.6
—英譯刊美國《亞特蘭大新聞》2017.1.20.

13. 墾丁冬思

與友港灣惜別後

我乘著夜之船

穿過海峽

就感覺到那沉默的沙灘，相依的手

是多麼溫暖——

如這冬日的木麻黃，等待於

光與石岸之雲的呼喚

我和妳一樣，自孩提起

就無畏於飄泊，也未放棄對完美的渴望

如今我已是半白的樺樹

任風攀緣我軀體

任枯葉散落我周圍

任思想獨落在鍵盤上

只把耳朵貼近土地的蒼茫

可我愉快於這三面環海之境

一個容易引起我們回到純真的地方

妹妹啊，妳聽，這寂靜的水域

潮聲不被俗事的繁重所打亂

世間塵埃網在天水之外

昔日的棉花田也已睡著

現在我願是披甲的武士，守候妳的陽光

－2013.12.22 作

註：墾丁位於臺灣本島最南端的恆春半
　　島，三面環海，東面太平洋，西鄰臺灣
　　海峽，南瀕巴士海峽。作者與杭州詩人
　　葦子〈張秀娟〉母子到墾丁遊後有感而
　　文。

－刊臺灣《人間福報》副刊，2014.2.18.

14. 相見居延海

我喜歡西海的暮雲
秋日的胡楊
它們的美麗與憂傷
讓千里戈壁為之動容
雪水的注入
牧者的祈禱
阿拉善的官兵在營房周圍
尋找自然的豐饒

我想橫渡黑河
看白鳥棲息，鴨浮碧波
那藍色的蒼穹
心靈所受的感動
源自一個深邃的古老的夢
哪怕路途迢迢
哪怕烈日風暴
西海，是我苦苦追尋的去處

—2015.7.8
註・居延海，位於內蒙古自治區阿拉善盟
　額濟納旗北部，漢代稱「居延澤」，後
　也稱「西海」。
—刊臺灣《臺灣時報》台灣文學版，
　2015.7.20 圖文。

15. 頌長城

春風
給長城帶來幽雅的涼意
它慢慢甦醒在暮色裡
那張輝煌的臉
撩起無數詩人的鄉愁

我夢見自己
輕輕觸及它剛毅的輪廓
如此自然
握暖了我的雙手
彷彿沉浸在莊嚴的芬芳裡

年年歲歲
它驕傲地立在沙丘之緣上
不朽的眼眸
深邃如夜空般的黑藍
無視大漠孤煙的寂寥

朝朝暮暮
它用絕世美麗的歌聲
激勵我奮勇前進
似彩虹鳥向四個方向飛去
只在夢裡才分外清晰

隨它飛吧！
飛入這長空澄碧
我在海峽和波浪間巡行
心繫北國，萬里雪飄
靈魂是一座孤獨的島嶼

—2016.3.3
—獲北京市，2016 年 "東方美" 全國詩聯
　書畫大賽「金獎」，頒獎於釣魚台賓館。
　--刊美國《亞特蘭大新聞》，2016.5.6
—刊臺灣《秋水》詩刊，第 168 期，2016.07，
　頁 51.

16. 我怎能停止爲你而歌

你說
每條巷弄都存著一種記憶
每個鄉親那麼溫暖樸真
瞧，這櫻花讓世上所有的星子
都跟我在瞬間靜默下來了
我怎能停止為你而歌

你那凝視的目光
從北方沿著黃河走來
喚醒了我的靈魂
在花的沉默面前
古老的琴弦
仍悠悠訴說著老城的舊事

而我從海上帶來
所懷的誠摯和鋪展的
夢，帶著夏日羚羊般的歡愉
我的心中，有你的驕傲

在你清美的水波裡
一切都變成了詩句

你說
我來了只是因為老城的等候
即使那山峰的水影遮住了我的視線
我也能看得見河上有船
我已遠行
在飛向一條詩河的地圖上

－2016.10.6
－刊臺灣《秋水》詩刊，第 170 期，2017.01，
頁 36。

17. 寫給鎮原的歌

1.

來自翟池的各種鳥兒
又飛向長綠壇的湖畔了
滿樹的杏花遮天蔽日
固守著不變的諾言

陽春已過，惹醉了綠柳
你的步容在暮色中旋轉
彷彿三仙女翩翩而來
親臨雞頭山吟誦

我願是座老城
在茹河響徹千年的呼喊
西風呵，我相信陽光
春天怎能遙遠

2.

你從遠方來

靜靜地。佇立於窗前
燭光照在老舊的書皮上
翻開的那頁
依舊是淡淡的憂傷
秋風在簷上搖晃
風雨樓上的琉璃瓦
雨聲很輕柔

　　這三岔黃酒多香甜
　　夢裡的詩在空中迴盪
　　熟悉的城啊
　　還有御爐前的香煙裊裊
　　把我從沉思中喚醒
也把石崆寺的泥塑神都叫醒了
而我只願伴隨這場雨
映照千頃茹河的盈盈淚光

3.
　　我好似一朵雲
在茹河岸上
在金針山嶺尋找
在梯田彎曲的步道

在土橋的山村尋找
在斑斕翻飛的杏花林
在柏山尋找
尋找一張臉色曾是美的不涸泉
而你隨風輕撫，隨風搖擺
彷彿開在樹下的忘憂草

啊，我的愛
循著你指示山丘的舊貌
大地的溫柔
已換成耀眼的高天厚土
我願與你旖旎共舞
祖先的傳承文化
仍在滋養我的血液，灌溉血管
你看，北石窟寺前綻開的花朵
是無與倫比的，而明日
我們將以語言和詩篇證實

4.
讓我做個甜夢吧
讓我看得到山水
記得住這裡的秋色

這裡的山川河流
它有著古文化的痕跡
也有獨特的地理風貌
彭陽古城，依山伴水
和風是我手心的芳香折扇

我無法遺忘
曾經看過社火隊的熱鬧
也聽過大嗩吶的滿街作響
風，古道上無垠的風
伸展翅膀
日夜飛翔
而我是秋日的最後花朵
諦聽著，故鄉的歌謠

　　　　　　－2016.12.22
　　　　　　－刊 美國《亞特蘭大新聞》），2016.12.30
　　　　　　圖文

18. 與菊城開封相會

菊城裡
我像一隻喜鵲
兜著圈子
唱歌。

時近重陽
夜裡
我從菊白堆裡撈出
　一首詩。

當殿前菊燈齊放
溫潤了老城
月傾斜，莫名的靜
撫慰著人心。

－2015.8.29
－刊臺灣《華文現代詩》，第 10 期，2016.08.
　頁 67.

19. 在初冬湖濱

聽，雪中雲雀的足音
梅朵輕嘆 兀自凋零
宛如夜行而過
急速消失的螢蟲
四野望去，儘是
空寂的淡色，只有
遠山帶著半黃
半紅的背影，引我步出了樹林

我，將粘上衣襟的湖光
還於金色的謐靜
走進夢想，且
讓過去的種種，化成
心頭的澄澈
當黎明升起 ——
我在水銀裏呼
吸，一股稻草甘甜的
清香，自空氣中凝聚

—2009.01.22 作，2017.1.9 修正原詩。
—原刊登全國中文核心期刊，山東省優秀
　期刊《時代文學》2009.2 期
—臺灣《人間福報》2009.9.4

19. On The Lake Bank In Early Winter

Listen, the voice of the lark in the snow
Plum blossoms sigh, withered lonely away
As if passing at night
swiftly vanished Firefly
Looking around, only the
Empty tinge, none but
The far off mountain with semi-yellow
Semi-red shadow , lead me step out of the woods

Me, return the ray of the lake on my shirt
To the golden quietness
Walk into the dream, and
Let the variety of the past melting
Into the clarity of the mind
When it dawns
I shall call from the quicksilver
Take in, the sweet fragrance of the straw
The faint scent, condensing from the air

（原詩由山東大學外語系吳鈞教授英譯）
（因義大利於 2017 年一月忽然下起大雪，我與義大利詩人
　Giovanni Campisi 交流詩作時，他預將此詩收編於他主編
　的《國際詩新聞》。原作已修改刪除三行詩及組距。）

20. 獻給湯顯祖之歌

風在演奏你的樂曲
那柳影沉垂靜謐
那小湖碧波的三生樓
那一段水袖流連的摺子戲
還是和往昔一樣
時光未曾衰老
而你的愛已生長成故鄉的星子
聚在牡丹亭上呢喃溫存
瞧，山茶花
在你的身旁唱起了歌
多少歲月過去了
又承載了多少悲歡離合的故事
重演這舞臺上的多少舊夢
以及那深深淺淺的離愁
多少次目光彌留在南城
你閃亮了東方的靈魂
就如雪松和大地輝耀

我好似一隻蝶兒

在秋日裡迷了路

在銀杏和紅楓林中漫舞

輕吻蘆葦旁的的燈芯草

忽兒吹來了園中桂花的芳香

忽而又送來了樹林的舞蹈

在我心中撫河靜臥成銀色

而你的身影朝霞般絢爛

一切是那麼熟悉

又那麼神奇

在波光的倒影中傲然屹立

溢滿鷗鳥的鳴啼

可我在風中

在遠方的綠野中穿行

啊，請同我乾一杯貢酒

你鮮活的碑表上

在臨川之鄉，刻著中國的莎士比亞之名

－刊美國《亞特蘭大新聞》，2017.1.13。

21. 寫給曹植之歌 （組詩）

一.

飄在冬凝橋的柳絲青青
　雨，不發一點兒聲音
閃閃爍爍的記憶
隨著你清韻之步
　流蕩，徘徊

遙思三國
夢裡的王孫在呼喚些什麼
　而暮暮朝朝的
曹植
　就這樣靠近了

我知道，你愛寂寞
　也將堅決地
哺養這片希望的田野
你呼喚，像勁風的蘆葦
　歌吧，搖醒江淮之夜！

二

秋日陵墓前古樹蔥蔥。
而你，
吟詠如壯士。

睡去的七步村多純真！
我却不願遺忘那年
土崗上出現了洞穴的史實。

登上八斗嶺。仰瞻。
啊我始終相信，你是
詩人中的詩人，不凡的一生。

靜靜的岱山湖

靜靜的岱山湖，
如拉斐爾手繪的聖母。
人在畫中走，
綠是一種顏色。
那裡群峰疊翠，出塵不染。
那裡清波蕩漾，荷影招展
在粧點華美的小舟上。
我凝神看了又看，
啊，就這樣——
放慢了腳步，依偎著繆斯笑了。

－2015.9.1
－安徽詩歌學會主辦，肥東縣文聯承辦，第二屆
　"曹植詩歌獎"華語詩歌大賽，林明理獲二等
　獎，獎狀及獎金人民幣兩千，2016.3.28 中國詩
　歌流派網公告。收錄安徽省詩歌學會主辦，合肥
　市肥東縣文聯及八斗鎮人民政府承辦，《第二屆
　「中國·曹植詩歌獎」獲獎作品集》，林明理獲
　二等獎新詩〈寫給曹植之歌〉組詩，頁 5，2016.04
　出版。

22. 米故鄉—池上

林明理畫

花田正值冬之美，
溪谷雨量充沛，
正月的霞光下，白鷺
　　輕掠
　　　再躍起
於天堂路的起點；
唯一渙渙的

　　水畔，
涵映殘絮般的雲天。

哦，只在夢中，
　　我的影子帶我，
游動如呼吸的
　　星子。
直到綠稻展揚前，
　　再把時間折疊
讓我回到最初吧，
那一個米國 ──
　　池上的晨輝。

註：台東池上位於花東縱谷中部偏南，在清澈甘甜的新
　　武呂溪所沖積而成的肥沃平原中，造就了聞名全台的
　　「池上米」；每年的一月中旬，沿途的油菜花田與隱
　　身其間筆直的伯朗大道，搭配藍天白雲，是不可錯過
　　的旅遊勝地。
　　　─2014.12.24 作
　　　─刊臺灣《人間福報》副刊，圖文，
　　　　2017.01.17。
　　　─美國《亞特蘭大新聞》，2017.1.20，圖文。

23.在難以表明的喜悅中

當耶誕樹花亮起
在難以表明的喜悅中
阿里山之美的影像
輕輕撩撥記憶的夢

那熟悉的光影與嘻笑
漸漸靠近
而我又踏上林鐵
沿著溪流唱吟

哪裡來的這般風景
心頭跟著歡快光明
哪裡來的採茶歌喉
讓我沉浸在幸福的一瞬

—2016.12.24 平安夜林明理感謝民視製作
　小組的辛勞，觀後感思。
—刊美國《亞特蘭大新聞》，2017.1.20。

24. 漫步在烏鎮的湖邊

漫步在烏鎮的湖邊

在夢幻似的大劇院傍

你的古樸滄桑

總是真實，沒有虛妄

那可是湍流之聲

是熟悉的白牆黛瓦

或是從那幽靜的

古巷裡瀉出的月光

我聽到輕微的花鼓戲聲

還有一顆星跟在我身後

是誰？或近或遠牽引著我

是誰？輕輕將我擁抱

這世界很美

我坐在橋街重溫舊夢

那熟悉的藍染

一如往昔樸素靜致

你的笑容使月嬌羞

比三白酒更醇厚清純

漫步在烏鎮的湖邊

在夢幻似的大劇院傍

我心宛似歌雀

在黑暗之中歡頌

你的古樸滄桑

不再憂愁，欣欣燃亮

註：烏鎮位於浙江省銅鄉市，是江南著名古鎮之一。
街道上民居以清代建築為主，保存完好。全鎮以河
成街，橋街相連。各式民居、店鋪依河築屋，即有
深宅大院、百年老屋，也有河埠廊坊，過街騎樓，
是江南典型的「小橋、流水、人家」。

－2015.10.3
－刊《華文現代詩》，第 10 期，2016.08.
　頁 67.

25. 珠江，我怎能停止 對你的嚮往

珠江，我怎能停止對你的嚮往
你有著最最美麗名字
孕育了多少個靈動的魂
青山點點錯落
銀波淼淼，江水絢爛
這白晝的序曲
像漂泊的詩行凝結在高塔傍
我怎能不投下一次次的驚嘆

那無以數計的帆
雖然一概寂默、蒼涼
但無論置身何處
嶺南依舊在那兒
散發著豐富的意涵
河海交匯的影跡
我又怎能從記憶裡一筆抹去

啊我就像一尾飛魚

在闌珊燈火處

就這樣幾小時地

靜聽珠江在夜裡的呼吸

當月光照在海印大橋中

有一種思念

正緩緩划過天空，跨越兩岸⋯⋯

註：珠江，又名奧江，全長 2400 公里，是
　　廣州的母親河；其下游的沖積平原是著
　　名的珠江三角洲，河海交匯，河網交錯，
　　具有南國水鄉的獨特風貌。
　－2015.10.5
　－刊美國（亞特蘭大新聞），2017.03.17。

26. 咏王羲之蘭亭詩

你來自百合和朝露
一隻蜻蜓戲弄了你的鵝池
你的筆就飛起來了
飛向濃密的竹林
林裡的鳥兒都開始為你而歌
你的眼睛，崇高而明澈
充滿了優美的言詞

你的形象，同日月相映成輝
完整地再現了藝術的見證
而夜來靜寂
秋聲颯颯，清水急流
只有微微酒香
和在曲水旁列座的詩人
舉起夜光杯，對著時間微笑

你的步容，俊朗清逸

使人想起藍色微風

風起了

我看著滿天星辰歌頌你

你行走

歌聲在風中蕩漾

好似在蘭亭，宴罷賦詩時

　　　　　　－2016.3.24
　　　　　　－刊美國《亞特蘭大新聞》，2016.10.14
　　　　　　　圖文

27. 秋 思

又是一個秋夜，幽深的長巷消融了小鎮的夜
聲，星野低垂，

遮沒了利吉惡地河谷，卑南溪和中央山脈樹
林……

啊，朋友，南疆飄下第一場雪了嗎？

我在這裡一切平和，有酒，足以重溫你我相知
的故事。

你說，一個傍晚，在崑崙山下的克里雅河畔迷
了路；一抬頭，

疏星朗月已在上空，有個安靜祥和的村落，它
有個神秘而迷人的名字，

沿著高大挺拔的白楊樹，你欣賞了于田拉依蘇
村美麗的夜景。

於是，我做了一個夢，彷彿跟著來到村頭，有
茂密的蘆葦在省道旁

隨風搖曳，隱約的茶香、包穀饢，一切都還在
返回鮮活的記憶中。

我激動——我擁抱，時而寧靜地繼續我朦朧的
詩興，時而懷著欣慕

渴望依著拉依蘇入眠。宇宙依然空闊，而時間
還在那裡，馳騁，發光。

當天鵝絨般的月光，蔓延開去成為山峰上潔淨
的煙霧，

它慢慢照進樹林，把夢的暗影投射到奇異的甜
蜜裡……

這時，雪水輝映著夜空的群星，朋友，我的靈
魂也樂於進入

林海的深處，在崑崙山的上空翱翔，在克里雅
河畔沉思，

並且可以輕聲告訴你，我獨自站在神的面前。
心卻已跨越地表的界線，

在永恆的友誼面前，永不疲乏地飄游到你的身
邊。

－2016.10.17-刊美國《亞特蘭大新聞》，
2016.10.28 圖文。

28. 草露

在冬季的牧場
我聽到咆哮東去的長河
那種不羈
讓我在星海的草灘
猛然驚醒

你呵，奔向無垠的大海
而我只有片刻的停留
除了有流雲招呼，蟲鳥相迎
沉睡的羊群和雨蛙的沼澤

若是春暖花開
水泊密佈
而月光輕吻如昨
我將回信寄予雪峰
與天地為盟

—刊泰國《中華日報》，2009.8.11。

29 耶誕卡素描

排排雪松覆蓋繽紛的夜，
彷彿來自北國的華彩，
那光與愛，輝耀遍野的星。

聖誕快樂
新年如意

為義〈非馬〉之群同賀
2016年

非馬博士寄贈耶誕卡

－林明理 by Dr.Lin Ming-Li2016.12.15 收到
Dr.William Marr 耶誕卡，有感而作。

Sketch of AChristmas Card

Rows of cedars circle the colorful night,
As if from the northern country
That light and love, glitter all over like stars.

－ written by Dr.Lin Ming-Li, 2016.12.15，
upon receiving Dr.William Marr's Christmas
card

－刊美國《亞特蘭大新聞》
－刊義大利埃采恩大學《國際詩新聞》，
2016.12.

Sketch of a Christmas Carol

Rows of cedars encircle the vivid night
as if from the north
light and love glittered all over
like stars.

－英國詩人諾頓博士 Dr.Norton Hodges 英譯

30. 故鄉，我的愛

夏蟲的嘶鳴，雨的輕柔
把我喚醒了。
西螺大橋一如往昔
在風中矗立，像個魁偉的騎士。
　　　是啊，塵世的榮譽如雲煙，
　　　如何追溯得了前塵舊事？
哦　曾經
你擁有最豐富的溪流 ——
　　　明朗　美麗　光燦。
田野在歡唱，小河在閃耀。
　　　多希望你來叩我的心扉，
回答我的所有冀望。
　　　多希望你悄悄說出一個字，
而濁水溪只對著我微笑。
啊迷濛的月光透過窗簾時，
　　　我聽得見
莿桐花樹哼著歌。
以及昨日校園的活潑景象。
　　　過去到底有什麼？ —— 因為想飛，我得離
開你麼？
　　　年復一年……
只在夢中，我的影子才會踏上
故鄉的土 —— 廣漠、熟悉、自由。

　　　　每一星光都使我驚喜，
　　　　每一市集的叫賣聲都讓我安寧。
有人叫我嗎？我不下千次地回想：
當月圓時分
我想飛入你寬廣的心，
再將你的影子
折疊入夢，像一朵幽潔的百合
　　　　放在胸前。
　　　　永久永久。
啊我的愛，
雖然未來無法逆料，
你的地景在快速的變動中，
但這一切變動，
終會使你更堅韌豐富。
　　　　只要閉上眼睛，
就能回到那些—
陽光璀璨的日子。
　　　　只要撩起時間的面紗，
就能看清你永恆的面貌。

　　　　　　　　　　　　　　　　－2015.8.1 作

　　註.故鄉雲林縣莿桐村，對我而言，它是永遠年輕的。我總是
　　　　會想起水田反映著雲和樹，想起離鄉前那些無邪的日子。童
　　　　年仍為思念之處，如在夏日早晨一樣充滿希望，在我胸懷中
　　　　仍反映著明朗的天空。

　　－刊台南市文化局《鹽分地帶文學》雙月刊，第 65 期，
　　　　2016.08.31，頁 196-197。

31. 從海邊回來

悠悠淡淡，晚歸的星
溜上冬青樹，風
拎著裙襬，沿著槐花巷
從黃牆的寺院跑回
隨鐘鼓，輕輕一敲
簷滴聲
不斷

幾隻舢舨，白濤閃耀
碎在浪峰的盡頭
在那被吹得彎彎的
平灘上，看見自己
影子的延展
伸到蒼海
又落在腳前

紅燈點點，葉灑石階
我是羞藏在夜露裡的綠草

告訴我
那八萬四千的詩偈
隨風低吟
是否也淌進遊子的心田
燃起另一種慈悲？

　　　　　　－2009.6.4

　　　　－刊臺灣《人間福報》副刊，2009.7.2.
　　　　－轉載山東省《新世紀文學選刊》2009.11
　　　　　期。

32. 龍田桐花祭之歌

今年四月間
我又走上桐花紛飛的舊路
妳舞在芳香的風中
把霧谷染白
在步道旁
似仙女輕撫青草
喚醒綠芽，讓繆斯甦醒

我在林間漫步
觀看穿著大衿衫的婦女跳舞
頓時被周圍的一切迷住
這是客家桐花祭
有音樂注入這片愛情之樹
還有孩童的歡呼
而妳的靜默是令人陶醉的頌歌

像不可忘卻的福鹿茶

杯沿上還殘留著一份甘醇

這是歌唱的山野

我站在這兒對妳凝神睇看

每一片花瓣都是故事

是詩

也是愛，像母親的叮嚀。

－2016.9.16

－臺灣《秋水》詩刊，171 期，2017.07。
－美國《亞特蘭大新聞》，2017.1.20。

33. 彼岸

一朵赤腳跑走的

雲，蒙塵之眼

些許濕熱；

風說，不是我，

從前我遲疑過躑躅過

現在幸有妳分嘗，

一如岩石和貝殼。

在遠方我聽見

海角之音——

那是天水相連著

經聲的雪影。

－刊山東省《超然》詩刊，總第 13 期，
　2010.06。

34. 珍珠的水田

淡霧中，我聽得幾滴清露

在竹葉上翻轉

那是一抹朝霞的微笑的沉默

於是我摘下天邊晨星，藏匿衣袖

草花跟著轉圈兒

雨珠濺得遠遠的

清澈的小溪也

永不歇著…

我沿著山徑，赤足繞過

凝望著半岩下的綠波，一群野鳩

驀地飛起

飛向一時忘記了那一片

珍珠的　水田

—刊臺灣《人間福報》，2009.11.11。
—轉載臺灣《新文壇》季刊，2010.01 春季
　號。

35. 給 *Bulgarian poet Radko Radkov* (1940-2009)

在如風般逝去的日子懷抱裡

任何天使之翼

也不能捎去我的訊息

枝上那隻夜鶯

已不再唱牠的妙曲

可是，就在這片刻之間

你從金馬車上翩然回首

在星辰中，堅韌如昔

身影從容優閒

彷彿回到玫瑰谷的重逢

註. Radko Radkov 是任教於保加利亞大學
教授，著名詩人。

35. To Bulgarian poet Radko Radkov (1940-2009)

Gone are the days like the arms in the wind

No angel's wings

Can carry my messages

The nightingale on the branches

No longer sings her wonderful song

Yet at this moment

You glances back from the golden coach

Among the stars,you are as tough as ever

And so calm

As if a reunionat theRose Valley

－非馬（馬為義博士 William Marr）英譯
－刊美國《亞特蘭大新聞》，2016.6.10 中
英譯詩及畫作

36. 你是一株半開的青蓮

你是一株半開的青蓮
在倒影的水中
如夢初醒的明媚
花朵上的朝露是
音樂，飄在空中
融入了岳麓山的無邊狂野

你的憂傷是西下的斜陽
藍色是記憶
紅色是思念
當山風拂過，四季流轉
你似喜似悲
用僅有的芬芳把大地擁抱

你的微笑是曲澗的飛瀑
在寺廟與潭水之間
庸容自在　充滿暖意
你聽風，聽雨呢喃
歌咏著偉大與渺小
聲調時疾時徐，真誠而美好

註.葉光寒是湖南師範大學客座教授、「葉光寒藝
術博物館」館長，集書、詩畫、譜曲於一身的名
家。近作荷花，十分生動，觀後有感而文。
－刊美國《亞特蘭大新聞》，2016.10.7 及水彩畫
1 幅。

37. 給月芳

仰望亞城的一角天空

我會看到妳帶著笑容

正直的靈魂，清澈如雪

－2017.1.9（許月芳主編是《亞特蘭大新聞》報社社長），本書詩作中共數十首刊登於她主編的《亞特蘭大新聞》，其中林明理詩作〈寫給蘭嶼之歌〉刊於《亞特蘭大新聞》，並由臺灣文化部贊助的【飛閱文學地景】製作後播出於 2017.11.19「民視新聞」，特此致謝。

－刊美國《亞特蘭大新聞》，2017.1.13。

38. 愛在德爾斐

蜿蜒的河流，獨留蒼鷹

不斷地重述德爾斐的憂鬱。

牠的歌聲中，鋪敘

許多古老的傳說。那是自由的音律，

比風笛還悠揚，

比詩還奇麗。

牠凌駕於山海與古城，

擁抱無垠的宇宙——

只為一個愛的許諾，翱翔於蒼穹。

> 註.傳說希臘宙斯曾經於相反方向放出兩
> 隻蒼鷹來測量大地，而它們相遇的地點
> 正是古代希臘的聖地德爾斐 Delphi。

　－2016.12.5

38. Love at Delphi

Meandering river, goshawks leaving again,

each time a reminder of Delphic melancholy

the birds sing the story

of the ancient legends and how we can be changed

more melodious than pan flutes

more beautiful than a poem

above the sea and the ancient city

embracing the universe

they soar in the sky simply for the promise of love.

translated from the Chinese of Lin Ming-Li
by 英國詩人諾頓 Dr.Norton Hodges 英譯

－刊美國《亞特蘭大新聞》，2017.1.20。

39.流蘇花開

一隻自由翩翩的歌雀
周圍是切割千面的翡翠
像片片溫暖的雪
淡淡的
輕拂
四月的雲天
風仍傳頌著
你的名和那些你喜愛的
紅杜鵑
在初夏微風的醉月湖
夜鶲拍綠了水畔
你的歌聲鳴囀，蕩漾
直等到移開我的視線
噢，我的雪雀
你是聖潔的詩人
輝耀在巍巍校園間

註.每次到臺大校園看到流蘇花開，都情不自禁癡
　迷於它的美！再一次信步來到它跟前，只想為它
　表白心跡。

－2016.5.11
－刊美國《亞特蘭大新聞》，水彩畫及林明理於台
　大校園照於2016.5.27。
－刊香港《圓桌詩刊》，第52期，2016.06，頁22.

40. 卑南溪

靜靜的卑南溪順水而流

線光穿刺天藍的夜色

從小黃山到岩灣河段

浩浩蕩蕩的尖壁望不到盡頭

到了這兒，我聽不見喧聲

到了這兒，我忘了自己身在何處

到了這兒，時間已無關緊要

到了這兒，愛情之樹常青

讓我緩緩地走向你

走在很久以前的傳說

多麼堅實的故土上

讓我駛入你深藏眼簾下的輕愁

飛入你寬廣的胸前

靜靜的卑南溪靜靜地流

你的憂鬱是我的戀棧

你的柔波是黎明在舞蹈

註.卑南溪是台東第一大溪，卑南之名是為了紀念卑南族
的大頭目。全長約 84.35 公里，流經台東七個鄉鎮市，
分別是台東市、卑南鄉、延平鄉、鹿野鄉、關山鎮、
海端鄉、池上鄉。流域面積約為 1,603.21 平方公里，
是灌溉台東平原的主要河川。日治時期興築「卑南大
圳」，引卑南溪溪水，是台東最大的水利工程。在卑
南溪最著名的景觀是山里至岩灣河段，該河段的西岸
地質景觀獨特，約有四公里的尖壁地形，常被稱譽為
台東赤壁或小黃山。

－2016.5.26 作於台東
－刊美國《亞特蘭大新聞》，2016.6.17 圖文

41. 二層坪水橋之歌

我歡呼當白鷺掠過

畫一道美麗弧線

我暢飲在鹿野

二層坪水橋的陽光

我凝視如海的稻浪

泛起一圈圈金色波紋

我知道溪流在舞蹈

天邊那片雲絮

已伴隨著一小抹晚霞消融了

當朦朧月在山頂上神秘地笑

我知道世界在寬廣的目光中

會變得更好，而我

竟忘記了年華的流逝

半個世紀過去了嗎

我將帶著這片活風景

再次找到希望的風帆

搖晃在航向故鄉的海面上

　　註. 台東鹿野鄉瑞隆村坪頂路旁，2016 年六月四日
　　　　為慶祝重新建造的「二層坪水橋」，特別舉行「稻浪
　　　　飄米香牽手護水橋」活動。據說，五十年前建造時，
　　　　當地農民憑著鋤頭、扁擔、畚箕，用人力挑土墊高水
　　　　路，艱鉅地完成了圳水輸送任務。但歷經半世紀，圳
　　　　路多已損壞。在農田水利會、水保局、鄉公所及當地
　　　　居民多方努力下，將原來的水橋改成拱橋加上古樸
　　　　風的仿古紅磚，水橋兩端的橋台擋土牆，則用陶板
　　　　凸顯了農村特色及先民開墾史。除了保有灌溉功能
　　　　外，橋拱下也加設燈光，營造為公園，長度達四百二
　　　　十三公尺。田野上，常能見到普悠瑪火車奔馳、白鷺
　　　　冉冉而過的身姿……迴首水橋，盡興踏影而歸。

　　　　　　－2016.6.20
　　　　　　－刊臺灣《笠》詩刊，第 314 期，2016.08，
　　　　　　　頁 69。

42. 在風中，寫你的名字

在風中，寫你的名字，像新月一樣

當它升到山巔同白晝擦身而過，

四周是歌聲，鳥語與花香的喜悅

而你是永恆，抹不掉燈火輝煌的故鄉。

－2016.6.21
－香港詩歌學會，《圓桌詩刊》）預稿

43. 給雅雲

我眼裡的藍山雀

像多年前那樣甜蜜的

歌著，家，對於她就是幸福

－2017.1.9 （彭雅雲是臺北市著名的文史哲出
版社發行人彭正雄之女，協助我出版書數
本，並上架於三民書局等銷售，特此致謝。）
－刊美國《亞特蘭大新聞》，2017.1.13。

44. 你的影跡在每一次思潮之上

啊讓我奮起翅膀

如鷹之姿，瞰整片海洋

歌聲中天堂也似的故鄉

一向是我最深的顧盼

深秋了，留下來的那輪月

是多少遊子的凝注

是多少墨客的讚嘆

我欣然

讀你騰躍而矯健的詩

讓文明之花馨香萬里

讓大地的淚變得聖潔而美麗

讓永恆的黃土芬芳綿長

啊，東方已曉——

你的影跡在每一次思潮之上

註.緬懷王羲之千古之誦〈蘭亭序〉，是書法
　　史上的豐碑，有感而文。
－2016.10.30
－刊美國《亞特蘭大新聞》，2016.12.9 圖文。

45. 永安溪，我的愛

野花，白鷺，蘆葦，溪灘
天藍如鏡，誰能知曉你的奧秘
風依舊吟詠 —— 送來你的名字
帆影點點，泛過閃耀的南峰

而你
聲音幽柔甜蜜，如戀人一般
我真想遠離一切空虛的迷惘
讓燃燒的夢想飛向月光下的故鄉

－2016.10.22
－臺灣（華文現代詩）第 12 期，2017.02
－美國《亞特蘭大新聞》），2017.1.20.

46.重到石門水庫

那年，夏風走過

大壩淼淼波光

林道上不見楓紅

卻喚起了我親切的情感與詩篇

百花開遍公園

綠潭與白鷺

唱出我最純粹的感動

山巒越發明晰，蟲鳴繞繚寂靜

啊，我願是飛遠的那隻灰鳥

重尋記憶裡青澀的童年

呼吸在遊艇上如此飄然

往事、歡悅還有歌聲 ——

沸騰了我的血

註.石門水庫啟用於 1964 年，耗資約 32 億台幣，位於桃園市大溪區、龍潭區、復興區，與新竹縣關西鎮之間的石門峽谷，採土石堤岸型壩體，攔截大漢溪溪水蓄水而成，是台灣第一座多功能水庫。園區內的景點包括大壩、遊湖碼頭、溪州公園、楓林公園、南苑生態園區等。每年秋末冬初，楓林公園及楓林步道，是最佳賞遊之處。

　　　—2016.6.30
　　　—刊美國《亞特蘭大新聞》，2016.12.16.及照片。
　　　—刊臺灣《臺灣時報》台灣文學版，2016.12.21及照片。

47. 在醉月湖的寧靜中

正月冬陽
在醉月湖的寧靜中
呼吸著綠蔭
瞧，白鵝藍鴨拍綠了水岸
把亭臺變得更加華美
那鐘聲依舊
杜鵑依舊
鳥聲聚集在
高傲的樹端彌留
而我們行進著
在緩緩而落的黃昏下
我又回憶起那段金色時光
是多麼歡愉

－刊臺灣《臺灣時報》台灣文學版，
2016.12.21 及照片。2017.1.11
－刊美國《亞特蘭大新聞》，2017.1.20。

48.東勢林場之旅

漫天櫻舞的春天
讓整個森林花園安靜下來
陽光在枝上舞動
隙縫中
我最為愜意
溪水環繞，鳥聲啁啾

當四季的芬芳由遠而近
在綠蔭間閃現
全都框進我的眼眸
在花蕾的影像投射於

林場的光芒
和流螢飛舞於草叢之中
你便抒情地揚起愉悅的歌謠

當時有快樂的境遇
未來也將被提起
而我像棵老樹
用心靈飛
因為我在浪漫的客庄大道
遇見一個美麗的邂逅

—2017.1.1　註.東勢林場是座美麗的森林花園，
古名「四角林」，東勢林場人稱中部的陽明
山，是中台灣最美麗的森林花園，位於台中
縣東勢鎮東南隅之大安溪畔，是台中縣市都
市近郊的桃花源。

—刊臺灣《臺灣時報》2017.1.5 圖文。
—詩〈東勢林場〉，《人間福報》2017.2.17 圖
文。

49.仲夏寶島號 (憶CT273)

夏風吹拂福爾摩沙
吹拂往日聯翩幻想
心卻跟在你前面飛馳
輕輕地牽引我越過山洞
越過無數綠野平疇
越過一甲子時光
像隻自由歡快的黑鳥
盡情飛騰
吹著高亢而悠揚的口哨
那麼響亮，最為動聽
是你
威武神奇的身姿
為生命而飛，溫暖而動容
讓我又重溫一次舊夢

註.台鐵 CT273 仲夏寶島號 Summer Formosa 是蒸汽火車
之王，與日本 C57 型車同型，是歷史上不朽的急行火
車。1942 年購入，1950 年代主要牽引西線特快車，1960
年改為牽引普通車，1984 年停用。直到 2010 年積極
修復下，2014 年 6 月 9 日鐵路節再度復駛，並於 2014
年八月首次開行於花蓮台東之間。台鐵正名為「仲夏
寶島號」。2016 年，CT273 重現舊鐵道風光，特別經
過基隆、瑞芳火車站，一路開到宜蘭冬山火車站。當
它噴大煙冒白色長龍時，不少鐵道迷跟民眾紛紛拿起
照相機、手機，只為捕捉那美麗的復古身影，留下讚
嘆不已的珍貴鏡頭與難忘的回憶。
—2016.7.2 寫於台東市

－2016.7.2 黃昏時，CT273 停在鹿野站，令我懷念起國
小畢業後離鄉往返於斗六至台北站，父親送別於月
台，汽鳴與迴首看到冒白煙的車頭...那熟悉的身姿與
搭乘它的美好記憶，因而為詩。
－刊《臺灣時報》台灣文學版，2016.7.6 圖文。
－（我的愛，台鐵 CT273）刊美國《亞特蘭大新聞》，
2016.7.8.圖文。
－〈憶 CT273〉刊臺灣《笠》詩刊，第 314 期，2016.8，
頁 68。

50.時光裡的和平島

為了愛，我又回來
你，純淨無邪的野百合
在回憶的波上
在我嚮往已久的岸邊踱步唱歌
高山阻檔不了你的魅力
峽谷隱藏不了你的柔情
河流帶不走你的憂鬱
大海為你永遠守誓
我在尋找你走過的路
岩縫間都長滿了苔衣
聽，金風蕭瑟，塵海起伏
那飛逝的季節裡
你仍是你
無懼驚世駭俗
多少冬夏與春秋
多少痛苦或歡笑
我愛你，天然的模樣
愛你不用讀唇的細語

愛你無需翻譯的沉靜
今夜，我是詩人
我看到了傳說中的傳說
看到了鷗鳥從岸畔飛起
瞬時，浪花有了節奏
隨你起伏跌宕
我看到了漁舟唱晚
心是如此幸福
當月兒停坐在尖石上
聆聽浪濤時
你的光芒湧動
而時間過去了，你的愛留了下來
讓記憶抵達過往吧
讓島嶼凝聚成祥和
重複講述你我相遇的故事
啊，tuman
光的細鱗在你四周
你的美麗
已戰勝了腐朽
秋波渺渺，暮靄重重
多少豪情在世間激蕩
多少淚水在世間漂流

你度盡風雨

又從火紅中孵出新綠

一如往年

島嶼的命運仍在轉動

當夜越顯漆黑時

你像玉山剛下的雪

白而光明

而我在懸崖的寧靜中

呼喚你

從這裡到光的盡頭

註.和平島是離台灣最近的離島，位於基隆港北端、港口東側，距基隆市約四公里，佔地六十六公頃餘。在清朝前期時稱「雞籠嶼」或「大雞籠嶼」，為北台灣最早有西方人足跡之地，也是基隆最早有漢人入墾所在之一。西元 1870 年，為了要與東北方海上的「小雞籠嶼」(即今日的基隆嶼)區隔，因此改名為「社寮嶼」，即凱達格蘭人大雞籠社房舍聚集之島嶼之意。最早島上的原住民為凱達格蘭族的巴賽人(Katagalan Basaijo)，稱此島為「tuman」，至 1949 年政府播遷來台後才被改名為和平島。因終年受到東北季風吹襲以及海浪拍打侵蝕的影響，島嶼有許多奇岸怪石的海蝕地形及景觀，如海蝕平台、豆腐岩、海蝕溝、海蝕崖、風化窗、萬人堆、千疊敷、海蝕洞、薑狀岩、獅頭岩、熊頭岩等，於 2012 年 6 月再度更名為「和平島公園」。而基隆嶼因孤懸海上，成為基隆與北海岸地區明顯的自然地標，2001 年正式開放登島觀光，島上有燈塔，採太陽能發電，原歸海關管轄，2013 年移撥交通部航港局。另有日治時期遺留之「楠田上等兵殉職碑」，用以紀念因工事殉職兵士。目前可由碧砂漁港與基隆火車站前小艇碼頭登船前往。附近海域是基隆外海有名的磯釣場，盛產白帶魚等豐富漁產，每到入夜時分，一艘艘海釣船停泊在基隆嶼附近，是基隆嶼夜晚最美麗的一面。

－2016.10.30 寫於台東

－刊臺灣《青年日報》副刊，2016.12.26.

51. 吹過島嶼的風

你日夜飛翔

在部落的靜寂天空上

那是我故里

是永不消隱的容貌

是祖靈聲聲低喚嗎

Luka，Luka——

叮嚀似繩索，繫我於心頭

註.2016.12.12 原視〈吹過島嶼的歌〉節目中
　胡德夫等原住民藝人感性地唱出部落的心
　聲及播放重返 1999 年「互助村部落音樂
　會」的回顧與沈思，有感而作。Luka 是「加
　油」之意。

－2016.12.12
－刊美國《亞特蘭大新聞》，2017.1.20。

52. 凝望

穿越巨浪
時間的海鷗
正叼走一頁滄史

—2016.12.15.Dr.Lin
Ming-Li

2016.12.14.M.L PAINT

52. *Gazing*

Through the waves
The seagull of Time
Is taking a page out of history

— 2016.12.15. Dr.Lin Ming-Li （ Translator ：
Dr.William Marr）
—刊美國《亞特蘭大新聞》，2017.1.13 中英譯。
—臺灣《秋水》詩刊，第 171 期，2017.07 預稿。

53.關山遊

我想畫一條溪
山巒夾著山坳
輕輕的
有白鷺掠過
或者
畫油菜花的靜默
一波波雲霧裊裊
但我框不住這片
青山
也框不住紅紅落日

我還想畫一縷炊煙
穿過灰鳥的方位
掬飲
一片幽雅的涼意
在祈求神明將我保佑前
悄悄地

將詩裡的小註
埋藏在閃亮的
褐色的土地裡

註.關山鎮土地肥沃水源充沛，因此開發很早，清
　　咸豐年間就有西部漢人李天送招佃入墾，今為台
　　東縣內工商較為發達的大鎮。鎮上的天后宮是當
　　地居民及臺東縱谷地區居民奉祀媽祖等各神明
　　的信仰中心。正門有雄偉高大的門樓，廟宇本身
　　為雙殿硬山式的建築，附近有市集、關山便當及
　　美食，是騎單車或旅遊的好去處。

－2016.7.15
－刊中國大陸《羊城晚報》，2016.7.26，副刊「花
　地」版。
－《青年日報》，2016.8.16刊登。

54. 睡吧，青灣情人海

睡吧，青灣情人海

你的音樂緩緩流過

我的血脈

那七彩的玻璃石

是光的寶藏

你歌中的每一句

都甜蜜自在

你眼底的清純

澄澈深邃

無論懷著關愛或憂傷

閃光的你

是春之憧憬

引我徘徊

　*在澎湖「仙人掌公園」附近的風櫃與青灣之間，有片約
　　長五十公尺的白色小沙灘，這沙灘由珊瑚遺體、貝殼、
　　石英砂、七彩的玻璃石等堆積而成。陽光下的玻璃石，
　　常呈現耀眼的光線，煞是迷人，因而吸引許多情侶在
　　此駐足，稱此地景為「青灣情人海」。

　－2016.7.18
　－刊《臺灣時報》台灣文學版，2016.7.22.圖文。

林明理旁白：澎湖的青灣情人海，常是許多旅人時不時
　　　地就要回憶起當時的情景。無論它是多麼地美，
　　　但憑著這一份純淨，就遠比在我的想像時刻裡幸
　　　福得多。因為每一個看到這裡的海景的旅人都在
　　　同樣地分享著這一快樂與感動！

55. 七股潟湖夕照

在夕陽下閃爍的潟湖

宛如一簇簇紫丁香

灰藍的影子沒入了

白鷺的喁喁情話中

而我回憶起大汛季年代

一窪窪鹽峰，晶耀如玉

依稀可以看見

包花布巾的勞工在鹽場奔忙

那紅樹林的每次顫動

都是美麗的靜默

也是我永遠的凝思

註.七股潟湖位於臺南市七股區境內，為臺灣第一大潟湖，面
積約 1,100 公頃以上，也是最大、最完整的濕地，由三
個沙洲所圍成，分別是頂頭額汕、網仔寮汕和青山港
汕。這裡蘊藏豐富的海產及植物生態，如魚、貝、蚵、
蟹、蝦、紅樹林、白鷺鷥，以及黑面琵鷺等二百多種
候鳥。當地人稱為「內海仔」或「海仔」，是台江內海
最後的遺跡。潟湖也有漲潮和退潮，但因為潟湖較平靜，
有鹽田、蚵架等景色，旅客可從龍山碼頭搭乘竹筏遊
湖。昔日鹽場最忙碌的季節是陽光普照、雨水較少的三月
至五月，鹽民稱為「大汛季」，收之可達年產量的一半。
－2016.11.15—刊臺灣《笠》詩刊，第 316 期，2016.12，頁 54.
－〈潟湖夕照〉刊臺灣《青年日報》副刊，2016.12.9.

56. 我的歌

在發生災難的
失眠時刻
你的傷痛隱藏於
天使的羽衣之下
如哀傷的銀鷗
長夜漫漫
世界有時變化無常
而我的歌
是熱血沸騰的回聲
穿過尼斯的月亮

註.2016.7.14 法國國慶日遭逢恐怖攻擊，死傷慘
重。我致電郵給 prof. Ernesto Kahan。所幸他安
好並回應說， "Dearest Ming –Li,Receive a big
huge perfumed with friendship. " 。因而為詩。

－2016.7.17
－刊美國《亞特蘭大新聞》，2016.7.22.圖文，
Translator：Dr. William Marr。

56. My song

In the event of a disaster
Insomnia time
To hide your pain
Under an angel's feathers
Sad as a silver gull
Long night
The unstable world
And my song
Is a passionate echo
From Nice through the moon

> Note .2016.7.14 Bastille Day aftermath of the terrorist attacks, the casualties. I call the Post to Ernesto. Fortunately, he responded well and said, "Dearest Ming -Li, Receive a big huge perfumed with friendship.". Thus poetry.
> --2016.7.17

附.2016 年 7 月 19 日於 8:27PM　Prof .Ernesto Kahan 回覆 MAIL

And my song
Is a passionate echo
From Nice through the moon

Dear Ming － li,
Your poem is a peaceful tenure for the victims
Thanks for sharing
Ernesto

57. 憶陽明山公園

一張舊照片，彷彿是昨天。

回憶帶著我穿越層層綠林，靜靜地，走進了舊夢。

蟲鳥爭鳴，泉聲叮咚，淺草裡有蝶，在叫我的名字。

櫻花不來，雨滴奔向泥土，蕩漾在偌大園區中。

花鐘旁的噴泉，沾著時光的濃墨，在空中書寫著離別與相遇的故事。

水花在風中飄散盤旋……以它優美的旋律。閃動的影子不就是我的相思麼？

在你的三月，那些掛滿枝枒的粉紅或醬紫，那些招展的花瓣與豐美的樹葉裡，

最精采的是投影在水面的天，藍得更清澈，白得更透亮。

而你的微笑，掠過了我的花園。

如今，我不知道芒花要訴說些什麼，但我知道它的孤寂悠遠。

噢，不，它不過是一瞥。假如驟然而落的風

是有情的，掠過這城市的輪廓，還有那熟悉的石

子小路，

　　那麼，你就呼喚吧，像是初次觀賞 —— 陽明山，

　　那些疊影，活在詩中，勾起了無數的仲夏夢。

> 註.陽明山原名草山，位於臺北近郊，泛指大
> 　屯山、七星山、紗帽山、小觀音山這一帶
> 　的山區，而非單指某座山峰，是臺灣著名
> 　風景區。

　　－2016.7.23
　　－刊美國《亞特蘭大新聞》，2016.9.2，林明
　　　理畫作及獨照。

58. A Song for Cordoba Synagogue

Dr.Lin Ming-Li

西班牙猶太教堂猶太教不朽的巧匠
邁蒙尼德（*Maimonides*）雕像

When I walk toward you, Cordoba,

Toward the city, toward the flowers Lane,

Toward the silent synagogue,

Toward the nine holy candlesticks,

Toward the desolate sound in the wind,

Near the statue of Maimonides,

When your silence descends like falling leaves,

And becomes the crystal spray.

58. 寫給科爾多瓦猶太教堂的歌

林明理 Dr.Lin Ming-Li

當我走向你，科爾多瓦，

走向古城，走向百花巷，

走向靜寂的猶太教堂，

走向聖潔的九燭台，

走向風中的荒涼聲響，

走向邁蒙尼德的雕像，

這時，你的沉默如葉飄落，

是我眸中晶瑩的水花。

Ah, God, my Almighty,

Thy mercy shines on the mortal world,

Thy gospel emerges from darkness.

Please help Thy people,

Heal historical wounds.

In this peaceful morning,

Listen to my silent prayer.

Amen.

Note Cordoba (Córdoba) in the Spanish autonomous region
of Andalusia, the Guadalquivir River, it is the capital of
Cordoba province, also has a lot of cultural heritage and
monuments of the city. Wherein the synagogue, ancient
and stately walls are carved with Hebrew from Jewish
craftsman Maimonides (Maimonides). Judaism has a seat
in the hall of his bust sculptures in the vicinity of the
flowers Lane also has a sculpture of his body, he is also
a famous Jewish philosopher, jurist and physician.

－2016.7.29（ TRANSLATOR：DR.WILLIAM MARR）
－英譯刊美國《世界的詩》《Poems of the world》），
2016.夏季號，頁 24。

啊，神啊，我的全能，

祢的慈悲光耀世道，

祢的福音在黑暗中浮現。

請支撐祢的子民，

撫平歷史的傷痕。

在這和平的早晨，

聽我無聲的祈禱。

阿門。

註.科爾多瓦（Córdoba）位於西班牙安達盧西亞自
治區、瓜達爾基維爾河畔，是哥多華省的首府，
也是一個擁有許多文化遺產和古跡的城市。其中
的猶太教堂，古老而莊嚴，牆上雕飾著希伯來文
是出自猶太人的巧匠邁蒙尼德（**Maimonides**）。
在猶太教堂內有座他的半身雕塑，在附近的百花
巷中也有一座他的全身雕塑，他也是著名的猶太
哲學家、法學家和醫生。
— 2016.7.29
— 中英譯刊美國《亞特蘭大新聞》，2016.8.5.圖文
— 英譯刊美國《世界的詩》（Poems of the world），
2016.夏季號，頁 24。

1985 年諾貝爾和平獎 Prof.Ernesto Kahan 幫此詩翻
譯成西班牙語

2016.8.11 收件者 於 1:18 AM
Dear Ming-li
This is my translation into Spanish.
Love
　　　　Ernesto

58. *A Song for Cordoba Synagogue*

Cuando camino hacia ti, Córdoba,

ciudad de flores en las calles,

hacia la sinagoga silenciosa,

hacia los nueve candelabros sagrados,

y hacia el sonido desolado en el viento,

cerca de la estatua de Maimónides,

cuando tu silencio desciende como las hojas que caen,

y se convierte en aerosol de cristal.

Ah, mi Dios Todopoderoso,

Tu misericordia brilla en el mundo de los mortales,

La Biblia emerge de la oscuridad.

en ayuda a tu pueblo,

y va a curar heridas históricas,

escucha mi oración silenciosa.

Amén.

59.冬日羅山村

走在羅山村，
大地如是純淨。
諦聽風中醉語，
我在土角厝屋簷下歇息。
啊，這大魚池，這瀑布，
這泥火山。
在孩童的歡笑中。
我享受著時光，
飯香和本地產的
豆腐佳餚。
融入
天空，鳥鳴，水聲。
冬日，午後靜而遠山暖。

註.花蓮縣富里的羅山有機村，有個生態驛站溫老太太開
　　設的「火山豆腐」，紅磚土角厝的老舍，古樸而懷舊。
　　另有濃郁的手工豆腐，是用當地泥火山的鹵水代替石
　　膏凝結豆腐，再以傳統老灶燒柴的方式將豆汁慢火熬
　　成豆漿，共要耗費六個多小時，才能製成泥火山豆腐，
　　口感綿密紮實，有淡淡的豆香味兒。當地居民多為客
　　家人，附近有羅山瀑布、木棧道、跨溪的拱橋，泥火
　　山步道、大魚池等等，風景原始自然而幽靜。
　　－2016.7.28.
　　－刊〈冬日羅山村〉刊臺灣《華文現代詩》，第
　　　11 期，2016.11，頁 87。
　　－美國《亞特蘭大新聞》，2016.8.26.及作者照片。

60. 二林舊社田龜夢

黃昏，我看到白鷺

成群舞躍

伴著收割機的聲響

自由輕啄

全村的農作物

都在田裡

我看到了

土地靜默的力量

落日降臨

在大池，在小鴨戲水的

悠遊時刻

如此美好。農舍也欣幸地睡覺

而月亮漫步著

傾聽耆老的訴說

註.彰化縣二林舊社是「田龜計畫」的故鄉，據史書的記
載，二林地區原為荒蕪之處，是平埔族的居住地，荷
蘭人進據臺灣之前，即有二林社，荷蘭人音譯為
Gielim，此字經過漢人的音譯，即成為「二林」。這
項計畫源於中山大學資管系退休的黃慶祥教授，為協
助當地農村再生轉型，並協助老農拓展農產品網
路銷售。「田龜」意指老農像烏龜般彎腰駝背在
田間工作，他想打造家鄉成為「全穀之鄉」，除
了鼓勵有機種植雜糧，還希望美化社區和編修在地歷
史。最近這項計畫的三夢想(田龜新產業、大池新生
態、廟宇新文化)，開始浮現成形。繼二林舊社故事
館成立、慈濟大愛電視台亦拍攝紀錄片《農夫與他的
田》，此外，新聞媒體也有所報導。如今，代安宮和
大池是田龜計畫的生態和文化中心。值得關注，因而
為詩。

　　　　　－2016.7.29
　　　　　－刊《臺灣時報》，台灣文學版，2016.8.11
　　　　　　圖文.
　　　　　－詩作貼於行政院農委會水保局官網
　　　　　　http://ep.swcb.gov.tw/EP/News.aspx

61. 你從太陽裡走來

還記得嗎
溪谷裡芒花開了
又謝
你從太陽裡走來
讓每次春光都帶來幸福的圖彩
啊，曾經走過的
每一塊壘石每一方泥土
都沾滿你樸實的氣宇
你看，這長巷
曾無數次召喚著，而
你從不與黑暗同在
心似把火炬
照亮了山川錦綉
燃起了覺醒的光芒

啊，讓我飛吧，像雲那般
向著你離去的方向
那四季的足音

似乎馱來了新的訊息
一切都將過去的———
無數悲喜和泣別
都在風中沉沉地睡去了
就像夜空下
奮力滋長的葉瓣與蟲鳥
是那樣生機昂然，在
這碑林前，我輕輕地
輕輕地
為你獻上一束雅潔的
花香

—2014.12.28
—刊安徽省馬鞍市《大江詩壇》，2015 中
國詩選，中國電影出版社，北京，2016.05
出版，頁 71.

62. 爲土地而歌

是誰？在歲月的黑暗中
以歌把生命獻給大地
是誰？喚醒群星舞躍
賜給族群永不失和諧
啊，朋友
當月光撫慰你們的苦難
當海平線四周
浪尖都成豎琴
你，我們的歌手
默默地
唱出憂傷與希冀
你，我們的夏日
何等光耀
何等雄健
這是為八月第一天
原住民族日
我決定再留片刻

融洽於
這場純真的讚美！

註：2016 年 7 月 30 日夜晚，台東鐵花村舊車站後面的
　　廣場，由「中華民國獵人學校協會」創辦人亞榮隆‧
　　撒可努文學家所主辦的一項【為土地唱歌，為尊嚴而
　　跑】公益音樂祭募活動，這項活動無任何政府補助，
　　是為 8 月 1 日「原住民族日」而起跑，主辦的意義在
　　於為土地而歌，為聯合族群融合，因為，連結的關係，
　　才有生命力，才能拉近彼此的心。當我看到各族群為
　　這場活動而努力，及原視幕後工作小組的辛苦，有一
　　種特異的感動與尊敬，因而為詩。

　　　－2016.7.31
　　　－刊美國《亞特蘭大新聞》，2016.8.12 圖文

63. 夏蟬，遂想起

夏蟬，遂想起家鄉，詩裡的童年，濁水溪畔，
釣青蛙於其中，螢火蟲於其中，可以從風中回去的。
黃昏的原野，水牛在遠方放牧，多農莊的房子，多
秧苗的綠田，
一切都離得遠遠 —— 人或景，地或天。
而今，逃了時間，失蹤了塵事，失蹤在驟雨的屋簷，
滂沱雨滴，斜斜地鞭笞窗櫺，擋不住我的視線。
夏蟬，遂想起莿桐花開，想起艷紅的花兒由枝幹端
詳我，
想起那麼多的麻雀，吱吱喳喳叫個不歇。
即使同樣雀躍，引領我朝向純真的歲月，
即使在早晨的生命裡，喊我，在後山這邊，又喊我，
等了無數個年。
即使一眼望去竟是百里之遙，在這蟬鳴季節，我又
追逐時間，
哪怕只留住疏落人群間的淡薄情義，哪怕喊聲剛
落，從思念中驚回。
時間在走啊走，可誰也沒發現。
我曾在那裡歡笑，也曾在那裡落淚。
老街的點點滴滴，都是腦海中幸福的記號。

--2016.8.5
--刊美國《亞特蘭大新聞》，2016.8.19.圖文。

64.黃昏，賽納河

你當記得，那天空
憂傷而美麗，波光與船燈互耀
而我癡迷於美的憧憬
癡迷於岸邊的街頭熱舞
周邊玫瑰色的彌蒙
那艾菲爾鐵塔，我所愛的王者
在充滿愛情的手中入睡
金色光座如聖體晃耀
一座座拱橋穿越夜的虛無
靜靜地養神中
在光影交織的大氣裡
噢，賽納河，我愛
你的閃光在我們之間交織
就像惜別時星辰的回眸

註.賽納河（**Seine**）是流經巴黎市中心的法國第
二大河，許多重要建築都圍繞著塞納河兩
岸，它也是巴黎的母親河。
－2016.8.4
－刊美國《亞特蘭大新聞》，2016.9.23 圖文。

65. 水沙連之戀

　　總想駕一葉輕舟，來到群巒浸拂著水霧的河岸，
去尋找你軀體裡彌漫的柔情與豁達。

　　那波紋暮光底下，遊艇徐徐緩緩。片片落葉，誕
生了朵朵漣漪，

　　都在你多情的懷抱裡。

　　總想聆聽各方風的呢喃，弄清各方魚的噤聲，

　　總想請時間的雨佇留，請歲月不再迅馳……

　　是的，在此休憩片刻吧。

　　就像這月光包裹著我，日月潭又名水沙連，彷彿
那片野薑花，

　　是一首抒情的詩。在老鷹之舞，在祭神與戰舞之
間，慢慢開展……

　　恍惚間，我已是伊達邵的一隻白鹿。

　　一隻白鹿，在水裡尋找生命的源頭，或者邵族的
根，根在這兒延伸，

　　枝繁葉茂，禽鳥們在拉魯島上得以快樂地飛躍。

　　一隻貓頭鷹，在枝頭看著我，也在蒼穹看著我，

像是要訴說什麼？

　　啊，沒有一種痛能夠將牠怠忽，沒有任何騷動能夠改變牠的言辭。

　　牠的寬容，如聖者，助族人習於堅毅，從黑夜到黎明，

　　在某個密葉裡安全地守護，在湖泊前，寂靜而耀眼。

　　不只在我心田種下了一湖新詩，還留下呼—呼的高音。

　　　　　　註.日月潭風景區位於南投縣中部魚池鄉水社村，自然生態豐富，因潭景霧薄如紗，水波漣漣而得名為「水沙連」，四周群巒疊翠，全潭以拉魯島（光華島）為界，南形如月弧，北形如日輪，遂改名為「日月潭」。旅遊區計有文武廟、孔雀園、拉魯島、青年活動中心、玄奘寺、慈恩塔、梅荷園，到達伊達邵（舊稱德化村）可觀賞鄒族部落的歌舞。也可在自行車道騎單車、湖濱步道散步或到碼頭搭船遊湖，坐纜車可達「九族文化村」。相傳邵族人祖先在山中打獵時，發現一隻白鹿，為追逐這隻鹿，一路翻山越嶺來到一片美麗的湖泊（即日月潭），這隻鹿隨即跳入湖中消失。這批狩獵隊因沒有追到鹿，只好獵捕山羌就食，無意中，卻發現這湖泊有取之不盡的魚。返回原鄉後，又帶來族人，從此在潭邊定居，日月潭就變成邵族人的故鄉。而貓頭鷹是邵族人守護神，被視為靈鳥。族人也喜歡表演杵音、老鷹之舞、野薑花之舞及祭神與戰舞等。

　　　　　　—2016.8.5
　　　　　　—刊臺灣《人間福報》，2016.11.11 及攝影一張。

66. 書寫王功漁港

風車在漁港中歌唱
漁港也在潮間中激響
望海寮上一艘艘竹筏搖擺
如整齊一致的黑武士

水鳥說話──紅樹林說話
招潮蟹更是說話
彈塗魚說話，濕地說話
而我，是靜默的島

從夜晚翩翩而來
佇在燈塔最高的視界
你所給我的
粼粼波光照影，曾是驚鴻

註.王功漁港位於彰化縣芳苑鄉王功村西濱沿海，瀕臨台灣
海峽，居民多以近海捕魚及沿海養殖為主，盛產蚵仔、
鰻魚、蝦、蛤蜊等漁產。王功漁火是彰化縣八景之一。
據記載，早在三百八十多年前，先民從福建渡海來台，
即在此定居。漁港裡黑白條紋的芳苑燈塔是台灣本島最
高的燈塔，還有十座風力發電機組、造型獨特的圓拱橋、
望海寮、濕地生態、竹筏、及夕照等景色。

─2016.8.6
─臺灣《華文現代詩》第十期，2016.08。

67. 美在大安森林公園

這條長長的步道
穿越了我數千個日夜
今晨，那熟悉的茶園儷影
竟瞬間擊中我的心
啊，新生的梔子花多麼嬌柔
憂傷的天空，無盡的奔馳！
而我溫柔的目光，凝注著紅土
記憶的空隙，漫無目的地飄浮
延著我的傘尖看去，幾度寒暑
大安森林公園——記錄我的憶念
在草木鳥獸，美麗的景象之中。

註.大安森林公園位於臺北市大安區，是座草木濃密的生態公園，被
譽為臺北市的「都市之肺」。公園內除有多層式綠籬景觀之外，
更有花壇處處，每逢花開時節色彩繽紛。公園外人行道則以綠樹
與道路區隔，計有竹林區、榕樹區、香花區、水生植物區、帶狀
林區、水池假山區、露天音樂台、兒童遊戲區、慢跑道、健康步
道和停車場等設施十分完善，西北口有座楊英風雕塑的觀世音菩
薩藝術像，為臺北市民最喜愛休閒場所之一。露天音樂台四周植
有玉蘭、梔子花、七里香、樹蘭、含笑、桂花等香花植物，園區
闢有自然水池、蓮花池，水池周圍及水中植有金露華、紅葉鐵莧、
美人蕉、軟枝黃蟬，並飾以薜荔懸攀石壁，池中錦鯉魚遊嬉其間。
雖四季之景略有不同，但協和的美，風姿綽約。
友人余玉照教授近日電郵告之：「我走在大安森林公園的紅土上散
步，有如走在家鄉農地上親切打拼的過往年代裡那般踏實、自
在、自得。」，有感而作。
　　　　　　－2016.8.16
　　　　　　－刊臺灣《臺灣時報》台灣文學版，2016.9.2，圖文。
　　　　　　－刊臺灣《華文現代詩》第11期，2016.11，頁87。

68.歌飛阿里山森林

我穿過白髮的
阿里山林鐵
去尋覓童年的純真

這山泉
是個愛唱歌的小孩
音色細而堅韌
神木旁　還藏有
遊客們笑聲

當火車汽笛吶喊出
嘹亮的清音
風的裙步跟著踏響了冬林
土地的記憶
也化成一片片寧靜

我把縷縷陽光剪下
鐫刻在櫻樹上

68. *Songs Fill the Forest of Mt. Ali*

Dr. Lin Ming-Li

Through the forest iron of Mt. Ali
Which is gray-haired
I look for my childish innocence

The mountain spring
Is a child who loves singing
In a reedy and tenacious tone
Near divine trees   hidden also
Is the laughter of travelers

When the train whistle produces
A loud and clear voice
The winter forest rings with the skirt steps of wind
The memory of land
Also turns into a piece after another piece of tranquility

Cutting down a beam after another beam of sunshine
I carve it on the cherry tree

它竟輕輕地
輕輕地
挽住了夕陽的金鬍子

啊，還有那雲海
從何時
已網住了我每一立方的夢境

————2012.8.9 作 左營
————《海星》詩刊，第 8 期，2013.06
————2016.8.22 錄影於民視「飛閱文學地景」吟詩專
　　輯的詩作，2016.12.24首播於民視新聞晚上六點。

And gently

Very gently

It catches the golden beard of the setting sun

Ah, the sea of clouds

Unawares

Has caught each cube of my dreamland in its net

（天津師範大學外國語系張智中教授英譯）

－刊美國《亞特蘭大新聞》，中英譯 2016.12.23.

　　及攝影照。

68. Songs Fill Ali Mountain Forest

In the forest of Ali Mountain
with its iron grey hair
I search for my childish innocence.

The mountain spring
is a child who love singing
in an unshakably reedy voice
under the sacred trees
while somewhere far off
travellers' laughter can be heard.

When the train whistle rings out
loud and clear
the winter forest echoes with the wind's encircling steps
the memory of land
piece by piece achieves tranquillity.

Cutting down one beam after another of sunshine
I carve it into the cherry tree
and gently
very gently
it catches the golden beard of the setting sun.

Ah, the sea of clouds
unawares
has caught each square of my dreamland in its net.

translated from the Chinese of Lin Ming-Li
（英國詩人 Dr.Norton Hodges 英譯）

69. 我的波斯菊

我的波斯菊
美麗的仙子
你的白色花瓣
高雅純潔
在我心頭開放
自由又暢快
在休耕的原野上
隨風搖晃相吻

是做夢嗎
我聽見了你的花語
來自何方
欲往何處
你什麼也不回答
像隻白文鳥
只留下短短一行字
朋友，珍重吧，心

註.雲林縣莿桐花海，連續三年結合當地休耕所種
植的向日葵、波斯菊等綠肥作物，不僅增進土地
肥力，又讓故鄉成為過年期間賞花的旅遊景點，
因而為詩。
－2016.8.17
－臺灣《秋水》詩刊，第 171 期，2017.07.
－刊美國《亞特蘭大新聞》，2017.1.20。

70. 寫給「飛閱文學地景」
製作之友

我期待你們

在八月火熱太陽下的午後

台東美術館

湖泊般靜謐

時有草木從土地深處萌芽

泊泊心泉，叮咚作響

閃亮的歌聲變成了輕輕的微風

你們的東岸旅程結束於

這座真樸的、最美山城

沒帶走的，是欣喜的淚與歡送的歌

註.繼人間衛視「知道」節目錄製第 110 集「以詩與畫追夢的
心──林明理」後，迄今剛好三年。今年暑假（二○一六），
民視（**FORMOSA TELEVISION**）《飛閱文學地景》節目
的編導涂文權、助理導演莊晨鴻、攝影邱立中、攝影助理吳
昆澧、空拍飛手張芳豪、梳化妝師黃心美等六人於八月二十
二日下午兩點在台東美術館錄製了我吟誦〈歌飛阿里山森
林〉及〈寫給蘭嶼之歌〉兩集。經過三個半小時攝影團隊的
精神與勞力──那是汗水與興奮之情的交匯！終於拍攝完
成，大家都鬆了一口氣，我的心裡充滿了感激。啊，錄影的
這一刻，我怎會忘記？因而為詩。-2016.8.22 夜

－詩〈寫給你們〉刊臺灣《臺灣時報》2016.8.26 及攝
影合照。
－詩〈寫給「飛閱文學地景」製作之友〉刊美國《亞
特蘭大新聞》2016.8.26，及合影照片 2 張，作者照
1 張。詩作及合照再刊於首版。
http://www.atlantachinesenews.com/News/2016/08/0
8-26/B_ATL_P08.pdf
http://www.atlantachinesenews.com/News/2016/08/0
8-26/ATL_P01.pdf
－刊臺灣《大海洋》詩雜誌，94 期，2017.01.頁 41。

2016.8.27MAIL
Dear Friend Ming-Li,
Thank you for your kinde e-mail and for
the poem. I translated it into French

70. Écrit pour vous

DR.LIN MING-LI

Je me réjouis en pesant à vous
Sous le brûlant soleil de cet après-midi d'août.
Le Musée d'art de Taitung
Est comme un lac tranquille
Quand les jeunes pousses sortent des profondeurs de la terre.
Bobo Xinquan, doux tintement,
Chant brillant dans l'aimable brise.
Votre voyage se termine sur la côte est
Où se dresse, toute simple, la plus belle des montagnes,
Elle, enchantée par les larmes que provoque cette chanson d'adieu.

Traduit en français par Athanase Vantchev de Thracy

Have a good day, dear Ming-Li

Athanase

71. 雨聲淅瀝…

雨聲淅瀝….
我看見鳥，哥兒般，在枝頭
啾啾響著。唱歌給河流聽。
無動於我的憂愁。

我想起貝加爾湖宛如煉獄
那野火使勁地燒
不再向人類細語吟哦。

我看見一片葉飄來，盪去。
輕如鴻毛。而我，
我心似松柏，不想嚎啕。

註·俄羅斯貝加爾湖〈Lake Baikal〉又稱西伯利
亞的藍眼睛，是旅遊盛地，但今年九月一場
野火讓原本如詩如畫的湖光山色成了人間煉
獄，有感而文。

－2015.11.21

71. Patter of Rain

Patter of rain…
I saw a familiar bird in the branches.
Its calls rang out, singing to the river,
indifferent to my sorrow.

I thought of the hell of Lake Baikal:
that fire burning wildly
no longer speaking the soft song of humanity.

I saw a leaf floating by,
light as a feather, but as for me,
my heart was like a pine tree and I could not cry.

Author's Note : Russia's Lake Baikal, also known
as Siberian Blue Eyes, is a tourist attraction, but a
wildfire in September 2015 meant that the original
picturesque lake became a hell on earth.
翻譯者： 英國詩人 PROF.Norton Hodges- English
－刊美國《世界的詩》《POEMS OF THE WORLD》，
2016.春季號，頁 26.

72. 摩洛哥之歌

在古城和沉思的海岸間，

我小小的夢漫遊著。我喜愛

造訪橄欖樹瀑布遠甚那些廣場市集，

所以沿它底部小道走，我將

憩止於小磨坊中歌聲之所在，

猶如乘著一彎彩虹，橫跨時空，

它歌給四季聽，噢，美麗的天堂島嶼

── 棕櫚、沙灘、紅土。啊，驚艷的摩洛哥。

註：摩洛哥 Morocco，是非洲西北部的一個沿海阿拉伯國家，
東部以及東南部與阿爾及利亞接壤，南部緊鄰西撒哈拉，西
部瀕臨大西洋，北部和西班牙、葡萄牙隔海相望。橄欖樹瀑
布位於阿特拉斯山區的拉勒省，高 110 米，不僅是摩洛哥最
美麗的瀑布，也是世界最美麗的瀑布之一。瀑布的名字
Ouzoud 因周圍的橄欖樹而得名，橄欖樹在當地被叫做
ouzoud 樹，因此命名為"橄欖樹瀑布"。

── 中英譯刊美國（亞特蘭大新聞），
2017.1.13.

72. The Song of Morocco

In the ancient city, on the pensive coast,

I let my imagination roam:

I travel to the Olive Falls,

far beyond the busy marketplace,

taking the trail as far as the mill

where I stop to listen to the very same song

the four seasons hear,

the song that rides the curve of the rainbow across time and space,

that speaks of a paradise island

of palm trees, sands and red earth,

a dream of unearthly beauty, of Morocco.

translated from the Chinese of Lin Ming-Li

（By 英國詩人諾頓 TRANSLATOR：
Dr.Norton Hodges）

73. 淡水黃昏

我偏愛淡水

偏愛碼頭

偏愛踏上的暮色

遠遠，帆影搖紅

有飛鳥逗著圈子掠過

風的輕漪，讓愛燃燒起來

霞光晃漾在長波裡

有人感到很幸福

有人陷入自憐或沉思

而我搖擺的記憶

隨風揚起，像蜿蜒的河

註.淡水河風景秀麗，為臺灣美景之一，並有『東方威
　尼斯』的美名。淡水一詞在昔日是淡水河口和淡水
　港的總稱，而滬尾一詞則是一個平埔聚落的名稱，
　音為『Hoba』、意為河口，漢人將它翻譯為滬尾，
　日治時期淡水以取代滬尾成為地區的代稱。淡水漁
　人碼頭的「情人橋」是美麗的新地標。淡水老街有
　古蹟巡禮、碼頭敘情，也可品嚐各式小吃。

—2016.8.27

—刊美國《亞特蘭大新聞》，2016.12.23.及水彩畫

74. 新埔柿農

黑夜裡，當九降風吹起，
在旱坑里山丘上，
……輕輕地喚醒柿農。
整個客家村開始忙碌。

這是黃金的隊伍。
這是薪傳的驕傲。
而風在低音區接續
一個又一個古老的故事。

月光下，他們徐疾有序，
屋簷內充滿
微笑、期待與知足。
那雙手的智慧，散溢著成熟的
甜甜果實，正是我心頭的歌。

新埔柿農 林明理畫

註：新竹縣新埔鎮客家村是台灣柿餅之鄉，每年的九月旱坑里九降
風吹起，直到十二月，是曬柿餅的季節。傳統的柿餅製作經由削
皮、日曬、脫水等程序後，排成黃金的隊伍在架上等熟成。柿餅
不僅原有的營養成分被保留下來，且更香甜，令人回味無窮。因
觀賞涂文權導演拍攝的影片《新埔柿餅》，有感而作。
　　　　　　　　　　　　　　　　　　　－2016.8.26

　　　　　－刊臺灣《人間福報》副刊，2016.10.24 圖文
　　　　　－刊臺灣《臺灣時報》副刊，2016.11.3 圖文
　　　　　－刊臺灣《笠》詩刊，第 315 期，2016.10.頁 61。

75. 民視「飛閱文學地景」
錄影記

我該如何形容這場錄影的過程？如何說出這驚人的地景與文學的結合？

假如我是攝影師，我想用各種角度拍出他們眉宇的汗珠和專注的雙眸。

假如我是個舞者，我想要以白鳥之姿，輕柔地用腳尖跳開，演出自己像一湖水，漾著溶溶的月。

假如我是朵雲，我想要輕飛，把黃昏染成一池沉碧的秋水。

然而，我笨拙如牛，只能以簡而婉約的文字，來描繪這場美麗的邂逅。

如同一隻歸雁，嫻雅地劃破天際，看到了蘆花的豐白，在槐樹轉黃裡隨風飄動，直想唱出我心中的歌。

但我沉思的心，在風前張望。我願意努力說出我心中所有的感動。

啊，朋友，我端凝地坐下來。

鏡頭對直，琴聲悠揚。詩裡的歡笑與離合，有我的情感，隨著空拍的動作，起了節奏！忽而低頭書

寫，忽而表現凝思；忽而朗讀，忽而漫步廊中。

　　我忘懷了世界，也忘懷了攝影隊友。只記得講說著蘭嶼與阿里山的優美詩歌。

　　至於，那空拍的畫面之美，我實在描繪不出。

　　但我知道，地景與文學結合的美妙之處，是去賦予一種新的審美形式或社會意涵，讓地景涵具更豐富的文化象徵意義。

　　若再有更詩意的說法，那就是謝謝你們的友誼與熱情，讓文學與台灣土地融為一體，帶我看見臺灣土地歷經歲月流逝的美麗與感動！

　　　　　　　　　　─美國《亞特蘭大新聞》，2016.9.2
　　　　　　　　　　及合照。

76. For Prof. Ernesto Kahan

You wore a draped glory,

In the crowd,

Like a laurel crown of the emperor.

I wish only the blue tits,

Fly to shine your window!

Ming-Li 2016.6.27

你披戴著一身榮耀，
在人群中，
像個桂冕的天子。
我願是隻藍山雀，
飛向你光耀的窗前！

註.賀 1985 年諾貝爾和平獎得主於 2016.6.25 獲得在巴
賽隆納「標題和皇家歐洲科學院醫生的院士殊榮並
發表一篇演講。照片由 Ernesto2016.6.27 Mail 給明
理分享其喜悅。
一刊美國《亞特蘭大新聞》2016.7.1.20。
http://www.atlantachinesenews.com/News/2016/07/0
7-01/B_ATL_P08.pdf

For Ernesto   2016.7.1.   U.S.A.   Ming-L

77. 西湖，你的名字在我聲音裡

　　西湖，你的名字在我聲音裡，來得多麼可喜，轉得多麼光潔；

　　就像秋月與星辰，不為逝去的陽光哭泣，只跟雨說話，為大地而歌。

　　我在風中，呼喚你，像新月一樣，升到山巔同白晝擦肩而過，四周是鳥語與花香的喜悅，而你宛若夢境，湖光把我的歌推向極遠處。

　　西湖，你的名字在我聲音裡，來得多麼輕快，轉得多麼遼闊；

　　就像飛鳥與狂雪，不為逝去的陽光哭泣，只跟風說話，為山谷而歌。

　　我在風中，凝望你，像雲彩一樣，升到深邃的繁星世界，輕輕搖曳，開始唱歌，而你在夢境邊緣，
——我是追逐白堤岸柳的風。

－2016.9.1

－刊中國《浙江日報》報業集團主辦，，美國版《僑報》「我與浙江的故事」徵文，第 410 期，2016.9.2。為 G20 高峰會議徵文而作。
　http://www.uschinapress.com/2016/0902/1077588.shtml
　http://www.usqiaobao.com/zhejiang/ 刊美國版「僑報網」的首頁版。
　http://epaper.uschinapress.com:81/#/issue/2027/15 -刊《僑報》C9 版《今日浙江》。

首页 › 浙江 › 新闻动态 › 正文

诗歌征文

2016-09-02 13:53　:来源: 侨报网　字号:【 大 中 小 】 已有2人浏览

西湖,你的名字在我声音里

林明理

西湖,你的名字在我声音里,来得多么可喜,转得多么光洁;

就像秋月与星辰,不为逝去的阳光哭泣,只跟雨说话,为大地而歌。

我在风中,呼唤着,像新月一样,升到山巅间白昼拂晓而过,四周是鸟语与花香的喜悦,而你宛若梦境,湖光把我的歌推向极远处。

西湖,你的名字在我声音里,来得多么轻快,转得多么迂回;

就像飞鸟与霏雪,不为逝去的阳光哭泣,只跟风说话,为山谷而歌。

我在风中,凝望你,像云影一样,升到深邃的繁星世界,轻轻摇曳,开始唱歌,而你在梦境边缘,——我是追逐白堤岸畔的风。

（作者系中国台湾人,现任台湾文艺协会理事、北京国际汉语诗歌协会理事）

浙江颂

梅卓祥

峰会名城人赞叹,浙江山水拓胸襟;

连云绿树仙间境,寛业杭州老外心。

国际花园砥盛放,东方港口客频临;

民风淳朴闻天下,华夏桃源百旅寻。

（作者系美籍华人,现居芝加哥）

78. 曇花的故事

昨夜，霧散漫如煙
秋又向我伸出雙手
千百年來
風雨中等候
冰雪中吟詠
而我
總是在黎明前
消失於霎時
難道
你未曾察覺
我在書頁裡用心寫著
在你途經的每次回眸
你可以再靠近一點
就會看個清楚
也許你　一無驚奇
也許我　仍在夢中

　　註.近日,詩友非馬傳來親種的曇花,恬淡絕塵的風采令我傾倒。相傳,曇花和佛祖座下的韋馱尊者有一段哀怨纏綿的故事,所以曇花又叫韋馱花。她原是天上的小花仙,卻愛上了每天為她鋤草的小夥子,玉帝知道後震怒,並把花神貶為一生只能開一瞬間的花,不讓他們相見,還把那個小夥子送去靈柩山出家,賜名韋馱,讓他忘記前塵,忘記花神。可是花神卻忘不了那個年輕的小夥子,她知道每年暮春時分,韋駝尊者都會上山採春露,為佛祖煎茶,就選在那個時候開花,希望能再見韋馱尊者一面。遺憾的是,春去秋來,花開花謝,韋馱終究不認得她了。因此,就有了「曇花一現,只為韋陀」的愛情傳說。有感為詩。

－2016.8.31

－刊臺灣《秋水》詩刊,第 170 期,2017.01,
　頁 36。

79. 布拉格之秋

千塔輝映著晚霞，
繆斯的眼眸繼續延伸。
被世界歌誦過無數的單詞，
從天文鐘塔塔頂飄到另一個國度。

一個詩人聆聽穿廊下飄揚的樂音，
讀到片片秋葉的心事。

－2016.9.13

－刊美國《亞特蘭大新聞》，2016.9.23。

80. 大灰狼的謳歌

當人們開始貪婪砍伐，
陽光顯得虛弱，天更憂藍；
難道人們已遺忘
大自然微弱的呼吸？
難道世界看不到
我的痛苦哀吟如昔。

看落雪覆蓋在山頂，
寒意習習：交錯的水系，
細長的峽灣，紛飛的眾鳥，
或鹿的蹄聲，暮色中的冰原……
一切在幻變，人們卻沒驚覺。

一片森林慢慢消逝，接著
又是一片，凍土慢慢消融，
極光如飄搖散去的淚。
而我，只是一聲凝眺遠方的嘆息，
也將在未來中飄散、消失。

　　—2016.9.13.為阿拉斯加原始森林慢慢消逝，憂心會影響
　　　大灰狼 timber wolf 等動物生存及生態環境改變而作。
　　—刊美國《亞特蘭大新聞》，2016.10.7.

81. 莫蘭蒂風暴

昨夜一場颱風
滿天烏雲擠壓著
好比野獸狂亂的雨腳
在等待黎明前
誰來揭掉島民心上的憂愁
誰來阻擋切膚入骨的風
啊，莫蘭蒂
妳像個潑婦，越洋而來
我們曾是海之勇士
而今，幾乎是一首悲歌
我們的痛又將如何填平
祖靈啊，請你守望著我們
請接受我們禱告
在這中秋團聚的重要時刻

> 註.莫蘭蒂 **Meranti** 是 2016 年西北太平洋最強的熱帶
> 氣旋，今年 9 月 14 日登陸後，在臺灣恆春海域轉
> 向，以強颱的姿態直逼呂宋海峽和廣東東部沿岸，
> 成為中秋節嚴重的威脅，致蘭嶼島民刮起十七級強
> 風及全島大停電的災情，因而為詩。
> －2016.9.14 寫於台東。
>
> －刊美國《亞特蘭大新聞》亞城園地，2016.9.16。
> －刊臺灣 Taiwan Times《臺灣時報》，台灣文學版，
> 　2016.9.21.圖文。
> －刊臺灣《金門日報》副刊，2016.10.22.

82. 紅尾伯勞

儘管是聒噪，

還朝著南方急進；

遙遠的未來，已幻成秋野的樂音。

—刊登四川省重慶市《中國微型詩》），
　　總第 17 期，2009.3.1。

83. 颱風夜

別呼嘯了。梅姬，妳
的急驟狂暴令我難過。
在妳眼中，難道只剩下最瘋狂的摧殘？
難道妳看不到島嶼的哭泣？
難道妳聽不見我們的禱告？
唉，太多的暴風雨
太多的悲情延續著。
在這漫漫長夜，
夠了，請無聲息地掠過──
把希望還給我們的家。

註.2016 年 9 月 27 日夜晚梅姬颱風襲台，造
　　成多處土石流及停水、大停電等災情發
　　生，因而為詩。

－2016.9.27

－刊臺灣《臺灣時報》，2016.9.30 圖文。

84. 佳節又重陽

當我老了真好，像茱萸
在初夏綻放而在秋天成熟
從花兒變成紫果
從歡顏變成孤傲
隨著遍處菊花，風箏
在孩童嘻笑聲中飄搖
我登高遠眺
讓心回歸自然
耳中飄蕩的是大雁歌聲
還有那悠揚多情的風
滔不盡萬里長江的秋色
朋友，萬物都讓我想起你
有酒
今夜你在這兒也許會聽到
月光盈滿老城的歡笑

－2016.10.2
－刊臺灣《人間福報》圖文，2016.10.11.
－刊臺灣《臺灣時報》圖文，2016.10.13.

85. 漫步黃昏林中

漫步黃昏林中

在咫尺之間的烏頭翁旁

秋風撩起

暴雨後的淒然

天空一片湛藍

鳥兒啊，欲往何方

請等等我——

你是優美的詩句

洋溢著愛情與希望

短暫的嘹音

既喜悅又帶些許傷感

—2016.10.3 寫於莫蘭蒂颱風過後，與友秀
　實同遊初鹿牧場，偶感而作。

—刊美國《亞特蘭大新聞》，2016.10.7 及
　攝影作一張。

86. 我的歌

我的歌在烈嶼吹響著
請用秋日注滿我的愛
流浪的風兒指給我看：
牛拖著犁靜靜地
跟著扶犁人前進
就這樣，引導我
宛如源自遙遠的
水頭聚落的聲波
至於，它的柔音像首詩
輕微地輕微地
在那兒奔馳
已無關緊要
在我腳步之夢的盡處
你的純樸孕育了我的哲學
像穿越金色麥田的月兒

－22016.10.14
－刊臺灣《金門日報》副刊，2017.1.10。

87. 在四月桐的夢幻邊緣

多麼美麗的初夏
我不停地尋思
像隻藍蝶找到了小瀑布
你彈著遙遠的琴音
在四月桐的夢幻邊緣
如鳴泉飛雨

輕輕
漫過林野，穿繞溪間
等待一個相約
在螢舞季節
懸在我耳畔，依呀作響

要是我能穿越時空
浸沉於台三線山谷的夜色
只有蟲鳴和水聲
從高處越嶺而來
啊，所有話語都無法描繪
你是獨奏的驚雪

－2017.1.5
－刊美國《亞特蘭大新聞》2017.1.20。

88. 獻給敘利亞罹難的女童

——為戰區的白盔志工致敬

再無人可以讓我哭泣
噢，我甜美的小女孩
如何讓妳重新唱歌
拂拭妳靈魂的憂傷
如何讓妳再度甦醒
默默地迎著親人走來

杏枝上掛滿了烏德琴
好似我流不住的淚
匯成空中的條條雨絲
讓我再貼近妳的小臉
比任何人都親
比任何人都把妳掛念

－2016.10.14

註 最近看到電視上有白盔志工男兒流下激動的淚，抱著
救出的敘利亞小女孩罹難的身軀，很感傷，因而為詩。

88. Dedicated to the girls killed in Syria

—tribute to the white helmets in the war zone

Dr. Lin Ming-Li of Taiwan

No one can make me cry
Oh, my sweet little girl
How to get you to sing again
To wipe awaythe sadness of your soul
How to make you awake again
Quietly to come while greeting your beloved ones

Apricot trees arecovered with a Oud
As if my running tears which can not stop
To form a line after another line of raindrops
Let me again get close to your little face
Closer than anyone else
I miss you more than anyone in the world

— October, 14, 2016

Remark: recently when I see on TV the white helmets in the war zone shedding hot tears while embracing the bodies of the girls killed in Syria, I feel sentimental, hence this poem.

－天津師範大學外國語學院所長張智中教授翻譯。
－刊美國《亞特蘭大新聞》，2016.10.21.

89. 倒 影

我曾夢想
為你搭起一座心房
那兒星光璀璨，林邊
到處飛舞著歌雀的翅膀

而我
是日日夜夜拂過的輕風
從繁花似錦的草原落到
你沉思默想的河畔

在我無數的回眸中
不管我立在東方或西岸
都將聽見一種曲調
那是水波激蕩著你唱吟的地方

－2016.10.21
－刊臺灣《海星》詩刊，第 23 期，春季號，
2017.03.01

90. 踏青詠春

金色楓林下，白雪木
團團簇簇
如聖誕初雪
路的盡頭
紅櫻藏身樹林
魚兒嬉遊野溪石縫

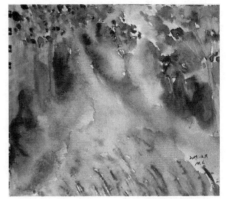

林明理畫

但我不能久留
春天的眼睛
閃爍著童稚的快樂
萬花又紅遍枝頭

而我聽見白冷圳
輕輕哼唱故鄉的小調

從賞花到玩踩水
從酒莊到虹橋
我聆聽薰衣草說話
也夢見那些原野和搖閃的
螢火蟲，幾隻白鷺掠過——
安然自得

－2016.12.30
－臺灣《青年日報》），2017.3.8.

91. 七星潭之戀

我喜歡聆聽大海，看慢舞的雲彩
一灣澄碧的水，浪花輕吻堤岸
在靜謐的月牙灣低迴

誰要是沒有領略過
旭日、沙灘和輕風
就無法理解歡樂或痛苦或漂泊的憂傷

我茫茫然回首，多少年後
會響起什麼樣的聲音
就像這風兒把愛輕輕寫在沙上

─2016.10.24
─刊美國《亞特蘭大新聞》，2017.1.20。

92. 憶阿里山

站在天堂也似的山上

清溪潺潺，天色泛紅

萬物都讓我想起你

還有那櫻花，晚霞，鐵道

奔馳的小火車

諦聽繽紛四季的風

讓我用羽翼貼近你

在山之巔，棲息在古木旁

悠然觀賞雲海變幻

四周的一切已然淡忘

看這水清山秀

看這怡人之鄉

漫步在山的雲端

我沉浸於你周圍的景色

你已撥動了我靈魂

像是在對我高歌

　　　　　－2016.10.31

　　　　　－刊美國《亞特蘭大新聞》），2016.12.2 圖文

93. 勇 氣

—祝賀川普（Donald Trump）

勇氣，親民，直言不諱

以及未受驚駭的選民

這些令你成了獲勝者

而多數人在經歷了同樣的震撼後

只能宣稱　覺得有句話還是

挺妙的！那就是讓人傳頌的：

「Make America great again！」

—2016.11.9
—刊美國《亞特蘭大新聞》，2016.11.11
　及水彩畫 1 幅。

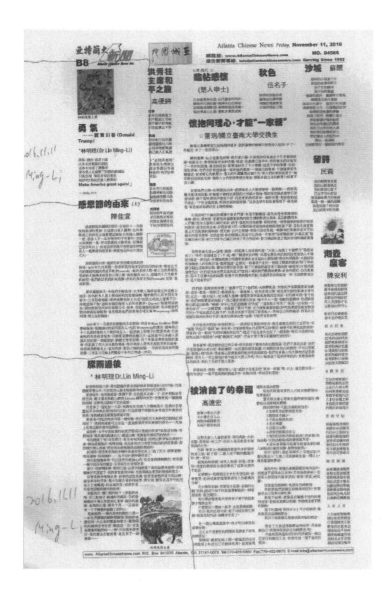

94. 你的故事：Η ΜΠΕΦΑΝΑ ΤΗΣ ΙΤΑΛΙΑΣ

神的恩典是多麼榮耀。

多麼公正，多麼令人意外與欣喜。

祂讓 Befana 具備了勇氣，

去實現心中的渴求。而

你的故事

與祈福家鄉所有善良女人的靜謐之情，

是愛，也是仁慈的心。

－林明理，台灣 2017.1.1-中英譯刊美國
《亞特蘭大新聞》，2017.2.24.

94. *Your story*

—（Giovanni Campisi：Η ΜΠΕΦΑΝΑ ΤΗΣ ΙΤΑΛΙΑΣ）

How glorious God's grace is.

How fair, how surprising and delighted.

He gave Befana the courage,

To achieve the hearts of the desire. and

Your story

And blessing home all the kindness of women quiet,

Is love, but also the heart of kindness.

By Lin Ming-Li ， Taiwan January 1, 2017

－英譯刊義大利 EDIZIONI　UNIVERSUM
INTERNATIONAL POETRY　ＮＥＷＳ（埃迪采
恩尼大學）《國際詩新聞》2017.1，林明理英譯。
作者收到由義大利詩人、出版家 Giovanni
Campisi 傳來一篇他寫的義大利故鄉一個貧窮的
女巫後來變成在耶誕節夜裡騎著掃帚分發糖果
給幼童的故事後，有感而作。

95. 聽　海

憂鬱的藍
像是起伏的心海
當它消隱之時
暮色旋踵即至
塔的幽影，玫瑰色的紅
還有浪濤砰砰擊響

啊西子灣
像母親的殷盼
哼一曲鄉居小唱吧
每當冬季來臨
你高歌如鷹
騰飛到我身旁

註.西子灣位於高雄市柴山西南端山麓下，南面隔海與
旗津島相望，是個以夕陽及天然礁石聞名的海灣。
　　－2016.11.17

－刊美國《亞特蘭大新聞》，2016.12.2 圖文，
攝影。
－刊臺灣《大海洋》詩雜誌，94 期，2017.01.
頁 41。

96. 蘭嶼情

──民視《飛閱文學地景》觀後

我總是愛聽達悟族的一切
那傳說中的傳說
總是任我極力馳騁的想像
而這些是我從來未曾見過的

正由於這緣故
前幾個月的一個夜晚
我為它譜寫成詩
而它也被製成一部影片紀錄
為表示由衷地嘆服
我目不轉睛地凝注著畫面出神

我默默地期盼
明年在東清部落
一起迎接第一道曙光
在土耳其藍的海水旁沉思

　　然後蹲坐在屋的一隅
　　聽耆老訴說悠悠歲月的往事

　　註：蘭嶼，（達悟語：Ponso no Tao），為臺東縣蘭嶼
　　　　鄉所管轄，四面環海，因其島上獨有的達悟族地土風
　　　　俗與自然景點，遠近馳名。島上的常見的生物有椰子
　　　　蟹、綠蠵龜、山羊、珠光裳鳳蝶、飛魚、角鴞（貓頭
　　　　鷹）、豬、夠貓及羅漢松等。從環島公路往東清灣岬
　　　　角附近的情人洞，為天然海蝕洞，是最美之景。2016
　　　　年 11 月 19 日午後三點五十七分，我看到了民視新聞
　　　　【飛閱文學地景】播出我吟誦出自美國《亞特蘭大新
　　　　聞網》的詩《寫給蘭嶼之歌》，螢幕中的蘭嶼，唯美
　　　　而浪漫。除了由著名書法家張炳煌親自揮毫題詩、配
　　　　合空拍的特殊技巧以外，一開始，有紙飛機輕輕掠
　　　　過……就好像引領著旅人的心跟著飛到蘭嶼，之後，
　　　　出現一整排的拼板舟、白燈塔如獵戶座般，閃耀於海
　　　　面的飄搖，美得太令人感動。接著，有婦人彎著腰在
　　　　礁岩旁工作、有泛舟及達悟族人歡愉地手拉手舞蹈……
　　　　當畫面最後逐漸消失在情人洞口的高點上，時空好像
　　　　跟著靜止了！直等到廣告的出現，我才回神過來。
　　　　啊，這是我的驚嘆，也是真實的心聲，我得把它永存
　　　　心底。而涂文權導演剪裁得簡潔有力，說出了詩語的
　　　　重點及訴求；背景音樂也能自然地流現高等感性。這
　　　　是我期盼了三個月餘，夢想中的蘭嶼，是幕後工作小
　　　　組的心血與努力。為表示由衷的嘆服，因而為詩。

　　　　　　飛閱文學地景　IV Ep 20 - 寫給蘭嶼之歌　林明理

　　　　　　－2016.11.22 夜於台東
　　　　　　－刊美國《亞特蘭大新聞》2016.11.25.圖文。

97. Write to you

Dr.Lin Ming-Li

Yes, my dear friend,

Your friendship bright as cedar,

Temperament like the general bright and clean snow,

How can I remove my gaze?

From a number of elegant manners ——

Close to the eyes of my praise!

$-$ 2016.11.27

97. 寫給妳們

Dr.Lin Ming-Li

是的，我親愛的朋友，

你們的友情亮潔如雪松，

氣質像雪一般明淨，

如何能移開我的凝視？

從諸多文雅的儀態——

緊貼著我讚嘆的眼睛！

註.旅美作家王克難女士電郵寄來近日聯誼會的一張
　　照片，並對於我吟詩（寫給蘭嶼之歌）的鼓勵，令
　　我感動，因而為詩。-2016.11.27
　－刊美國《亞特蘭大新聞》，2016.12.2 攝影。

98. Ode to the Orchid Island

The land has its memory
Like the melody of waves
From year to year
It is singing myriads of songs
In the morning or at dusk
When Dawu people climb up to live in the mountain
Or return from the sea
It gives an echo of history
What is soul-stirring
Is the howling sea
And the forms flashing in sea waves

In the years where they are watching the sea
When they want to again penetrate the waves
These yearnings, like clouds floating in the sky
But the land has its memory
And it will never forget
On clansmen the pain of land being destroyed
And the shouting of warriors in tidal waves
Whenever the dawn comes
It repeats our song time and again

by Dr. Lin Ming-Li

IPN

2016. 11.

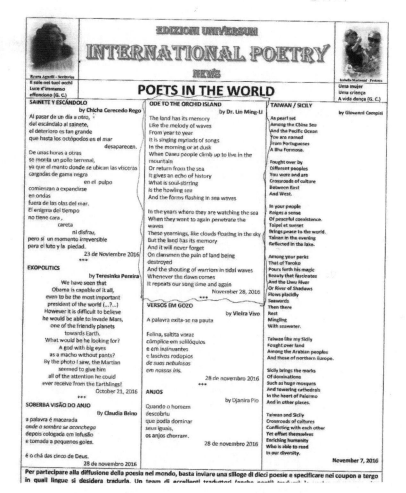

－刊英譯刊美國《Poems of the World》季刊，2016.秋季號
－刊義大利 EDIZIONI UNIVERSUM INTERNATIONAL
POETRY ＮＥＷＳ（埃迪采恩尼大學）《國際詩新聞》
2016.11，林明理詩〈Ode to the Orchid Island〉，張智中
教授英譯。

—美國《亞特蘭大新聞》2016.12.2 首頁網可點播視訊林明
理吟詩〈寫給蘭嶼之歌〉。
http://www.atlantachinesenews.com/News/2016/12/120216.html

98. 寫給蘭嶼之歌

土地是有記憶的
正如浪花的弦律
歲歲年年
歌咏著億萬種詩句
清晨或暮靄時分
當達悟人上山
或出海返航
它就發出歷史的回聲
那震人心魄的
是大海在狂呼
還有海浪上閃耀流逝的身影

在他們望海的歲月裡
在他們想再次穿破浪頭的時候
這些渴望，如雲漂浮太空
但土地是有記憶的
它不會忘記
族人身上留有土地被破壞的痛

留有勇士們在潮水中的吶喊
每當黎明到來
它便重複著重複著我們的歌

－2016.7.24 寫於台東

*此詩的創作第一句啟蒙於山東大學吳開晉教授名詩
〈土地的記憶〉），有感而作。

－刊美國《亞特蘭大新聞》）圖文，2016.7.29.
－2016.8.22 錄影在台東美術館錄影於民視「飛閱文學地景」
節目，林明理專輯吟誦的詩作之一，2016.11.19 晚上六點
民視新聞首播。可由 GOOGLE 點播民視「飛閱文學地景」
節目
YouTube https://www.youtube.com/playlist?list=PLf2VRok0uR
O0_VqLv_fPoGHtNe3fAMUSz
YAHOO Video https://tw.video.yahoo.com/fei-yue/
https://www.facebook.com/WenHuaBu/posts/1174239905989277
臉書

98. Ode to Orchid Island

The land has its memory
like the melody of the waves,
year after year
its sings myriads of songs
in the morning or at dusk
when the Dawu　people
climb the mountain
to find a place to live
or return from the sea
the land echoes with history
what stirs the soul
is the howling sea
and the figures　flashing in the waves.

There are years when they watch the sea
or when they want to go to sea again
their yearnings are like clouds floating in the sky,
but the land has its memory
and it will never forget
the pain of clansmen laying it waste
or the cries of warriors in tidal waves,
and when dawn comes
its song is heard
again and again and again.

From the Chinese of Lin Ming-Li
－英國詩人諾頓博士 Dr.Norton Hodges 英譯

99. 無比崇高的泰米爾詩人

——To Dr.Vaa.mu.Sethuraman

你忽地出現在我面前
滿面含笑
彷彿聖殿中的蓮花
受難化現的尊者
在悠悠歲月裡
你用心靈之光
譜寫世界和平的詩
都交織成菩薩的淚花
點點
滴入泰米尔人民的心田
而篇篇永恆的話語
與不滅的愛
如雨露和天地合一
讓全球村庄靜默

－2017.1.6 寫於台灣

99. The lofty Tamil poet

— To Vaa.mu.Sethuraman

Dr.Lin Ming-Li

You suddenly appeared in front of me
Smiling
As if the lotus in the temple
Of the Venerable
In the long years
You use the light of the mind
Compose poetry of world peace
Are woven into the Buddha's tears
Little
Tamil the hearts of the people
The chapter of the eternal discourse
And the eternal love
Such as rain and the unity of heaven and earth
Let the global village quiet

－2017.1.6 written in Taiwan
－英譯刊《亞特蘭大新聞》，2017.1.20。

100. 寫給包公故里──肥東

是怎樣的企盼，怎樣的憧憬？讓我飛越海洋的邊界，

泊在巢湖之畔，等待無比明顯的希望之城──肥東。

是的，你就像心中的巨人，堅毅而平和。

這裡美麗超出了想像，雨後大地更有麥香的味道。我懷著格外強烈的情意，再一次俯視這座石塘古鎮。

若不是從高處遠眺，怎能親近岱山的湖光山色，又怎能在風中歇息片刻，在奔向文化園路途上就有我的停留？

你說：「跟隨我吧！我是你的舵手。」

如果我往你身邊走，迎著的這股風，散發著彼處和遠方的芳菲──聽稻浪的柔音，還有那如海似的翠微。頭頂參天老木，這裡只剩下美和真。美在皖中腹地，真在耕者鋤禾裡。

輕快的白雲，群山和寧靜的沃土……都在我的血液中搏動。

溪流在岩邊跳著舞，古民也唱出心中的歌。它突破

了語言的疆界，歌裡飽含著透徹的靈魂，使我聯想起自己久別的故里，沒有任何虛妄，但我驚訝於它如何歷經千年依然為世人所傳頌？

啊，是你，使繆斯唱吟，是你震撼我的心靈，帶給勞動者心的力量。

如果我閉目靜聽，就會聽到河湖的低語，如果我凝望著那藏在山谷外的藍霧，這對我來說，彷彿是豐富的饗宴。

今夜，我依舊做著旅人的夢，夢裡用眼睛尾隨著飛逝的船隻，我感到莫名的幸福。當我目光與你對視，是你甜柔的歌聲，讓所有野花開放。

你屬於永恆，而我懷著這樣的深情，在我隱秘的心底，世上再沒有什麼樂音，讓我鼓舞地駛過萬頃波浪。

如果你看我，我就帶著江淮之間的夕陽和唇邊一朵微笑，邊哼著歡樂的小曲，駛向黑石咀的金色沙灘，在天宇間漫步，與你吟咏荷花塘。

－2016.12.06
－刊美國《亞特蘭大新聞》，2017.02.03.

101. 那年冬夜

你的憂懼巨大
而蜷伏
我的恰似
月下草上失足的孤星

生命
正從身邊溜過
什麼時候我重生
哪裡是我夢中的雲影

我們的記憶
是淺鑄的
一面
淚鏡

—2014.8.30
—臺灣《海星詩刊》，2014.12，第 14 期，頁 94。
—詩作〈那年冬夜〉應邀於《海星》詩刊【詩的影像】現代詩
　與攝影聯展，2017.2.4 於台北市長官邸藝文中心參展。
文化部 i culture：　http://cloud.culture.tw/frontsite/inquiry/
eventInquiryAction.do?method=　　showEventDetail&uid=
586f3b1acc46d8fa6452ca16

102. 諦 聽

小小島嶼，
無論悲傷或美麗，永遠擁抱著大海。
那歷史的斷片，撩撥我的思古。

－2017.1.13

林明理畫

Listen

Dr.Lin Ming-Li

Small islands,
Sad or beautiful, always embrace the sea.
The fragments of history, deeply provoke my thoughts.

（Translator：Dr.William Marr）
－美國《亞特蘭大新聞》，2017.1.20.圖文。
－義大利《國際詩新聞》，2017.02.

103. 燈下讀《田裏爬行的滋味》

謝謝，你生命的溫情

彷彿曙光下綻開的

百合

在你無瑕的思想裡

慈悲與憐愛贏過一切

　這是你生命之歌

樸真而堅定

與世長存

我把你的記憶與愛

存於胸中，讓夢想無限馳騁

余玉照著

附註：2016 年 10 月 26 日，欣喜於台大余玉照教授寄贈《田裏爬行的滋味》，深感榮幸；此書除了把作者自幼在農家經歷的事描述得十分感人以外，還能身教言教，讓讀者對農家及食物多分敬意。我深信，他的成功並非偶然，而是一步一耕耘；而在農地裡苦過、打滾過，所衍生的生活智慧，與力爭上游的骨氣，令人敬佩，因而為詩。

　　—刊美國《亞特蘭大新聞》，2017.1.13。

104. 獻給青龍峽的歌

誰打開了神秘的魔盒

靜謐

靜謐的煙波浩渺

浩渺於山峽的雲臺山 ——

光影裡一幅幅山水畫卷

畫出中原第一峽

畫出七彩潭和倒流泉

畫出瀑溪和雄峰

畫出溶洞和植物群落

但畫不出

看谷不見谷，聞水不見水的模樣

瞧瞧千年的椰樹

還有古牌坊和樓閣

似等待依序而來的日子

在蟲鳥唧唧的奏鳴中

靜聽‾

我在遙遠的遠方獻上一束詩

向長谷的頂巔呼喊

這裡看起來的確像天堂

把世界帶進青龍峽吧

啊我願再次與你相擁，像隻蒼鷹

在望龍瀑的肩膀上長吻

> 註：青龍峽風景名勝區位於河南省焦作市修武縣，是
> 河南雲臺山世界地質公園主要遊覽區之一，被譽為
> 「中原第一峽」。

－刊美國《亞特蘭大新聞》，2017.1.13。

105. 給 LUCY

讓我們一起詠嘆吧
那是山海交織的頌曲
妳側了身，像顆不願夢醒的朝露

林明理攝

105. To Lucy

Let's sing together

Of mountains and the sea

You turn your body, like a morning dew

Unwilling to wake up from its dream

－2017.1.15（DR.WILLIAM MARR 英譯）
－刊美國《亞特蘭大新聞》，2017.1.20.
　及攝影照。

106. 炫目的綠色世界

大黑麥田，農場和馬房

從空曠到金色的海面

我無法一一盛裝

翩翩而來的春天

就像思鄉的弦懸在耳畔

林明理攝

－2017.1.13
－刊美國《亞特蘭大新聞》，2017.1.27，圖文。

The dazzling green world

Lin Mingli

Large black wheat fields, farms and stables
From the open to the golden sea
I can not dress them up one by one
Spring on her dancing feet
Is like homesickness ringing in the ears

－2017.1.13Translator：Dr.William Marr
－美國《亞特蘭大新聞》，2017.1.27 圖文。

107. 日月潭抒情

那年冬天。

我讀你的名字，Lalu。於是，蜿蜒在涵碧半島的森林氣味氤氳而來，開始有了難忘的牽掛。一葉船屋，在某些小灣上，一份閒適圍繞。

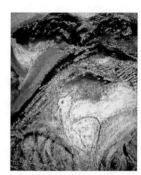

林明理畫

這是個充滿古老傳說的名字，在我腦海似有若無，低調、親切，泛起遐思。

在月光照耀的落葉上，稀微光芒倒影的湖面，彷彿一座聖潔的水晶連橋。

每當漫步林間，偶見五色鳥、山紅頭、繡眼畫眉在隱約的樹蔭裡活潑跳躍，我便止不住內心的激動，有一種生命的喜悅經過我的身體。

我被水意和晨曦引領著。行至潭畔，眺望蔚藍色的雲朵，看白鳥剪水，看堤堤上綠草如茵。啊，Lalu，你是如此素美和富饒。

我願是展翼的歌手，聽你訴說邵族的傳說。那白色水鹿輕輕默默走過，沒有引起任何騷動，就像你生命的溫柔脈動，我只想無拘無礙在此逗留。

當明銳的陽光斜影在冬天的伊達邵碼頭，你的名

字是手中的小鳥，落霞中，若隱若現……沿著堤岸在粼粼波光之上戲耍，在樹林間來回穿梭，在啁啾鳥聲中愉悅地歌詠著邵族鄉民。

我想站在北極星斗下採擷四季的風，讓倒映的鬱綠拴住我心深處。讓記憶裡的潭畔，穿過時空，接通了夢想。

我願做一尾魚，迎向起風的岸，浮雲在天上，也在湖中。而我將一種相思鑲嵌進我的詩裡，在碧波之上騰挪……

黎明前，朝霞像某段記憶，過濾著群山之上的風與雨。我願聆聽歲月低語，在雨後的黃昏，鑑賞雨霧繚繞的歡笑。你那朦朧的臉龐，忽而清晰起來，空氣中還存有一絲涼意。

你是水做的島嶼，我照見你籠在一朵朵私密的雲海裡，可濃可淡，可墨可彩。每當落入潭中的天，藍得那麼純淨，銀波森森。

啊，Lalu，你這美麗的鳥，漸去漸遠如夢般，漫不經心地來，風中，可有我的信息？可有我為你高亢的歌？

註.拉魯島（邵語：Lalu）是一座位於南投縣日月潭中央的小島，當地居民習慣稱為珠仔山，是邵族傳說中祖靈安息之處，也有「心中聖島」之意。傳說，邵族的祖先由於打獵時發現一隻白色水鹿而沿路追逐到日月潭的拉魯島。但白鹿瞬間變成一棵白茄冬樹矗立在島上，所以邵族的祖先也從此在潭畔定居下來。因此茄冬樹成了邵族的聖樹。　　　　　　　－2016.12.9

－《鹽分地帶文學》預稿。

108. 玉山頌

站在雪地上，仰望、傾聽。
我期待你的歌聲，堅毅
深情如母親河。

－2017.1.16（新聞報導，臺灣最高峰的玉山
下了第一場雪，因而為詩。）

林明理畫

108. *Ode to Yushan*

Lin Mingli

Standing on the snow, looking up, listening.
I look forward to hearing your strong voice
Affectionate as the mother river.

－2017.1.16 (Recently, Taiwan's highest peak
of Yushan had its first snowfall.)
－美國《亞特蘭大新聞》，2017.1.27。圖文，
DR.WILLIAM MARR 英譯。

109.張家界之夢

1.

我是雲，我曾走向你
那一座座拔地而起的石崖
塗染太陽的顏色
啊，這比世上什麼夢還要逼真
也許要走過許多彎路
也許也不那麼勇敢過
但為了能飄搖著
尋找歇息的帳篷
我停下，是為了飛騰的激情
我歌著，是為了古老的龍王洞
如何去裝扮那蒼涼的天穹
如何想起你深深的一吻
輕輕地，我攀著砂岩峰林
飛繞月宮
讓周圍的一切都變得無關緊要
而後
慢慢回到你的懷抱

有誰知
我飄搖著，感到自在消遙
還把你的形象寫在我的日記之中

2.
你是大地母親的寵兒
遠望著這個世界
偶爾捎來神鷹
喚我穿越海峽向你走去
從千峰萬壑傳來
從運行的星球上傳來
你展示了巨大的存在
頂破億萬年封閉的地殼
在東方兀自站起
太陽給你七彩的靈光
雲霧給你神祕的長袍
八方的風挽起你的手
雕刻著武陵源的形象
大海退得遠遠的
為的是襯托你的成長
你來自遠古生界
拋出了美麗的銀瀑和林帶

我總忘不了
黃獅寨和砂刀溝
時時刻刻，都超凡而奇妙

3.
那金鞭溪是你美麗的軀體
穿行在
峰巒幽谷間
偉大的岩石似人似物
默立的岩石似鳥似獸
但癡情的雲啊可仍記得
你是怎樣調皮
又是怎樣歡跳舞蹈
是怎樣踏出了一串串新韻
又是怎樣不息的勞作
種植出彩色的所有音符
是你透明的心音
讓我看盡了你奔騰的歡樂
也許，有一天
你會突然醒來
像小孩子奔下山澗
一路上張望

同時逗著我
啊遠方的朋友
讓我為你唱首歌，只在夢中

4.

月亮跳進十里畫廊
沾一身琴音
它輕輕地問採藥老人

如何踏著萬頃湖波
把千古舊事
化入
刻骨的相思引向藍天
如何把絲絲縷縷的秋雨
從天的源頭
敲到人們的心頭

5.

用衝越天子山的峰牆
跨過千丈寒風的肆虐
用不老的禦筆之奇
畫開一匹匹武士馴馬

你這峰林之王
正指揮著百鳥的合鳴
盼仙女漫步而來
橋上神兵聚會
橋下唯一的語言
是綠色

6.

你，披散崖下
日夜擁抱著這群奇峰
從九天玄梯奔過來
從乾坤柱的岩頂奔過來
像奧運運動員，一躍而過
啊，龍泉瀑布
你那迷人的歌聲
是欣喜，是祝福
從不保留什麼
如遙遠的夢

7.

夜晚的沱江
努力向前，靜靜地流

河畔燈光閃爍，歌聲迷濛
啊，你是中國南方最美麗的
鳳凰古城
那青石板街，新砌的城牆
還有吊腳樓
阿拉營趕場的叫賣聲
民族風味濃厚
萬名塔上的風，掠過虹橋
在歷經三百一十二年滄桑後
燦然地笑了

　　　　　　　　—美國《亞特蘭大新聞》，2017.1.27.

110. 春歸

轉瞬間
雪變成了馥郁的季節
我在草綠間尋覓
飛掠而過的蝶影
吻走最後一滴星淚

--2017.1.24

The Returning of Spring

Lin Ming-Li

In an instant
I find the snow has become a season of fragrance
In the green grass I look for
The shadows of flying Butterflies
Which will kiss away the last teardrop from the stars

－刊美國《亞特蘭大新聞》，2017.2.3，馬為義博士譯。

附錄 1. 1985 年諾貝爾和平獎得主 Prof. Ernesto Kahan 翻譯林明理詩

詩〈寫給科爾多瓦猶太教堂的歌〉為西班牙語詩

西班牙猶太教堂猶太教不朽的巧匠
邁蒙尼德（*Maimonides*）雕像

A Song for Cordoba Synagogue

Dr.Lin Ming-Li

When I walk toward you, Cordoba,
Toward the city, toward the flowers Lane,
Toward the silent synagogue,
Toward the nine holy candlesticks,
Toward the desolate sound in the wind,

Near the statue of Maimonides,
When your silence descends like falling leaves,
And becomes the crystal spray.
Ah, God, my Almighty,
Thy mercy shines on the mortal world,
Thy gospel emerges from darkness.
Please help Thy people,
Heal historical wounds.
In this peaceful morning,
Listen to my silent prayer.
Amen.

Note Cordoba (Córdoba) in the Spanish autonomous region of Andalusia, the Guadalquivir River, it is the capital of Cordoba province, also has a lot of cultural heritage and monuments of the city. Wherein the synagogue, ancient and stately walls are carved with Hebrew from Jewish craftsman Maimonides (Maimonides). Judaism has a seat in the hall of his bust sculptures in the vicinity of the flowers Lane also has a sculpture of his body, he is also a famous Jewish philosopher, jurist and physician. — 2016.7.29

寫給科爾多瓦猶太教堂的歌

林明理 Dr.Lin Ming-Li

當我走向你，科爾多瓦，
走向古城，走向百花巷，
走向靜寂的猶太教堂，
走向聖潔的九燭台，
走向風中的荒涼聲響，

走向邁蒙尼德的雕像，
這時，你的沉默如葉飄落，
是我眸中晶瑩的水花。
啊，神啊，我的全能，
祢的慈悲光耀世道，
祢的福音在黑暗中浮現。
請支撐祢的子民，
撫平歷史的傷痕。
在這和平的早晨，
聽我無聲的祈禱。
阿門。

註.科爾多瓦（Córdoba）位於西班牙安達盧西亞自治區、瓜達
爾基維爾河畔，是哥多華省的首府，也是一個擁有許多文化
遺產和古跡的城市。其中的猶太教堂，古老而莊嚴，牆上雕
飾著希伯來文是出自猶太人的巧匠邁蒙尼德
（*Maimonides*）。在猶太教堂內有座他的半身雕塑，在附
近的百花巷中也有一座他的全身雕塑，他也是著名的猶太哲
學家、法學家和醫生。　　　　　－2016.7.29

－2016.8.11 收件者今天 於 1:18 AM
Dear Ming-li
This is my translation into Spanish.
Love
　　　Ernesto

A Song for Cordoba Synagogue

Cuando camino hacia ti, Córdoba,
ciudad de flores en las calles,
hacia la sinagoga silenciosa,
hacia los nueve candelabros sagrados,
y hacia el sonido desolado en el viento,
cerca de la estatua de Maimónides,
cuando tu silencio desciende como las hojas que caen,
y se convierte en aerosol de cristal.
Ah, mi Dios Todopoderoso,
Tu misericordia brilla en el mundo de los mortales,
La Biblia emerge de la oscuridad.
en ayuda a tu pueblo,
y va a curar heridas históricas,
en esta mañana pacífica,
escucha mi oración silenciosa.
Amén

－中文詩刊美國《亞特蘭大新聞》，
2016.8.5.

附錄 2.林明理博士古詩三首

林明理畫

1. 亭溪行

晴巒樹石雲浮空，悠緩炊煙連山濛。
四面晚風掩村舍，回眸亭溪已成翁。

2.黃陽隘即景

楓紅泣古隘，怎不憐曉天。
苔綠穿老樹，又眺石階前。

3. 寄霍童古鎮

霍童抱線獅，甦醒映雪月；
為我伸展手，如聽冰崖水。
客心織夢景，有幸話當年。
再聚支提山，冬風念故人。

> 註：傳說周朝時有霍童真人，居霍林洞，由此得名。境內
> 不僅植被良好，以國家森林公園、峽谷瀑布和眾多植物
> 園著稱，霍童下街還保存著較為完整的明清風格的老街
> 區，散佈著各種各樣的古跡，如全國道教四大名宮之一
> 的鶴林宮、「不到支提枉為僧」的宗教聖地──支提山
> 華嚴寺和省級文物保護單位隋代古水渠等。

> ─刊美國《亞特蘭大新聞》，2016.10.14 圖文

附錄 3.林明理博士中英法簡介

林明理簡歷
Dr. Lin Ming-Li

　　林明理，1961 年生，臺灣雲林縣人，中國文化大學大陸問題研究所法學碩士，美國世界文化藝術學院榮譽文學博士（2013.10.21 頒授）。曾任屏東師範學院講師，現任中國文藝協

會理事、中華民國新詩學會理事，北京「國際漢語詩歌協會」理事，詩人評論家。2013.5.4 獲第 54 屆「中國文藝獎章」文學類「詩歌創作獎」。2012.9.9.人間衛視『知道』節目專訪林明理 1 小時，播出於第 110 集「以詩與畫追夢的心—林明理」。2016.8.22 文化部贊助，民視『飛越文學地景』拍攝林明理兩首詩作錄影〈歌飛阿里山森林〉（2016.12.24 民視新聞首播）、〈寫給蘭嶼之歌〉（2016.11.19 民視新聞首播）。著有《秋收的黃昏》、《夜櫻--詩畫集》、《新詩的意象與內涵--當代詩家作品賞析》、《藝術與自然的融合--當代詩文評論集》、《湧動著一泓清泉—現代詩文評論》、《用詩藝開拓美—林明理談詩》、《林明理報刊評論》、《行走中的歌者—林明理談詩》、《海頌—林明理詩文集》、《林明理散文集》、《名家現代詩賞析》。以及詩集《山楂樹》、《回憶的沙漏》（中英對照）、《清雨塘》（中英對照）、《山居歲月》（中英對照）、《夏之吟》（中英法對照）、《默喚》（中英法對照）、《我的歌》（中法對照）。她的詩畫被收錄編於山西大學新詩研究所 2015 年編著 《當代著名漢語詩人詩書畫檔案》、詩作六首被收錄於《雲林縣青少年臺灣文學讀本》，評論作品被碩士生研究引用數十篇論文，作品包括詩畫、散文與評論散見於海內外學刊及詩刊、報紙等。中國學報刊物包括有《南京師範大學文學院學報》、《青島師範學院學報》、《鹽城師範學報》等二十多篇，臺灣的國圖刊物《全國新書資訊月刊》二十六篇，還有在中國大陸的詩刊報紙多達五十種刊物發表，如《天津文學》、《安徽文學》、《香港文學》等。在臺灣《人間福報》已發表上百篇作品，在《臺灣時報》、《笠詩刊》與《秋水詩刊》等刊物也常發表作品，另外，在美國的刊物《世界的詩》或報

紙《亞特蘭大新聞》等也有發表作品。總計發表的創作與評論
作品已達千篇以上。

　　Dr. Lin Ming-Li was born in 1961 in Yunlin, Taiwan. She holds a
Master's Degree in Law and lectured at Pingtung Normal College. A
poetry critic, she is currently serving as a director of the Chinese Literature
and Art Association, the Chinese New Poetry Society, and Beijing's
International Association of Chinese Poetry. On the 4th of May, 2013, she
won the Creative Poetry Prize in the 54th Chinese Literature and Arts
Awards. On the 21st of October 2013, she received a Doctor of Literature
degree from America's World Culture and Art Institute. On the 9th of
September 2012, the World Satellite TV Station in Taiwan broadcast her
interview, "Lin Ming-Li: The Heart that Pursues a Dream with Poetry and
Painting". On the 22nd of August, 2016, FTV (FORMOSA
TELEVISION) videoed two poems by her, namely, "Songs Fill the Forest
of Mt. Ali" (2016.12.24 premiere) and "Ode to the Orchid Island"
(2016.11.19 premiere).

　　Her publications include *An Autumn Harvest Evening, Night Sakura:
Collection of Poems and Paintings, Images and Connotations of New
Poetry : Reading and Analysis of the Works of Contemporary Poets, The
Fusing of Art and Nature: Criticism of Contemporary Poetry and Literature,
The Gushing of a Pure Spring: Modern Poetry Criticism, Developing Beauty
with Poetic Art: Lin Ming-Li On Poetry, A Collection of Criticism from
Newspapers and Magazines, The Walking Singer: Lin Ming-Li On Poetry,
Ode to the Sea: A Collection of Poems and Essays of Lin Ming-Li,*

Appreciation of the Work of Famous Modern Poets, and *Lin Ming-Li's Collected Essays.*

Her poems were anthologized in *Hawthorn Tree, Memory's Hourglass,* (Chinese/English), *Clear Rain Pond* (Chinese/English), *Days in the Mountains* (Chinese/English), *Summer Songs* (Chinese/English/French) , *Silent Call* (Chinese/English/French) and *My song* (Chinese/French).

Many of her poems and paintings are collected in *A Collection of Poetry, Calligraphy and Painting by Contemporary Famous Chinese Poets,* compiled in 2015 by New Poetry Research Institute of Shanxi University. Six of her poems are included in *Taiwanese Literary Textbook for the Youth of Yunlin County.* Her review articles have been quoted in theses by many graduate students. Over a thousand of her works, including poems, paintings, essays, and criticisms have appeared in many newspapers and academic journals at home and abroad.

Le Docteur Lin Ming-Li est née en 1961 à Yunlin, Taïwan. Titulaire d' une maîtrise en droit, elle a été maître de conférences à l'École Normale de Pingtung. Critique de poésie, elle occupe actuellement le poste d'administrateur de l' Association Art et Littérature chinois, de l' Association Nouvelle Poésie chinoise et de l'Association internationale de poésie chinoise de Pékin. Le 4 mai 2013, elle a obtenu le Prix de Poésie créative lors du 54ᵉ palmarès de littérature et d' art chinois. Le 21 octobre 2013, l' Institut de la Culture et des Arts du Monde d' Amérique lui a attribué le titre de

Docteur. Le 9 septembre 2012, la Station Mondiale de télévision par satellite de Taiwan a diffusé une interview d'elle intitulée « Lin Ming-Li, le cœur qui poursuit ses rêves par la Poésie et la Peinture». «Célèbre poésie moderne Appréciation». " Lin Ming-Li Collected Essays ".22/08/2016 FTV (FORMOSA TELEVISION) vidéo LIN MING-LI deux poèmes (chansons volent Alishan Forest) (2016.12.24 première) et (Orchid a écrit la chanson) (Première 2016.11.19).

Ses publications comprennent les titres suivants : « Soir de moisson d'automne», « Nuit des Cerisiers - recueil de poèmes et de peintures», «Images et connotations de la Nouvelle Poésie - lecture et analyse des œuvres de poètes contemporains», «Fusion de l'Art et de la Nature - critique sur la Poésie et la Littérature contemporaines», «Le Jaillissement d'une source pure － étude sur la poésie moderne», « Rehaussement de la Beauté grâce à l'Art poétique - Lin Ming-Li au sujet de la poésie», «Recueil de critiques tirées de journaux et de revues», «Les Chanteurs errants - Lin Ming-Li au sujet de la poésie» et «Ode à la mer － recueil de poèmes et d'essais de Lin Ming-Li». Ses autres livres de poésie sont: «L'Aubépine», «La clepsydre de la mémoire» (bilingue: chinois － anglais), «L'Étang de pluie claire» (bilingue: chinois － anglais), «Jours passés dans les montagnes» (bilingue: chinois － anglais), « Chants d'été» (trilingue: chinois － anglais － français) et «L'appel silencieux» (trilingue: chinois － anglais － français), «Ma poésie» (trilingue: chinois － français) .

.

Certains de ses poèmes et peintures figurent dans le *«Recueil de poésies, calligraphies et peintures des plus notables poètes chinois contemporains»* publié en 2015 par l'Institut de Recherches sur la nouvelle poésie de l'Université de Shanxi.

Six de ses poésies figurent dans le *«Manuel de littérature taïwanaise pour la jeunesse du comté de Yunlin»*. Ses articles publiés dans différents magazines ont été cités dans les thèses de nombreux diplômés. Des milliers de ses œuvres de poésie, de peinture, d'essai et de critique ont eu l'honneur des colonnes de revues et journaux du monde entier.

得獎等事項記錄：

1. 2011 年臺灣「國立高雄應用科技大學 詩歌類評審」校長聘書。
2. 詩畫作品獲收入中國文聯 2015.01 出版「當代著名漢語詩人詩書畫檔案」一書，山西當代中國新詩研究所主編。
3. 2015.1.2 受邀重慶市研究生科研創新專案重點項目「中國臺灣新詩生態調查及文體研究」，訪談內文刊於湖南文聯《創作與評論》2015.02。
4. 《中國今世詩歌導讀》編委會、國際詩歌翻譯研討中心等主辦，獲《中國今世詩歌獎（2011-2012）指摘獎》第 7 名。
5. 獲 2013 年中國文藝協會與安徽省淮安市淮陰區人民政府主辦，"漂母杯"兩岸「母愛主題」散文大賽第三等獎。2014"漂

母杯"兩岸「母愛主題」散文大賽第三等獎、詩歌第二等獎。2015"漂母杯"兩岸「母愛主題」詩歌第二等獎。

6. 新詩〈歌飛霍山茶鄉〉獲得安徽省「霍山黃茶」杯全國原創詩歌大賽組委會「榮譽獎」榮譽證書。

7. 參加中國河南省開封市文學藝術聯合會「全國詠菊詩歌創作大賽」，榮獲銀獎證書〈2012.12.18 公告〉，詩作〈詠菊之鄉─開封〉。

8. "湘家蕩之戀"國際散文詩徵文獲榮譽獎，散文詩作品:〈寫給相湖的歌〉，嘉興市湘家蕩區域開發建設管理委員會、中外散文詩學會舉辦，2014.9.28 頒獎於湘家蕩。

9. 獲當選中國北京「國際漢語詩歌協會」理事〈2013-2016〉。

10. 獲當選中國第 15 屆「全國散文詩筆會」臺灣代表，甘肅舉辦「吉祥甘南」全國散文詩大賽，獲「提名獎」，2015.7.26 頒獎於甘南，詩作〈甘南，深情地呼喚我〉，詩作刊於《散文詩·校園文學》甘南采風專號 2015.12（總第 422 期）及《格桑花》2015"吉祥甘南"全國散文詩筆會專號。

11. 2015.08 中國·星星「月河月老」杯（兩岸三地）愛情散文詩大賽獲「優秀獎」，詩作〈月河行〉。

12. 北京新視野杯"我與自然"全國散文詩歌大賽獲獎於 2015.10 獲散文〈布農布落遊蹤〉及詩歌〈葛根塔拉草原之戀〉均「二等獎」。

13. 河南省 2015 年 8 月首屆"中國詩河 鶴壁"全國詩歌大賽，獲「提名獎」，詩作〈寫給鶴壁的歌〉。

14. 2015.9 中央廣播電臺、河南省中共鄭州市委宣傳部主辦"待月嵩山 2015 中秋詩會詩歌大賽"獲三等獎，新詩作品〈嵩

山之夢〉，獲人民幣 1 千元獎金及獎狀。

15. 2012 年 9 月 9 日人間衛視『知道』節目專訪林明理 1 小時，播出於第 110 集「以詩與畫追夢的心－林明理」。http://www.bltv.tv/program/?f=content&sid=170&cid=6750

16. 雲林縣政府編印，主持人成功大學陳益源教授，《雲林縣青少年臺灣文學讀本》新詩卷，2016.04 出版，收錄林明理新詩六首，〈九份黃昏〉〈行經木棧道〉〈淡水紅毛城〉〈雨，落在愛河的冬夜〉〈生命的樹葉〉〈越過這個秋季〉）於頁215-225。

17. 北京，2015 年全國詩書畫家創作年會，林明理新詩〈夢見中國〉獲「二等獎」，頒獎典禮在 2015.12.26 人民大會堂賓館舉行。

18. 福建省邵武市，2015.12.15 公告，文體廣電新聞出版局主辦，邵武"張三豐杯海內外詩歌大賽"，林明理新詩〈邵武戀歌〉獲「優秀獎」。

19. 安徽詩歌學會主辦，肥東縣文聯承辦，第二屆"曹植詩歌獎"華語詩歌大賽，林明理獲二等獎，獎狀及獎金人民幣兩千，2016.3.28 中國煤炭新聞網公告。http://www.cwestc.com/newshtml/2016-4-2/406808.shtml http://www.myyoco.com/folder2288/folder2290/folder2292/2016/04/2016-04-22706368.html 來源：肥東縣人民政府網站發佈時間：2016-04-22。

詩作（〈寫給曹植之歌〉外一首）刊於中共肥東縣委宣傳網 http://www.fdxcb.gov.cn/display.asp?id=37800

20. 北京市寫作學會等主辦，2016 年"東方美"全國詩聯書畫大

賽，新詩〈頌長城〉，榮獲「金獎」。

21. 2016"源泉之歌"全國詩歌大賽，林明理新詩〈寫給成都之歌〉獲優秀獎，中國《華西都市報》2016.6.16 公告於 http://www.kaixian.tv/gd/2016/0616/568532.html

22. 2016.11.19 民視新聞（FORMOSA TELEVISION）下午三點五十七分首播「飛閱文學地景」節目林明理吟誦〈寫給蘭嶼之歌〉。https://www.youtube.com/watch?v=F95ruijjXfE https://v.qq.com/x/page/e0350zb01ay.html 騰訊視頻 http://www.atlantachinesenews.com/ 2016.12.2 美國《亞特蘭大新聞》刊

　　民視【飛閱文學地景】林明理吟詩〈寫給蘭嶼之歌〉於首頁網，可點播

　　http://videolike.org/video/%E9%A3%9B%E9%96%B1%E6%96%87%E5%AD%B8%E5%9C%B0%E6%99%AF

　　【飛閱文學地景】video

　　https://www.facebook.com/WenHuaBu/posts/1174239905989277 文化部 臉書

23. 2016.12.24 民視新聞晚上六點首播（飛閱文學地景）節目林明理吟誦〈歌飛阿里山森林〉。

　　https://www.youtube.com/watch?v=3KAq4xKxEZM

　　http://www.woplay.net/watch?v=3KAq4xKxEZM

林明理專書簡介：

1.《秋收的黃昏》。高雄市：春暉出版社，2008。

2.《夜櫻-林明理詩畫集》。高雄市：春暉出版社，2009。

3.《新詩的意象與內涵-當代詩家作品賞析》。臺北市：文津出版社，2010。

4.《藝術與自然的融合-當代詩文評論集》。臺北市：文史哲出版社，2011。

5.《山楂樹》（林明理詩集）。臺北市：文史哲出版社，2011。

　　6.《回憶的沙漏》（中英對照譯詩集）。臺北市：秀威出版社，2012。

7.《湧動著一泓清泉——現代詩文評論》。臺北市：文史哲出版社，2012。

8.《清雨塘》(中英對照譯詩集)。臺北市：文史哲出版社，2012。

9.《用詩藝開拓美——林明理讀詩》。臺北市：秀威出版社，2013。

10.《海頌—林明理詩文集》。臺北市：文史哲出版社，2013。

11.《林明理報刊評論 1990-2000》。臺北市：文史哲出版社，2013。

12.《行走中的歌者——林明理談詩》。臺北市：文史哲出版社，2013。

13.《山居歲月》（中英對照譯詩集）。臺北市：文史哲出版社，2015。

14.《夏之吟》（中英法譯詩集）。英譯：馬為義（筆名：非馬）（William Marr）。法譯：阿薩納斯 · 薩拉西（Athanase Vantchev de Thracy）。法國巴黎：索倫紮拉文化學院（The Cultural Institute of Solenzara），2015。

15.《默喚》(中英法譯詩集)。英譯：諾頓 · 霍奇斯（Norton Hodges）。法譯：阿薩納斯 · 薩拉西（Athanase Vantchev de

Thracy）。法國巴黎：索倫紮拉文化學院（The Cultural Institute of Solenzara），2016。

16.《林明理散文集》。臺北市：文史哲出版社，2016。

17.《名家現代詩賞析》。臺北市：文史哲出版社，2016。

18.《我的歌》。臺北市：文史哲出版社，2017。

http://blog.sina.com.cn/june122333
june122333@yahoo.com.tw

附件1.個人部落格：

http://blog.sina.com.cn/june122333　AINA 新浪博客 林明理博士 Lin-Mingli

http://blog.xuite.net/june1223333/wretch 隨意窩博客　Dr. Lin Ming-Li 林明理博士

附件2.相關官網參考資料：

1. 中央研究院圖書館林明理作品資料
   http://sinica.summon.serialssolutions.com/search?s.q= 林 明 理 #!/search?ho=t&l=en&q=林明理

2. 臺灣「國家圖書館」期刊文獻資訊網
   http://readopac.ncl.edu.tw/nclJournal/index.htm 林明理作品資料

3. 美國《亞特蘭大新聞》Atlanta Chinese News 2016 年 1 月 15 日巴黎出版書訊《默喚》=SlientCall=L'appelsilencieux/林明理及中英法簡介
   http://www.atlantachinesenews.com/News/2016/01/01-15/b-05.pdf

4.法國巴黎出版林明理三語詩集《夏之吟》轉載于非馬Dr.
William Marr（馬為義 博士）
http://www.weibo.com/p/2304185b34806b0102w6g0
由非馬英譯，法國詩人薩拉西法譯。

5. 2013 年 9 月 9 日電視專訪人間衛視《知道》節目【知道 110
集】以詩與畫追夢的心—林明理
http://www.bltv.tv/program/?f=content&sid=170&cid=6750
節目介紹：林明理老師，以法學碩士身份，跨界到藝文界
從事創作。2007 年她在《笠》詩刊發表了〈雨夜〉，至今
五年間，詩文評論作品豐富，發表的刊物橫跨兩岸。她同
時繪畫，配上自己的詩，意象清晰，給予的境界也更為無
窮。今天知道節目，讓我們一起來探究，林明理老師跨界
創作的故事。

6.2016 年 8 月 22 日電視錄影民視「飛閱文學地景」節目，2016
年 11 月 19 日播出吟詩〈寫給蘭嶼的詩〉。
YouTubehttps://www.youtube.com/watch?v=F95ruijjXfE
臉書 FACE BOOK Videohttps://youtu.be/F95ruijjXfE
蘭嶼，在觀光開放的影響下，達悟族人的生活空間與傳統
文化，近年來屢屢受到外界的關注。希望政府相關單位能
夠多正視這個問題，也是林明理老師創作這首詩的靈感來
源，而這塊美麗的島嶼是過去達悟族人的祖居地，也是未
來達悟族人維繫傳統文化與生活方式的土地。

7. 臺灣師範大學網公告 2013.5.4 獲第 54 屆中國文藝獎章新詩
創作獎-林明理
資料來源/青年日報/報導日期：2013-05-05

http://pr.ntnu.edu.tw/newspaper/index.php?mode=data&id=14466

8.山東大學文學院吳開晉教授書評〈以詩為文妙筆探幽〉《人間福報》2010 年 3 月 14 日

http://www.merit-times.com.tw/NewsPage.aspx?unid=171758

9. 中國「國家圖書館」存藏林明理著

http://opac.nlc.gov.cn/F/FM74YKUAAY69XM7L7B6DTBBMJHNK8KK88VNCUHEC8PX11C6FKR-00650?func=short-jump&jump=1

著名法國詩人、翻譯家
Dr.Athanase Vantchev de Thracy
簡介

　　阿沙納斯‧凡切夫‧德‧薩拉西是五十多部涵蓋了整個詩歌體裁包括古典詩和自由詩的作者。他還出版了一連串的專題論文和一篇博士論文【保爾‧魏爾倫詩中的輕象徵主義】。阿沙納斯還用保加利亞文寫了對偉大的伊壁鳩魯派的貴族、尼羅的親信、諷刺小說《薩迪利空》(Satyricon) 的作者佩特羅尼烏斯 (Petronius Arbiter elegantarium) 的研究，又用俄文寫了碩士論文‘杜思妥也夫斯基作品中的詩學和形而上學’。以他對古代文物的廣泛知識，阿沙納斯‧凡切夫‧德‧薩拉西寫了無數關於希臘詩和拉丁詩的論文。在突尼斯度過的那兩年當中，他連續推出了三部關於布匿時代(Punic-era)突尼西亞的兩個城市，‘*Monastir-Ruspina － 光之臉*’，‘*El-Djem Thysdrus － 蔚藍的未婚妻*’以及 ‘*Thysdrus 的鑲嵌圖案*’。

　　當他在敘利亞、土耳其、利比亞、沙烏地阿拉伯、約旦、摩洛哥和毛利塔尼亞度過的那段期間，他同回教的邂逅深深打動了他，因此花了好多年的時間去研究東方宗教史。這階段開始了他把穆斯塔法三世的歷史性著作 ‘季諾碧亞，巴爾米拉的女王’（*Zenobia, Queen of Palmyra*）改編成法文。

他把他在俄國停留的那兩年(1993-4)全部花在研究俄國詩上。一大批特出詩人的翻譯者，阿沙納斯・凡切夫・德・薩拉西獲得了國家及國際上許多有名的詩獎，包括下列這些國際大詩獎：法國的索倫紮拉（Solenzara），俄羅斯的普希金，阿爾巴尼亞的 Naim Frashëri，希臘的亞歷山大大帝，以及烏克蘭的舍甫琴科（Chevtchenko）和也是烏克蘭的果戈爾。他是法蘭西學院的桂冠詩人，保加利亞藝術和科學學院、巴西文學學院、烏克蘭高等教育學院、和歐洲科學藝術文學學院等的會員，保加利亞 Veliko Tarnovo 大學與巴西文學學院的榮譽博士，法國外事部的桂冠詩人，法蘭西筆會的會員，法蘭西文學與文學人協會和作者與文學之家的會員，世界詩人國際運動組織的會長和日內瓦的環球和平大使。

保加利亞政府曾頒給他 Stara Planina 勳章的最高榮譽。他的詩被翻譯成多種文字。

Biography

Athanase Vantchev de Thracy is the author of over sixty volumes of poetry in both classical and free verse, which cover the entire spectrum of prosody. He has also published a series of monographs and a doctoral thesis on *'Light Symbolism in the Poetry of Paul Verlaine'*. Athanase has also written, in Bulgarian, a study of the great epicurean patrician Petronius (Petronius Arbiter elegantarium), favourite of Nero and author of the *Satyricon*, and, in Russian, a Masters degree dissertation on *'Poetics and Metaphysics* *in the Work of Dostoevsky'* . With his extensive knowledge of antiquity, Athanase Vantchev de Thracy has devoted numerous articles to Greek and Latin poetry. During the two years he spent in Tunisia, he brought out three successive works on the two Punic-era Tunisian cities, *'Monastir-Ruspina – the Face of Light'* , *'El-Djem Thysdrus – Fiancée of the Azure'* and *'The Mosaics of Thysdrus'* .

During periods spent in Syria, Turkey, Libya, Saudi Arabia, Jordan, Iraq, Morocco and Mauritania, he was deeply impressed by his encounter with Islam and spent long years in the study of the religious history of the East. From this period dates his remarkable adaptation into French of Mustafa Tlass' s historical work, *'Zenobia, Queen of Palmyra'* .

The two years he spent in Russia (1993-4) were spent entirely in the study of Russian poetry. Translator of a pleiad of poets, Athanase Vantchev de Thracy has been the distinguished recipient of numerous national and international poetry prizes, including the following Grand International Prizes for Poetry: the Solenzara (France), the Pushkin (Russia), the Naim Frashëri (Albania), the Alexander the Great (Greece), the Chevtchenko (Ukraine) and the Gogol (also Ukraine). He is a laureate of the Académie Française, a member of the Bulgarian Academy of Arts and Sciences, the Brazilian Academy of Letters, the Academy of Higher Education of Ukraine, and the European Academy of Sciences, Arts and Letters, Doctor Honoris

Causa of the University of Veliko Tarnovo, Bulgaria and the Brazilian Academy of Letters, laureate of the French Ministry of Foreign Affairs, a member of French PEN., a member of the Société des Gens de Lettres de France, and the Maison des écrivains et de la littérature, president of the international movement Poetas del Mundo and a Universal Ambassador for Peace (Geneva).

He has been decorated with the highest honour of the Bulgarian state, the Order of Stara Planina. His poetry has been translated into many other languages.

Biographie

Athanase Vantchev de Thracy a écrit plus de soixante recueils de poésies (en vers classiques et en vers libres) couvrant presque tous les spectres de la prosodie.

Il publie une série de monographies et une thèse de doctorat sur *«La symbolique de la lumière dans la poésie de Paul Verlaine»*. Athanase rédige, en bulgare, une étude sur le grand seigneur épicurien Pétrone surnommé Petronius Arbiter elegantiarum, favori de Néron, auteur du *Satiricon*, et une maîtrise, en langue russe, intitulée *«Poétique et métaphysique dans l'œuvre de Dostoïevski»*.

Grand connaisseur de l'Antiquité, Athanase Vantchev de

Thracy consacre de nombreux articles à la poésie grecque et latine. Lors de son séjour de deux ans en Tunisie, il publie successivement trois ouvrages sur les deux cit é s puniques tunisiennes: *«Monastir-Ruspina ‒ la face de la clarté», «El-Djem-Thysdrus ‒ la fiancée de l' azur», «Les mosaïques thysdriennes».* Pendant ses sé jours en Syrie, en Turquie, au Liban, en Arabie Saoudite, en Jordanie, en Irak, en Egypte, au Maroc et en Mauritanie, il fait la connaissance émerveillée de l' Islam et passe de longues années à étudier l' histoire sacrée de l' Orient. De cette période date sa remarquable adaptation en français de l' ouvrage historique de Moustapha Tlass *«Zénobie, reine de Palmyre».*

Il consacre entièrement ses deux années passées en Russie (1993-1994) à l' étude de la poésie russe. Traducteur d' une plé iade de poètes, Athanase Vantchev de Thracy est distingué par de nombreux prix littéraires nationaux et internationaux dont le Grand Prix International de Poésie Solenzara (France), le Grand Prix International de Po é sie Pouchkine (Russie), le Grand Prix International de Poésie Naim Frashëri (Albanie), le Grand Prix International de Poésie Alexandre le Grand (Grèce), le Grand Prix International de Poésie Gogol(Ukraine), le Grand Prix International de Poésie Chevtchenko (Ukraine), etc. Il est lauréat de l' Académie française, membre de l' Académie bulgare des Sciences et des Arts, membre de l' Académie des Lettres du Brésil, membre de l' Acadé mie de l' Éducation supérieure d' Ukraine, membre de l' Acadé mie européenne des Sciences, des Arts et des Lettres, Docteur honoris causa de l' Université de Veliko Tarnovo, Bulgarie, docteur honoris causa de l' Académie des Lettres du Brésil, lauréat du Ministère des Affaires étrangères français, membre du P.E.N. Club français, membre de la Société des Gens de Lettres de France, membre de la Maison des écrivains et de la littérature, président du Mouvement international Poetas del Mundo, Ambassadeur universel de la Paix (Genève), etc.

Il est décoré de la plus haute distinction de l' État bulgare, l' Ordre Stara Planina.

Ses poésies sont traduites en plusieurs langues.

附錄 4：林明理散文 13 篇

1.墾丁遊蹤

　　整個冬季一過，風不再凜冽，院子裡原來蟄伏了一段時間的百合、風信子，終於在泥土中開始復甦。而牆垣上開滿了攀藤玫瑰，夢幻般的色彩，使我思想也隨之飄忽搖曳。

　　那是融融的春日，車行約一個半小時，抵屏東。一路上，

小孩在後座像麻雀一刻地歡愉聲，使我感到欣悅。

復行半小時，抵社頂自然公園，它位於墾丁森林遊樂區旁。一下車，綠蔭如蓋，極目遠視，長在礁石上的樹木受到東北季風的吹襲，雕塑出自然盆景狀的藝術。園內更有豐富的動植物、石灰岩洞、以及礁岩裂縫造成的「一線天」。在深林的枝葉中，穿梭在珊瑚礁石裡，頗有探險的意味。

閒步墾丁公園，這裡清麗幽靜，可以說是本島最南端的名勝，三面環海，東面太平洋，西鄰台灣海峽，南瀕巴士海峽。海域清澈且特有植物衍生，包括：瓜葉馬兜鈴、紅豆樹、鵝鑾鼻大戟、恆春鐵莧、南仁五月茶、金線蓮、石斑木等百餘種。幸運的話，每年十二月至初春，在恆春西海岸的海口附近，還可遇見鯨魚及海豚的蹤影。

最令我心馳神往的是，每次來到它的懷裡，它給我的永遠是一份悸動，一種壯闊，一種熟悉，無以言喻的美。它的柔和的漣漪或蔚藍海岸如油墨大地，那粼粼波光常帶給我永不抹滅的幻想，也照澈了我的夢。在山綠海藍的光影中，再往前行，公園兩旁綠樹成蔭，鳥聲清脆，好一個人間潛藏的桃花源。

猶記前年我站在龍磐公園礁岩上，面對遼闊的太平洋，隨處可見白芒翻飛，莽莽蒼蒼，如此活潑、自由而好奇！詩人卞之琳在《斷章》中寫下：

你站在橋上看風景，

看風景的人在看你，

明月裝飾了你的窗子，

你卻裝飾了我的夢

思之思之，彷若電影的切片，一幕幕回憶裡的風景，清晰如昨。公園內有大草原，可從陡峭的崖邊遠眺，瑰麗壯觀，很適合賞日出及星海。

告別了龍磐大草原，遂驅車往龍坑。它位於恆春半島東南端岬角，介於太平洋和巴士海峽交界處，有許多特殊少見的濱海植物。其中有幾種使我印象特別深刻。其一是「濱斑鳩菊」，全台灣除了蘭嶼之外就只能在龍坑這裡看得到。其二是花瓣只有一半的「草海桐」，有刺的「飛龍掌血」，還有遠從大溪地飄洋過來的「橄樹」都是龍坑特有的濱海植物。

若在大尖山山頂也可俯瞰恆春半島全境，以及青蛙石、船帆石等景點。浩瀚的大海不見邊際，偶有小船駛過，濺起了細碎的水花白浪。小雨後，遠山青蔥，近鄰翠綠。沐浴在灰藍的海上，靜靜諦聽小海鷗在拍岸的沿線上空盤旋飛翔……。

行約半日，車過白沙灣，它在貓鼻頭西北方的海岸線上。這一帶得天獨厚，擁有一段長達百公尺的沙灘，由純白的貝殼砂所組成，以沙白水清聞名。

登上貓鼻頭居高臨下的觀景高台，貓石正靜靜地趴在海面上，也可遠眺巴士海峽。這裡珊瑚礁受到長時間的波浪侵蝕、沙礫鑽蝕及溶蝕等作用，產生了崩崖、壺穴、礁柱、洞窟等奇特景觀。

而我看見海岸線恰似百褶裙般風情萬種地披散開來，就這樣盡享這般的美好景致。聽說在夏夜，更可看到南十字星緩緩

的從海平面升起。但此行過而未能一睹，真是遺憾。

　　若說墾丁公園之寶則當然就是鵝鑾鼻燈塔了。它是全台最南端的白色燈塔，於 1898 年重建。二次大戰時被美軍炸燬，戰後依原建築修復迄今。塔身為圓柱形，白鐵製，塔高 24.1 公尺，是臺灣八景之一。難怪詩人余光中為它吟唱，以訴衷曲：

　　　我站在巍巍的燈塔尖頂，
　　　俯臨著一片藍色的蒼茫。
　　　在我的面前無盡地翻滾，
　　　整個太平洋洶湧的波浪。
　　　一萬匹飄著白鬃的藍馬，
　　　呼嘯著，疾奔過我的腳下，
　　　這匹銜著那匹的尾巴，
　　　直奔向冥冥，寞寞的天涯…
　　　驀然，看，一片光從我的腳下，
　　　旋向四方，水面轟地照亮；
　　　一聲歡呼，所有的海客與舟子，
　　　所有魚龍，都欣然向臺灣仰望。

　　是的，詩人已為鵝鑾鼻之美建造了一座詩的殿堂。晚間，在恆春老城住宿的老闆說一定要到墾丁夜市大街看看夜景。走著走著，短短的九百公尺內的，大小的攤販近百攤，還有許多知名的商家、飯店，霓虹閃爍。每到旅遊旺季，人頭攢動，就真不知該用什麼來形容了呢？

　　在墾丁夜市飽飲後，終點是恆春大街的民宿。那晚的月色如水，讓我整夜不覺得寒意。而以往每想起墾丁，總會跟著想起余光中（銀夢海岸）詩中美麗的描寫，記載著對墾

丁海，如愛情般的深刻：

> 今晚的海岸，該怎麼說呢？
> 遠方，是藍幽幽的天色
> 近處，黑闃闃的地形
> 只有中間閃動着一片
> 又像是水光又像是時光
> 從一個吹笛的銀夢裏
> 滿滿地流來

多美的詩境啊！能夠如此享受月色，不正應該是這樣幸福的嗎？

　　翌日早晨，出恆春東門往滿州路上左側，不多久，抵達一處名為「出火特別景觀區」，地面上經年燃著火焰，下雨更會形成水火相容的奇景。但當日停車場上十分冷寂，只有一、二處空擺著的小食攤，雖然晨光照在樹林間很有點美感，卻是靜得有些落寞淒涼……。

　　回程到了參觀的終點「南灣」，此地因海水湛藍，又稱做藍灣。沙灘全長約 600 公尺，弧線美，沙質潔淨，經常有許多遊客在此漫步，戲水等水上活動。往後壁湖邊去，只需十幾分鐘也可以順道去核三廠參觀。

　　原來簡單的快樂，就是知足。遠眺墾丁，碧波在望，果然不負詩人之所譽。在高爽的空氣下，墾丁，更顯然最美麗的景像。啊，墾丁，我的愛，我要用一生的時間來讚美你，端詳你，你可與我的靈魂同徜徉？

－2016.3.18 寫於台東
－刊臺灣《人間福報》副刊，圖文，2016.4.20.

2.美濃紀行

　　好不容易盼到個假日，出了高雄市，上十號高速公路盡頭，車過旗山，就是美濃鎮前的鄉道，沿途是波斯菊田野，引人欲醉。這是正月下旬的花海季，在陰涼的天空下更覺秀麗。汽車開不遠，就到了這古樸民風的小鎮了。

　　原來所謂美濃，舊稱「瀰濃」，地形上為山區平原地形，人口約四萬七百餘人。這裡是客家六堆中的右堆，是著名的客語區之一，也是觀光小城。

　　這秀毓的鄉村，像甘甜的

門樓紅磚．古色古香。

酒。那綠得要凝固的水波,山巒的親切與多情,真令我莫名的感動。而美濃鎮的淳樸和優雅,又像翩翩起舞的紫斑蝶,使我靈魂深處被觸動了。這裡原來正是鍾理和作家的故鄉啊!

談談說說,不禁已開到了美濃鎮尖山山麓,在黃蝶翠谷與朝元寺入口附近,距離鎮街約七公里,有一座鬱鬱蔥蔥的「鍾理和文學紀念館」矗立著。這是一個涼爽的冬日,我和家人來到這裡參觀鍾理和晚年生活、寫作的故居。這棟二樓建築,館後是笠山,前後都由樹林果木包圍,極清幽寧靜。

從我初次與鍾理和的《原鄉人》、《笠山農場》等作品接觸的那一刻起,我的生活中就多了一個謎。我感到深藏在他心中、那種觸摸不到的文學力量又重新回到我身邊。這種力量在我童年讀許多外國文學書籍的記憶中是永遠不曾有的。即使後來當我長大了些,生活中值得細細回味的台灣文學作品也寥寥無幾。而現在的初次相會仍能感到一種激動與神奇。

這位臺灣文學的作家鍾理和,生於日據時代(一九一五年),因肺結核病逝,享年僅四十六歲。我一邊參觀,一邊默默思忖著。這就是他——戰後第一代重要作家鍾理和給我種下的印象。僅管比大多數作家的經歷更坎坷,這我們也瞭解。但他生平以心靈和愛去關懷臺灣社會與文學,那淳厚堅毅的風格與不妥協的人性尊嚴,的確為後代作家樹立了楷模。

當我走出館外，那座令人遐想的花園時，慢慢的打開了他那些著名的短篇小說《草坡上》、《野茫茫》…的畫面，心裡也有點兒酸酸的。

他愛護動物，尊重生命，作品也擅長描寫農民生活，是具有悲憫襟懷的人道主義者。雖然在他生前只有一部作品集《夾竹桃》印行，但憑著對文學的鍾愛與不悔，終能寫出一篇篇以生命的真實和真誠無偽的作品。

我敢說這位熱血青年，他是用自己的方式在愛著家人，愛著臺灣這片地土，也愛著貧苦的百姓。他的目光充滿了悲傷，也有著文人的自豪。他的後半生雖然纏綿病榻，但在困阨窮苦之際，仍堅持創作的理由到底是什麼呢？

我想鍾理和先生寫作的本意是想讓自己變得更堅強，去勇敢的面對生活中的起起伏伏。儘管他那顆真誠的心不容易被當時的環境所發現，但有很多次我都看到它仍閃閃發光，而且是為臺灣文學發展而閃光。

我在紀念館裡找回自己內心的平靜，靜靜的凝視著那一張張老舊而佈滿歷史的照片。暫時忘卻了自我和生活中的瑣事，獨自沉浸在書香與那片特殊土地上棲息著的蟲鳴鳥叫之間。

想到這裡，抬頭仰望天空，真想大聲的說出了多年來一直埋在心裡的話。

「尊敬的作家，鍾理和先生。你被上天選中去給後代作家指引光明之路。我以您為榮。」

我知道鍾作家從未聽過我說的這些話，但我一直想親自對這個紀念館講。即使現在也不算晚！花園中央有一隻漂亮的鳥兒向下好奇的望著我們倆，唱著動人的歌。不知覺中，牠已扇動著翅膀向空中揚長而去了。

這是一個訊號。是啊，在我心中，鍾理和那些創作的文字，故事，依然珍貴，因為這些都是臺灣文學的饋贈。而我的心魂，也在向上騰動著……就像那隻漂亮的鳥兒飛過了高大斑駁的樹枝，飛過了那思慕的故里的水田……聽風吹落葉聲，眸光裡也流露出一些思念。

冬日的美濃鎮天空，更加藍得可愛。繞過街巷，除了見證了美濃繁榮與發展的永恆記憶，由西側的敬字亭開始直到東門樓，處處都充滿了古樸懷舊的氣息。

當陽光逐一的照亮了遠處的山巒，也照耀著這條已歷二百年歷史的永安老街，不禁升起了一絲喜悅。這是當年開發最繁榮的街道。相傳是清朝年間，原居屏東里港的客家人渡過荖濃溪，來到美濃月光山建立了「瀰濃庄」。開庄時十六姓先民在此建造了二十四座夥房，並以永安街命名祈求永久安居之意。

我還一直記得非常清楚。一棟棟古色古香的客家建築都有著完整的門樓紅磚，其中最具特色的，是菸業大王林春雨的房舍。若走累了，還可以品嚐各種客家美食、擂茶，或到客家文物館深入了解。

美濃當地特產，除了稻米，還有油紙傘。在早期客家庄裡，由於客家話「紙」與「子」諧音，故客家女性婚嫁時，女方通常會以兩把紙傘為嫁妝，意含著「早生貴子」和「祝福幸福美滿」。當然我也和其他遊客一樣興奮，在店裡酌一杯擂茶，再拿把大紅的油紙傘攝影留念。今既遊美濃，才知此地的讀書風氣確實與藝術有著共同的氣質。聽說在清朝年間有許多文魁、進士在這裡誕生，因此這些紀念牌樓正載明著美濃小鎮又有「大學搖籃」的稱號呢。

此外，風景區還有德勝公壇、宋屋學堂、伯公祠、客家藍衫店、美濃舊橋、水圳、還有許多看不盡的門樓、夥房，訴說著兩百年來滄桑而美麗的故事，令人頓感心胸曠遠。

一路走下去，這裡有許多歷史的文化遺產，走完永安老街，等於幾乎認識了貌似平淡卻以其深厚的歷史文化感見勝的美濃呢！它是那樣的樸實而清麗，真令人留連不忍離去。

參觀既畢，回程遂轉往旗山糖廠稍為休息，大口地吃碗紅豆冰淇淋，就驅車返家，很快天就黑了下來。我這才體會到正因為美濃鎮遠看平凡，要待深入探索，才能知每一飛簷，每一

回眸，都是一份悸動。而美濃鄉民齊心以率真熱烈的感情，努力開拓出敦樸淳厚的世界，著實讓我的懷念更深了。

－2016.4.9

－刊臺灣《人間福報》副刊圖文，2016.6.8，
　　水彩兩幅。

3.大龍峒保安宮紀行

記得幾年前的一個秋日，與友人胡其德教授、何醫師從護國禪寺、孔廟，一路遊歷到保安宮；回想起來，歷歷在目。廟外，混著香火味，還有遊人陣陣的笑語，都在微微潤濕的空氣裏醞釀。我的視界無由伸展，可以看到廟前石雕裝飾中的盤龍柱，神氣活現，扮演著守護建築物的象徵。還有一對古樸而精雅的石獅，特別表出。相傳這對石獅，一隻是仁獸，一隻是法獸，立在廟前，是在呼籲天下，重視法律，施行仁政。在這兒，給人一種神秘的、莊嚴雅靜的美質，一種原始的宗教情感竟油然而生。

林明理博士於臺北市
大龍峒保安宮

返身入殿，從廊前四處看，心胸為之一闊。傍走進去，清潔高敞。經過天井來到正殿，可看到主奉神明保生大帝神尊。保生大帝是福建省同安縣人吳姓名吳本，字華基，醫術極精湛，相傳大帝升天後，依然時常顯靈，

為民除害、醫治百姓疾病。所以宋高宗在西元 1151 年為祂建廟，宋孝宗在西元 1171 年封為「大道真人」，因此保生大帝又稱「大道公」。另外，兩邊奉祀的是 36 官將神像，是西元 1829 年，聘請泉州名師許嚴來台，前後費時 5 年才完成的雕作，神儀俊朗。同時，還可注意到牆壁上有七幅珍貴的彩繪，分別描述中國民間故事，實為難忘的意趣，予人舒展的、文雅的氣息。

我特別喜歡奉祀的註生娘娘，色彩明麗，背景圖畫成功地再現了客觀的自然美。兩旁有十二婆姐，分掌 12 個月，主管婦女的懷孕、生產。後殿又稱神農殿，主祀農業醫藥業祖師神農大帝。相傳在一百多年前，台北好幾個月不下雨，所以住民就虔誠祈求神農賜雨。果然，沒經過多久，就下了一場大雨，所以住民就恭迎神農大帝到保安宮後殿奉祀了。每年 農曆 3 月 15 日 ，為慶祝保生大帝聖誕，特別舉辦結合宗教祭祀、民俗技藝、古蹟導覽、藝文研習、美學競賽、家姓戲、繞境踩街、過火等一系列活動；是目前北臺灣最盛大、最熱鬧，人氣也最旺的廟會活動。

大龍峒保安宮雖不如臺南安平古堡有顯赫的歷史，但也因未經那麼多戰禍，加以精工的整修，故能完整地保存了下來。在建築上，它是屬於富麗型的，其內部的裝飾趣味包涵一種獨特歷史背景的餘韻，遂而成為遊客觀光的薈萃點。從外部空間結構看，視線由入口的兩只石獅開始，其間裝飾藝術，如龍柱、花鳥柱、剪黏、泥塑、交趾陶、木雕、彩繪壁畫等，形象逼真

且輕鬆諧趣，予人以精神性及感官上的愉悅，亦有文化薰陶之效。各種縈迴盤繞的動物雕塑，除了飄逸的裝飾作用外，還具有另一層意義，例如：蝙蝠代表「福」氣、四隻蝙蝠有祈求「賜福」之意，鹿表示「祿」位、鶴代表「長壽」。這些浮雕、透雕、線雕、陰雕等等遠近馳名的石雕藝術瑰寶，每一件都具有歷史及藝術的價值，是保安宮不可多得的傑作，深受民間喜愛。

保安宮在日據時期的重修，曾延聘大稻埕第一木匠郭塔及陳應彬兩位匠師，以廟宇的中軸線劃分為左右兩邊，各自發揮其建築技巧。當年陳應彬負責東邊的木雕，擅長於斗拱，尤以螭虎的造型最為獨特，充蘊著純中國風的雄偉形象。而負責西邊的郭塔特色是較為西式風格，建築雕痕造型優美，表現出渾圓的質感。據傳陳應彬獲勝後，郭塔無法認同，遂而在作品裡悄悄的留下了「真手藝無更改」、「好工手不補接」的話語來暗諷對手，留下一段百年佳話。

此外，保安宮正殿東側，兩屋簷間的水車閣設計上有幅郭塔的「八仙大鬧東海」的作品，然而陳應彬確認為不需要有多餘字在上頭，於是就成了今日我們只見西側「鬧東海」三個字，這些對應的彩繪畫面，十分奇趣。其間，剪黏、泥塑或交趾陶、木雕，都透露出畫匠強烈的主觀感受及深沉飽和的情思，它是一種美的形式，而這種良性競爭就是當時流行的對場作。因此欣賞保安宮的裝飾藝術時，亦可同時欣賞左右兩邊、不同匠師的作品。

　　接著，正殿迴廊牆壁上的 7 幅壁畫，給人的美感享受就更濃烈了。這是國寶級彩繪大師潘麗水的作品，它表達了忠孝節義等傳統美德的民間故事或神話傳說、歷史故事等文學典故，也能顯示出畫師的獨特藝術風格。主題分別為：「八仙大鬧東海」、「花木蘭代父從軍」、「朱仙鎮八槌大戰陸文龍」、「鍾馗迎妹回娘家」、「韓信胯下受辱」、「賢哉徐母」、「虎牢關三戰呂布」。其中，印象鮮明的是，黑面鍾馗身著藍衣柔軟自然、眼珠親和地與外甥互動；令一旁十分畏懼鍾馗的小鬼一臉狐疑的表情，形神逼肖，氣韻生動，讓此幅浪漫的想像，兼具靈巧與詼諧之趣的畫作，賦予彩繪壁畫一個嶄新的詮釋角度。而大戰陸文龍畫壁圖中的左右兩匹駿馬呼之欲出，讓觀者的每一縷生命纖維，都想跳躍；更加豐富了色彩的對照。轉彎後廊的花鳥柱似乎都在歌舞，每一雕塑都有其脈搏與呼吸，正吸引著遊客們的吟笑，也組成了一幅幅有聲的畫。

　　目光越過了殿後，步子不得不放慢，漸漸端詳起四周的奇景。起初我當然不懂保安宮的時代意義，完全是從友人的口中聽熟的。保安宮內，我虔誠默站一會兒，也求得一上籤。秋日傍晚，偶飄細雨，信徒們祈福的背影漸漸含糊。廟中仍絡繹不絕，如雨入湖。嬝嬝上升的爐煙如霧、檜柏濃蔭，莊嚴的佛像，巍然端然。登上殿樓，眼前盡是紅瓦，掩映雲天之下，調節著我的鼻息。我開始變得舒適，宛若一個悠然朝拜的信士，期以達致一種平遠而放逸的華嚴真境。

　　大龍峒保安宮重建以來雖經過多次整修增建，但由於建造年代已久，更遭風吹、日曬、蟲噬，嚴重影響建築本體。為了維護文化資產，自西元 1995 年起，再度決定重建以來規模最大的修復工程，保安宮自力籌措全部經費，並自行統籌、監造，成為全國首宗民間籌資主導古蹟的案例；歷時 7 年後，花費高達 2 億 6000 萬元、動員 60 位工匠才大功告成。特別感慰的是，修復工程更於 2003 年獲得聯合國教科文組織「2003 年亞太文化資產保存獎」。這幅銅製獎牌也置於正殿牆面，因而豐富了保安宮古蹟的建築藝術，引人生發崇敬的審美心理。

　　這時瞧見，一些香客們圍著拍攝最美的姿勢。我臨走前依偎著石欄張望，只見暮色中開始降著柔軟溫暖的疏雨，樹葉子卻綠得發亮，紅瓦烘托出一片安靜與平和，這是一次難得的生活體悟。那天傍晚，當我裝滿行囊的視覺形象，已告結束。我回頭看了一眼西天，昏黑的雲邊，馬路上，撐起傘慢慢走著的人，那裏，一個古老寺廟的餘暉在揮手。

　　我深深感觸的是，世間堂皇轉眼凋零，喧騰是浮生。保安宮似乎足以成為一種淡泊而安定的意象表徵，它較之於顯赫對峙的大型寺院，保安宮比山林間的茂樹更有生命力及建築美。還保留和標榜著一種超塵的靜謐，讓生命熨貼在既清靜又舒展的角落。在我心中，它就是一種宗教性的人生哲學的生態意象。它足以反襯出一個清幽而不死寂的美的境界，它又穿插著一種合乎人性的光明的重建，而這動與靜的對立的統一，正是如實地表現自己感動的過程。

　　在今夜，我打開了一扇透視靈魂的窗口。我似乎聽到了保安宮的敲鐘聲，輕輕的，隱隱的，卻聲聲入耳，灌注全身，如遊故地，踏訪著一個陳舊的夢境。我到過的保安宮，閉眼就能想見，一座座雕刻精緻的石雕，穿過簷前到樓庭，我寧靜地坐在那裏看著過往的香客。保安宮少了那種滄桑之慨，多了一點暢達開明。它保留下多少遺跡，也就有多少歷史的浩歎。然而，它的歷史路程和現實風貌都顯得平實而悠久，就像經緯著它們的盞盞紅燈籠的宮前。一點點黃暈的光，烘托出一片安靜而和平的夜。

　　我想起保安宮給人以親切感，還有別一原因。歸結來說，在於它是當地民俗、文化、信仰有機地配合在一起。再遠的都要到這裏來參觀，也不能忘情於這裏的寧靜；再苦寂的，只要觀瞻這裏的一角秀色，就會變成一種治療心靈的藥劑。其雕塑藝術深奧的理義可以幻化成一種知性的導覽方式，而背著行李來到保安宮朝拜的我，眼角時時關注著寺廟內外建築的藝術功力。我們三人沿路談著，走著。保安宮，是古風蘊藉、文氣沛然的。我想，短暫的旅程也像人的一生，在起始階段總是充滿著奇瑰和險峻，到了中年後的我，未來怎麼也得走向平緩和實。在這兒，那無數雙藝術巨手把我碎成輕塵……保安宮，像母親的手撫摸著我，晚風起了，它帶來些淡淡的檀香味。

——刊美國《亞特蘭大新聞》2016.5.20 及作者彩照 2 張。

刊美國亞特蘭大新聞"2016.5.20

4. 海濱散記

五月下旬的某個午後，頭頂是微妙展開變化的天空，富港碼頭沒有什麼風濤，遠處的海面一片灰藍。我俯瞰前方，看著那可能是被我迷住的停船處，看漁舟泛波偶起的浪沫！而我環視了一下天際路，無論是清晨或黃昏，益發顯得完美無瑕。

關於富岡漁港的詩篇，關於迦路蘭的風……對我來說是非常值得回憶，非常美好的——正如草坡上沾濕的露珠那樣，透明閃亮。即或過去我的想法不同，此刻我已能在這座島嶼之上一動不動地凝視著天邊，那澄澈的藍！那光豔的海！就連一隻飛鳥翩然而過對我都是幸福的。

極目四望，從此處至海面的一帶平蕪，這海，是纖巧的。雖然空曠，卻美得像首精緻的小詩。

富岡漁港是興建於 1954 年，又稱伽蘭港、加路蘭港或臺東港，因鄰近阿美族部落「加路藍社」而得名，老一輩人這麼說。它是綠島、蘭嶼等離島的交通唯一港口。位於台東市富岡里，距市區約六公里，東臨太平洋，是僅次於成功漁港的台東縣內第二大的漁港。

不管來過多少次，這個以深邃和清澈為名的漁港，應值得加以描摹。它與親潮、黑潮交會，帶來豐富的魚群。也就是說，

它具有大自然的惠贈，一年四季都富有夢幻的風貌。

倘若，允許我把燈塔當作無畏的戰士，那麼，乳白的流雲就是出塵的仙人。還有中央山脈緜延的峰巒，像大地的戀人，沉靜、溫柔——這一帶的海岸線，多像一曲飄散的牧歌啊。

「妳知道嗎，」友人對我說，「我不敢相信我真到了這個地方，因為這裡，不是我的幻想吧？！妳瞧，碼頭旁，那些漁船！在藍盈盈的海呦！還可以看到那燈塔。這完全像是電影畫面裡才有的夏日的午後……那波光粼粼，耀得我眼睛都花囉！」

我回過頭去，看到了她不時露出興奮的眼神，看到了那無拘無束地、海的碧波……有一刻間，我們停住了腳程，久久地諦聽著拍浪，也可猜出那海水有多麼澄淨！多麼撫慰人心。

友人一邊忙著拍攝，一邊聽著。太平洋越來越遼闊地包圍著我們……浪聲忽近忽遠，似有若無。我們一邊遙望著高居於山脊的邊緣，就這樣沐浴在海濱與藍天之間……

同是東岸風韻，這海卻勾起我的一種激情。我們沿著港灣緩步而行，清靜，幽寂。雖然沒有花蓮賞鯨的驚嘆，熱烈。但可以很容易的看見水面數呎下成群的小魚，甚至可以很容易的輕輕觸碰海水或看寄居蟹玩耍。在我的感覺與印象上的確是再有趣不過的事了。

沿著台十一線，驅車再往北岸，不多時，便可看到隆起的奇岩怪石及巨大的珊瑚礁群。這片宛如鬼斧神工的雕刻，個個

像是沉思的哲人，只有風，不時書寫了它的心事……而岩上也有蔓蓉生長。

這裡，因和新北市野柳風景區景觀相似，故被稱做「小野柳」。不僅海濱植物種類和花期各異，而且裝置藝術或建築和海色，都洋溢著南國的氣息。沿途可欣賞遍生的白水木、黃槿、林投、海棗等罕見植物。看著浮雲的幻變，光陰，搖碎在樹影裡。

再沒有比從棧道上，看上去更迷人、更清晰的。在這裡，原始林木森嚴茂密，讓人無法感到單調。我閉眼也可想像，空氣中好像都能聞到甜甜的芬多精，而茂盛的馬鞍藤特別艷麗醒目……所有這些天然的石雕或珊瑚礁岩，都帶著勇士般的狂烈，都致使小野柳的風物極富於變化。

然而，太平洋的浩瀚與神秘，才是最具代表性的部份，使人更接近神與繆斯的聖殿。這般的深澈與廣袤無垠，正是海的生命。儘管這季節旅客並不多，但這裡的山珍海味，有飽享黑潮和日光饋贈，是當地漁夫的驕傲。

在靜靜的黃昏後，雨絲忽然開始打在平靜的海面上沙沙做聲，鬱鬱青山也籠著一層薄薄的煙……我願是人間的畫師，風之使者。即使我的筆墨微不足道，也不知歌兒該怎麼唱？但我期盼能在此佇足，描摹出這山海帶給我一種純潔堅定的力量。雖然，我真是無法用言語道盡的。

－2016.5.24 寫於台東
－刊中國《羊城晚報》，2016.5.31.副刊。

5. 森林公園香頌

五月的黃昏，雨季不來，夏陽初熾，我在臺東森林公園又走上熟悉的舊路。

乍乍綻開的朵朵燈籠花，迎著一張張旅人欣喜的面容，靜靜沁入我寂然的心胸。

熱情的三角梅錯落地倚懸於棚架，像是雲端飛翔的鳥……整個公園攏著濃郁的幽芳。

淡紅的粉葉金花也一朵朵地落滿一地。它們光燦著，似熱戀中的情侶，默默地躺在樹蔭那裡。

我也躺在樹屋的長椅上睡著了。

在無邊無際的冥思中，聽蟲鳴鳥囀。不同於昔日的，是任由思維緩緩地流，流灌過一些曾有的夢。

喔，風的瀟灑、浪花的飛濺，總為我吟唱著歡樂的歌兒……是的，那來自太平洋的風，已在我嘴角的微笑上浮動著。

當湖泊與我比肩坐在一塊兒時，一隻小白鷺躡手躡腳地走到我跟前，親吻著我的小詩。

魚兒們也好奇的想知道，詩裡到底說了些什麼？

一隻野鴨正睡在媽媽的懷抱。向星空奏樂的樹蛙，也把我的憂傷偷了去呢。

然後我拾起一朵杜虹花，在落徑與飛來的雉雞為戲，聽蜜蜂嗡響。我也成為風景的一部分，宛如一只小小的貝殼倘伴於憧憬的、閃爍的沙灣之中——

　　沿途的阿勃勒一如既往地看上去非常調和，亦一如既往地努力地綻放！

　　但是我知道一旁的台灣紫珠，始終保持著舞蹈者一般曼妙而自由的步履。它的手勢，浪漫而舒緩。

　　我總想著。假如我變成了一隻夜鴞，我願回到開闊的森林。在樹葉和微風之中，聽滿天星斗如海潮般傾訴。

　　儘管有許多故事在繼續。那醉臥月光中的湖，我已準備好吟詠和親吻了。

　　啊，這裡的湖，純美、瑩澈，像一堵堵翡翠屏風。每時，每日，像愛人忠誠的眼睛，全流進了我的靈魂。

　　它的陰鬱與光華，似一首纖柔的詩，是大自然送給我最珍貴的禮物。

　　註.臺東森林公園，地緣遼闊，林木鬱蔥，舊稱「黑森林」，位於臺東市北郊，卑南溪出海口。由防汛道路進入並與海濱公園接壤，距離市區僅幾分鐘車程或沿著馬亨亨大道亦可到達。先民為防風災而在此區域種植木麻黃，遠看林相漆黑，因幽暗神祕而得名。內有三座湖泊，分別為地下湧泉所形成的「琵琶湖」，是距離台東市區最近的天然湖泊，有極珍貴的河口海濱濕地。鄰近尚有原本為沼澤濕地，後來經過整治的半天然湖「鷺鷥湖」，又名「鴛鴦湖」，物種十分豐富，有鷺鷥、野鴨、樹蛙、雉雞、魚類等在此棲息。而「活水湖」是一個規則性的長條形人工湖，它連接卑南溪出海口的溼地，北起石川圳、大石堤防，南至台東大堤及馬亨亨大道，西以台東大橋為界，深線六公尺處，是每年舉辦龍舟競賽或各項鐵人比賽的場地，也是森林公園內最大的湖。這是當地民眾休閒及旅客享受與自然共舞的好去處，也是我喬居台東最常散步之地景。因而為文。

—2016.5.26

　　—刊《臺灣時報》台灣文學版，圖文，2016.6.22
　　—刊美國《亞特蘭大新聞》，2016.6.24，攝影兩張。

林明理攝/臺東森林公園/琵琶湖

6.明天過後

　　強颱過後，我的原鄉，清冷而靜穆。尤其是山區偏遠地及綠島、蘭嶼，遭遇這樣大浩劫，如死寂般的村鎮，一幅荒棄的樣態，卻表現這樣的大氣魄，這樣的從容。有堆積如山的垃圾，有狼藉的街道，有搶收作物的老農，有無家可歸的傷痛。而這裡所有的，卻奇怪得很，是勇於接受的沉默。這和我夢境差不多美的台東，只不過遭逢百年來最嚴重的風災，竟已罩在烏雲密佈的陰霾底下了嗎？

　　它曾具有像熱汽球般馳騁的夢想，也有過許多族民一起歡舞與熱情……通過它的道路、縱谷、綠野、溪流、海洋、山脈，是閃爍的、奔跑的，是我夢中最感動，最嚮往的。而如今，它依舊是這麼與眾不同的，——那使我感到溫暖的東西，是它顯示於居民的堅韌和互助，純樸和無私的那種鮮明而與城市的浮華有著多麼不同的對照。而受創最嚴重的族民是那麼的無助——又那麼那麼地多！

　　今晨，勉強將庭院打掃清理後，驅車到鯉魚山買菜。我看到一個個老人仍蹲坐在地上等待顧客的招呼，這是我在他們身上從來不曾看見的果敢。原來這個城鎮的聲音和光耀，是要我見識見識這些老農努力背後的辛酸，是要我感受到外界不斷的關懷與救援不再是那麼緩不濟急。

中華路口，向來是被如雲的旅客所擁擠，無論春夏秋冬，總有最熱鬧的街景，但此刻所有的店都忙著，或關著，有許多穿著綠色軍服的阿兵哥忙著開著軍用車四處清理道路、倒下的路樹及垃圾。有許多霓虹燈及廣告招牌懸空在那裡晃著或掉落滿地，有許多鐵皮屋被掀起或屋頂、門窗破損。離島也有無數個等待與絕望的心，正在一秒一秒的將受災戶趨向崩潰邊緣……

當我看到這麼一幅景像，總以為台東原是那麼獨出而快樂的，然而，你倘使知道，這些受災而需要救助的人兒，也是我們善良的同胞，血液裡也有我們引以為傲的族群。你就得思考，或者為這意外的不速之客——尼伯特而感到揪心了。這的確是一個破紀錄的颱風，所有這裡面，受苦最深的還是災民。但受災戶都振起了殘餘的勇氣，繼續為重建而努力著。等強颱走了三天後，電視畫面都清清處處地播放出來了。那是令人心碎的，幸虧台灣族民的心是不易被擊碎的；而勇士們堅毅，在黑暗的生存中發光。有許多勇敢的心，也跟著生存的渴望燃燒起來！

黎明後，曼妙的夏蟬，聲嘶力竭地鳴著，這是歷經數年在黑暗中最漫長的等待。牠在曙光下短暫的歌頌，聲音在我的身後慢慢地掠過高高的枝上，沒有被折彎的一片葉梢。溯這歌聲而上就像回到重創前的台東，那高大植物在地上盛長，一片深沉的寂靜，美麗的森林、湖泊、沙岸、河流……空氣依然清新，

寬闊的卑南溪穿過一群滋長著林木的島嶼。我遵循著新站前習慣的路走──然後停下來聽著。是啊，在未來的日子中，危險也許仍無可避免，但只要心中存有希望，生命中真正持續的是成長，就像這幾天的我一樣，必然會發現伴隨而來的是災難過後更懂得惜福的心情。

－〈強颱過後〉刊美國《亞特蘭大新聞》
　2016.7.15，圖文
－〈明天過後〉刊《臺灣時報》2016.7.13 圖文。
－（曙光）-臺灣《人間佛教》學報/藝文，2017
　年預稿，佛光山人間佛教研究院出版。

7. 蘭陽藝術行

　　火車抵達宜蘭，已近中午十一點。出站後，但見幾米廣場，和對面的童話公園，好多小朋友玩耍……使人立刻感到愉悅。

　　新月廣場即在公園近側，紅樓的接待人員與我們相互寒喧幾句，用餐後，隨即漫步去搭車直往礁溪，行數十步到溫泉街，放眼一看，四處矗立的飯館與商店林立。尤其夜晚時分，霓虹燈耀眼，人潮擁擠，各式各樣餐飲，一覽盡收。

　　我也很喜歡溫泉的氣味。不僅在知本溫泉如此，我在各處溫泉鎮都嗅到了各種不同的溫泉氣味。然而，這礁溪溫泉，水質透明無味，屬於中性碳酸氫鈉泉。我們一家人循水道間小徑而行，抵達飯店泡湯，果然疲勞盡解。

　　次日，打開臥室的窗扉，在給礁溪披上粉妝玉琢的淡灰色的清晨，總算是告別了喧囂，卻還原其素淨的美。背景是剛睡醒的山丘，年青的綠。

　　「要是蘭陽博物館也是這麼個好天氣，我們就出發去踏青吧！」女兒說。
　　這是夏末的事。

　　如箭矢似的，一下子就抵達頭城，和平街是頭城最早發展，也是碩果僅存的老街，古稱「頭圍街」，它保存不少了昔日的遺跡，也可看到清代及日治時期的建築。如「十三行」，是清代頭城首富盧家的倉庫，國小校長宿舍、慶元宮、源合成商號，老紅長興等等。漫步其中，彷彿走入時光隧道，靜待旅人的片刻駐足。

　　我面前是何等雄偉的建築！原來座落於頭城鎮烏石港區的「蘭陽博物館」向以建築美稱著，這座建築歷經十餘年的籌備與興建，於二〇一〇年十月十六日開館。主體建築以「單面山」為幾何造型規劃，屋頂與地面夾角為二十度，尖端牆面與地面則為七十度，令人感覺彷彿由地面竄出，並與頭城地區獨有的單面山山形地景融合。其外牆則使用多重質感的石板，配合前有大波池倒影，藉以呈現這蘭陽平原四季山海交融的景緻。

　　想起來了吧，書裡記載，宜蘭平原，又稱蘭陽平原、噶瑪蘭平原，是僅次於嘉南平原及屏東平原的臺灣第三大平原。平原南北端各有烏石漁港及蘇澳港兩處港口。其中以宜蘭市、羅東鎮為中地，四周各有規模較小的鄉鎮聚落。

　　沿著博物館前湖岸行走，鴨戲水聲乘風而來，白鷺在湖面飛飛落落……

在如鏡的水波上，一陣風刮起了階梯的塵土、有類似日本太和鼓陣的旋律，值得引入博物館之中。這是由宣揚日本沖繩文化和三味線演奏法為職志的「太陽之子」東風平高根先生所組成的「當代樂坊　童玩節慶樂團」，他們除了展現出親子演奏和歌唱的魅力，也演出安里屋之歌、島之歌、淚光閃閃、沖繩之舞等。別人對這飛揚的樂團可能沒有什麼特別感觸，可是它使我感到快樂而單純，也使旅人的心情為之激動。

至於館內典藏文物及各界捐贈的文物、史料記錄，彷彿宜蘭縮影。美哉，蘭陽博物館，幽清雄奇，溶身山水之間。怎不令人激賞？回眸遠山，不禁悵然若失。我見過那都蘭灣的明淨的藍天，但這裡蘭陽平原的天空更加活躍、更加蘊藉。它像詩人的眼睛，懂得微笑與悲。

歸途，我們在羅東車站下車，聽說，羅東地區在未開發前是山林地帶，尤其是有很多野生猴子群居於森林。「羅東」這個地名緣起於當地原住民噶瑪蘭族將「猴子」（rutung）稱為「老懂」，及後清代漢人開墾蘭陽平原，因而沿用其名，稱此地為「羅東」。搭乘手扶梯出站後，街道熱鬧無比。午後兩點，便搭火車轉回台東。

揮別宜蘭，風中，一抹清輝浮動。車窗外，天空是背景，山巒縣延、秧苗的水田與農作物，相依在雨和光影中，帶給我最初的靜穆，更令人心曠神怡。

　　我常常感到雨後花東縱谷格外的美。白色的霧靄盤旋在山谷間飄浮，濛濛細雨，白鷺也翩躚，恍如把心事遺忘在田野裡一般。車過玉里，又轉晴了，也看到關山鎮的米國學校和建物。放飛我的思想吧！只想跟隨黃昏裡的翅，獨享這片刻的寧靜。

　　「看，好多隻白鷺在飛呀！」

　　記得多年前的一個夏日，我的小孩也同樣對我說了這麼一句。近旁，一個小男孩也拿起相機，抓緊時間按下快門。我總可以看到車窗外那一畦畦水田延展伸向遠方，而鐵軌也在夕陽之下閃亮。老農彎腰耕作的背影擦邊而過——在那裡，土地面貌中最純樸的部份無法用言語表述，它猶然迴響耕耘者播種的餘音。

　　可是，這次在礁溪老街看不見一輪大滿月，也看不見稱得上是美麗夕暉晚照的景象。因為它的週遭都是人潮。但此刻，中央山脈的山巒上紛紛披上了晚霞，青山淡淡，白雲悠悠。我多想是隻信步原野的飛鳥，心中裝滿大自然閃動的影子。

　　住在台東新站，雖不像礁溪之夜的熱鬧，但彎曲的河流、那邊的小黃山，峰巒嶙峋的利吉惡地，也另有一番賞心悅目的樂趣。我經常散步在水圳公園上凝望著靜謐的卑南溪，尋找那出海口，心情則像空氣般澄清。

看鳥兒飛過曠野。有時候三兩隻聯翩飛翔。美，正在於此。在漸去漸遠如夢般的夜裡，旅人啊，請帶上自己的眼睛，卸下心中的重負，和我一樣，擁抱大自然的寶藏吧！此刻，我以無限的深情回想走過的宜蘭景色，每當聽到心靈深處的鳴泉，我就找到了思念的窗口。

人人說，大自然是最偉大的藝術師；那麼，人類窮盡一切是否就為了靠近那渾然天成的美？累了，苦悶了，便到大自然的懷抱裡換換氣，把沉重卸下。或者說，追求也是一種幸福。

－2016.8.11

－刊臺灣《臺灣時報》，2017.1.13，圖文。

8. 有隻松鼠叫小飛兒

後山，這季節，已經是九月。然而，暑熱並未退盡。天剛
亮，魚肚白色的曙光裡，空氣甜淨，大街上也開始多點兒喧嚷。
我走出庭院，環顧了一下，裝滿水電材料的貨車正停在屋前紅
綠燈，從我身邊駛過。昨夜的雨珠兒，仍在草尖兒上閃閃爍爍。

朝霞微露，幽藍的天空不見一片雲朵，整個新站越發安
詳，生氣中又帶點柔美，還有夏蟬高鳴著。忽而，我看到那隻
熟悉的身影竟在我家石牆上晃動了一下，便跳進欖仁樹頂上的
樹枝丫，並轉身望我。但吃驚的並不是牠——我的小飛兒，恰
恰是我自己。牠卻毫不掩飾，眼裡藏著狡點的目光、頻頻翹起
尾巴，嘴唇卻貼在行道樹幹上，看上去又逗趣又可笑。可我沒
有笑，只定睛地望著光光的樹梢上。

「喂……小飛兒，你在玩什麼呢，」我叫了一聲，並予以
高度歡迎。

後來呢？
後來這黑色的松鼠也不理會，就匆忙逃開，鑽進樹幹上一
個洞窟，就是牠唯一的巢穴。咦，牠還要找尋什麼？我像一個
傻瓜，等一個來無蹤去無影的小孩，卻要我無限牽掛。但牠毫
不遲疑，又前一腳後一跳踏著步子飛行起來。那雙小小的、窺

探的黑眼睛，好奇地探索世界，有多真真切切啊。

　　但，也只是片刻時間，蒼穹下一片靜寂，風，又開始聚集著烏雲。在烏雲和大樹之間，我的小飛兒像黑衣的閃電俠。一會兒，做著眉眼，靈巧至極。一會兒，左顧右盼，箭一般的飛竄在巨樹挺直的軀幹，一棵緊挨一棵，讓我目不暇給。

　　牠奔躍著……從容自在。這個靈敏的小精靈，在紛紜世界裡勇敢地求生，烏雲也感染了歡樂。我盡可以在每個晨昏盯住牠的身影，只要小飛兒回頭看我一眼，我就會眼勾勾望著，欣喜不已。

　　這次，我折回頭，從客廳矮櫃邊上趕緊帶上照相機，我小跑著，拚命尾隨牠，牠卻拐了一個彎之後，一晃又消失了。我感到有些惆悵，忽而記起一首歌謠：

　　泥娃娃，泥娃娃，一個泥娃娃……我做他爸爸，我做他媽媽，永遠愛著他。

　　這時，紅屋瓦上又停了隻流浪的鴿子，咕嚕咕嚕地叫著，一隻鳳蝶在風中輕輕顫動。是啊，有多少年沒見過這樣感動了？風沒有應答。我只好自言自語。
　　信步走回，每走一步，雨越加集密了。濕透了髮絲，卻澆不熄這場豐盛的景物。好久沒有這般自在了，我深深吸著林蔭下清新的氣息。路上靜悄悄的，好一個清幽的所在。其實，生

活可以很簡單，不必多想什麼。一隻看不見的雀鳥在飛簷上啼鳴，喚起我童年一些溫暖的記憶。而烏黑的柏油路上沒有一個車影，也沒有一丁點聲響。

回到書房，我仍興奮得走來走去，身不由己，踮起腳尖，窺視窗外。那深深的山影裡，像一幅幅著色的水墨畫。而反反覆覆的雨點，落在泥土，落在變了灰暗的屋頂上，連院子楓葉上一兩片淺紅的小葉子也在抖動著。

原來是秋姑娘來了。

－2016.8.29

－刊美國《亞特蘭大新聞》，2016.9.16.圖文。

9. 三仙台心影

九月的一個上午，從新站出發，沿著台十一線，約莫五十分鐘就抵達成功鎮市集了。我自己也說不清楚，為什麼選在陰霾的天出發到這裡來，但巧就巧在碰到一個推著三輪車賣各式各樣草仔粿、紅龜粿、碗粿的客家籍年輕人，他的住家店舖已經營六十年，傳承到第三代，東西看來分外好吃。我不覺走了過去，閒談中更指引了我們沿著海岸公園驅車直往三仙台。於是，幾分鐘後，就站在停車場上環顧。

我信步走著，左側有塊大標示，記載著這樣一段文字：三仙台原名「比西里岸」（阿美族語：Pisilisn，意為養羊之地），是早期部落族人養羊的地方，也是族人長期以來捕魚及採集大海時鮮的場域。瞧，周圍有隆起的珊瑚礁分布。島上也處處可見林投、白水木、台灣海棗、濱刀豆等濱海植物。

之後，當我坐在海岬北側的礫石海灘上，昂首向天，風兒雖吹亂了髮絲，但舒爽而適意。看著前方潮水和海浪翻湧沖刷的海灘，真希望自己是那奔流不息的大海中的一朵浪花，它不規則的飛濺散逸，與岩石激撞所發出震撼的聲響，總能打動我給我留下深刻的記憶。

視線的右方，巨龍般的八拱跨海人行步道橋興建於 1987 年，因波浪的造型優美，宛若蟠臥在海上，已成為矚目的地標。相傳八仙

中的鐵拐李、呂洞賓、何仙姑都曾在這島上停憩，且在山上留下三仙足印，故名三仙台；而阿美族人則流傳著三仙台藏有守護神「及發烏安」海龍的故事。由於長期受到風化和海水侵蝕，這裡有許多造型奇特的海蝕地形，如海蝕柱、壺穴和隧道型海蝕門，也蔚為大觀。

遠望，位於三仙台和台灣本島白守蓮之間的海域設有定置漁網，可看到有三兩艘膠筏停泊在基翬漁港內。如站在跨海拱橋上及白守蓮海岸遠眺的感覺又不一樣，隱約可見到漁網的浮標在水面上晃動、載浮載沉。

沿比西里岸漫遊，走著走著，找到一隻木雕的羊。再往前，走到村子的盡頭，幾十戶人家。眼面前出現灰牆上幾米故事裡的彩繪人物跟花貓，這種視覺的確令人愉悅，會造成一種寧靜。最有趣的是，兔子吃草的竹雕，裝置得可愛，有一種粗獷美。

在堤岸上站了一會，只有帶著澀味的海風迎面撲來，靜寂而憂傷。不多時，灰黑的雲在頭頂上開始奔馳，我望著對面的霧雨來臨前的八拱跨海步道橋，海面上，這會兒連船影都沒有。但潮聲在心裡喚起的感動，竟讓我出神凝望。不禁恍感置身於仙山，羽化遨遊於天際了。大自然就是這麼神奇的調色盤，我這才體會到正因為它的峻偉與壯闊，讓我感受它的寧靜與純粹，才能讓我倍感勇氣。

　　回程前，空中飄著細雨，不知怎地，又止不住去望它。我穿過巷子出來，有些飛簷上斷殘的瓦片，斑駁朽頹的牆壁，又喚起某種情感。我取出相機，隨意拍下了風景，也紀錄下最美的瞬間。終於消失在小路的盡頭，像是個美麗的邂逅，又像是夢。

－2016.9.24

－刊《金門日報》，副刊，2016.11.1，轉載金門縣海洋教育資源中心，《金門海洋文學》2016.11.7
http://ocean.km.edu.tw/wordpress/index.php/2016/11/07/n-345/#more-2820
－刊中國《羊城晚報》，副刊，2016.9.27.
http://ep.ycwb.com/epaper/ycwb/html/2016-09/27/node_23287.htm
http://ep.ycwb.com/epaper/ycwb/html/2016-09/27/content_151573.htm#article

10.記得文學錄影處

八月二十二日午後，進了台東美術館，轉入展覽會，室內冷氣特別涼爽。我未曾想到的是，攝影隊員竟已一個個湊上前，親切地招呼。瞬間，消除了我忐忑不安，也沒想到會談得這樣自然。不一會兒，與涂文權導演寒暄幾句後，立即輕鬆下來。

在錄影前，終於看到晨鴻，年紀輕輕，這位來自澎湖的青年，卻已當上助理導演，一臉稚氣，更顯得謙恭有禮。據說，他以幽默浪漫微電影拍攝出「戀動愛島」的澎湖之美，贏得讚賞。這部作品或許是他心靈的歌吟，讓澎湖之勝與濃郁的人情味，一覽盡收；而我也看到了一個遊子對故鄉熾熱的心！雖在電話中聯繫過出訪的行程，但這回近距離望了他一下，我們都會心笑了。而我期待的正是這燦爛的笑容。接過他遞來的一杯冰紅茶，滿是感謝。

一個多小時之後，終於步出了門口，導演開始講到如何拍攝外景，還需再捕捉幾個特殊鏡頭，我專心聽著。繼而，我在迴廊下走幾步後再回頭，恰好看到一隻夏蟬棲息在樹幹上，似

乎不願斷斷續續的嘶鳴了。這時，並沒有風。大夥兒的汗珠，一滴一滴，落在臉頰。又兩個小時過去了，太陽已經偏西，可屋簷下還有些燥熱。乘休息時，我在草地的石階旁，找個地方，在晨鴻給我的記事本子上記上一筆詩作的手稿。剛蹲下，目光就可以看得很遠。建築物上空的暮色間，幾隻飛鳥掠過，低垂的枝丫彷彿也感受了這周遭的美，將繽紛的花兒開遍樹下，就這樣靜悄悄展現它綠意盎然的美色。沒有比這黃昏的寧靜，詩歌在心裡喚起的感動，更貼進又遙遠的鳥鳴更自然的了。

於是，我又翻開另一紙頁，用鋼筆寫下：「飛閱文學地景帶你看見臺灣土地歷經歲月流逝的美麗與感動！」就在我注視一對祖孫兒在前方牽手走過的那會兒，我聽見導演喊叫了一聲，原來正趕上錄影完工了。

我在記憶中努力搜索這一路辛苦錄製的影像，剎那間，記憶變得更清晰了，工作人員的畫面從腦海中一閃而過。我想，這多颱的秋季過後的夜晚，屋外街道那麼安靜，靜得令我擔心。看到電視上災民的苦痛，不禁深深嘆了口氣，但窗外只有嘩嘩水聲和偶爾汽車急駛而過的濺水聲。我拉開點窗戶，颼颼涼風吹著。再次端詳手邊這張合影照片，讓我突然生出一個願望，由於種種機緣促成這次的偶然，如果這兩集詩歌吟詠能吸收製作的意念和涵義，或者能對蘭嶼與阿里山的地景賦予一種新的社會意涵的話，我心懷敬意。

　　現在，這節目已製作完成一百多集，得以介紹臺灣美景的成就，實是一件快慰的事。當然，學無止境，詩藝也無止境。但至少就這次錄影而能獲得一些難得的經驗與無名的喜悅，是無疑的。

2016.10.18 作

－刊《臺灣時報》台灣文學版，
2016.10.26.，合照一張。

11. 驟雨過後

　　趁著雨來臨之前，我在臨窗的書桌前舒展身體嗅著秋日的空氣。夜幕還籠罩著山谷，只有海岸山脈末端被那冉冉初昇的月兒照亮。

　　推窗望外，竟毫無睡意，便擱下筆，索性起來走動一下，信步到院前等候狂風。剛才讓我那般心醉的 Fabrizio 鋼琴的音色，彷彿變成一種纖細的情愫，這都怪這陰晴不定的氣候。

　　夜更深了，遠近無一人影。風開始從四面八方襲捲而來，任我再怎樣豎起耳朵也無法聽到雨的沉默，可我即便不想聽也會穿過空中濃密的濕氣，陸陸續續透過簷溜傳進耳鼓。

　　漸漸地，閃電從地表的那一端疾馳，雨已拖起它冗長的尾巴開始狂掃地面了。透過玻璃窗可以看見一盞盞整整齊齊灰濛濛的燈光——馬路上落葉也被吹得四處騰起。

　　這時候，太平洋的波濤將給我們帶回什麼樣的歌聲？我無從知曉。可我知道，風急遽地躍過岩石，躍過山巔，而濤聲將

湧起夜的悲涼……

可你聽清了嗎？夜雨滂沱，來去匆匆何處往。雨的沉默穿梭在無垠宇宙，無論是慌亂的、喧嘩而過，或是使勁用力地落到地面的調皮模樣，都根植於我心深處，帶給我的視覺總是浪漫而傷感的。

剎那間，我想要把雨的多種形象畫在筆記本上。過了許久，雨聲淅瀝，時而清晰，時而隱約……也不知什麼時候停息了。

雨的記憶誰都有，但記憶有些是傷心的，有些是模模糊糊的，有些是一種不甚分明的懷念，有些則比什麼都珍貴。

翌日，我睜開眼睛，風雨已過，白雲仍俯視著下面的島嶼與族群。在福爾摩沙天空底下，我將常常感到幸福，也會偶爾品嘗我的憂傷與思念。

沿著馬路旁慢慢走著，迎著的這股秋風，散發著彼處與遠方的山巒，還有東岸的芳香。風中也飽含著我的凝思。我知道，驟雨永遠不可能完完全全地離開。但這場雨後，卻讓我意外看到這幅田園式的景物：

灰藍的天，欖仁樹的枝丫上清脆的鳥鳴，有三隻相守、躲過昨夜風雨，仍和樂融融的牛隻正依偎地吃著草，細碎的蟲

聲，低飛的白鷺曙光乍現……這畫面竟一下子擄獲與感動了我的心。

　　毫無疑問，一種向著我的歡快力量——卻在我激動的眼眸裡顯現。我始終這麼認為，大自然的豐富與偉大，動物間的和諧與從容自若，眼前這一切，才是最真實與純粹的……啊，生命是多麼美好。我的意志在增長著，並且多了一絲羨慕……

－2016.10.19

－刊臺灣《人間福報》副刊，2016.12.20，
攝影一張。
－刊美國《亞特蘭大新聞》），2016.11.11
圖文，水彩畫 1 幅。
－文〈驟雨初歇〉刊臺灣《臺灣時報》，
2016.11.18，圖文，水彩畫 1 幅。

12. 迦路蘭東遊記

　　秋末初冬的一個午後，我們一行九人沿著杉原海岸沙灘漫步。這之前，真怕颱風再來攪和，直到露西帶著艾梅、美生母子、蓮蓮夫婦、余老師夫婦等友人千里迢迢來到台東，心裡方才踏實。抬頭望著湛藍的雲天，腳下感受礁岩縫隙的小魚兒悠遊之樂。

　　在東岸住過的人，看太陽從太平洋地平線上升落，本不是什麼鮮事；然而，對飄洋過海來的遊子或首度踩在都蘭達麓岸部落屋的旅人來說是興致勃勃的。

　　而後，在迦路蘭空曠的廣場上看綠島，尤其在陽光特別燦亮，把對岸的島嶼山影照得都顯眼的時候，友人們都無比的興奮，我當然渴望一種特異的感動，將來哪一天，忽然回憶起這一幕情景與異國他鄉是有所不同的。

　　果然，我聽見浪濤拍岸的聲音，蓮蓮先生遠遠地呼喚，且高聲叫著，聲音那麼清晰，那樣深情。接著，我就看見了這對恩愛五十多年的夫妻背影，站在望海坡的頂端，目光拋向在水一方，定定地回過頭來，看著我們就那麼燦然笑了。

　　是啊，年輕的感覺，就在這一剎那都復活，而宇宙彷彿只是——郁郁青青的，我的界線四下，每個生命都是永恆的開端，每道風景都動人心弦，而我們的友誼與傳達了宇宙靈氣無遠弗屆的愛也在彼此心中悄悄地滋長…….

　　等到留心回覽，還想看得更遠……已近黃昏。除了深深的山影裡，平鋪著瀰漫的雲氣開始聚集，在夕陽西下前，隔著中央山脈山頂上還剩一抹殘霞，我們已折了回來，在秀泰影城休憩，欣賞鐵花村夜景的美妙，直到返回民宿，向夜星道別。這也許就是我們渴求重回大自然原始黑暗的懷抱與感動吧？

　　翌日，清晨五點半，余老師起了個早，除了趕上觀利吉惡地與小黃山以外，在朝旭未露前，雲輕如棉，緩慢而又柔和地翻騰、起伏。寂寥的卑南溪，水聲潺潺，風車徐徐緩緩的轉……有隻水鳥在飛，但是涼風從岸上來，可以聽見偶爾而過的老農掠過的車聲，卻聽不見那近處河道上水鳥的叫聲。

　　從水圳公園涼亭上遠望，明晃晃的海面有些變得模糊，雀屏似的金光正從雲層中射出奪目的霞彩，終於臨照在天空，普徹了四方。而我只能在原地，不想挪開一步。我聽見卑南溪水流動，就整個沉浸在這靜謐之中。

　　讚美啊，這大自然的奧妙，我忽而想望里爾克的頌詞：

　　美為最初、天然。一切正在形成當中的，皆會變美。只要

人們不去干擾它。

　　我想，在這寂靜的公園的週遭裡獨自體會一番，同誰也不必說話，就消融在這都蘭山下風光水色合一的環境裡倒也不壞。回到民宿，包車抵達鹿野高台，品茗甘醇的福鹿茶，又驅車直往「米舖」大啖一番客家料理。午膳之後，一路直奔池上鄉大坡池，伯朗大道上看白鷺輕飛田野、掠過阡陌人家，漸漸遠去……聆賞古典音樂片及稻浪成熟美景。返家的車上，余老師開始以高亢的歌聲唱誦起來，最後一首客家小曲，贏來了許多掌聲，那是何等的幸福呀！

　　第三天清晨，卑南文化公園的天空，更加藍得可愛。修整的草地上，傳來新鮮的剛除過鐵線草的香味。大葉雀榕枝Ｙ上的飛鳥歡唱著，地上已無昨天午後飛起的塵沙。早餐後，我們又重返水利公園做最後的巡禮。近午，大家餓了，就往我住家弄些湯品、水梨跟池上飯盒來吃。這次的聚首，已隨著普悠瑪車班的來臨，而在月台前──話別了。

　　此刻，戶外時有蕭索的秋風吹來，紅楓也被風搖撼，我在鍵盤前整理攝影的合照時，眼睛忽而紅潤了起來。如今他們八人已各往各的家鄉奔。朋友，咱們再會不知何年又何時呢？

　　我伸出食指，輕輕觸了一下收音機上的 CD，琴聲瞬間響起，我移動身體，伸手從書架上摘下藍晶送我的《草原之歌》那本書，將書頁慢慢翻閱……書裡細訴了一位海外的學子擁抱

自然與其生命之歌，它代表的是歡笑、希望與夢想，字裡行間有她美麗的回憶與哀愁。而秋風裡的亞城，有多少離鄉的遊子，跟她一樣，時刻不忘、惦記著哺育他們的故里，思念似水，綿延無盡……想到她的友誼之愛，心裡不覺充實了起來。

　　秋一深，打字到這裡，我歡喜於這三天充滿驚異的交流與邂逅，這或許是命中註定的相逢，彷彿前世的同窗演完一章，但願今生再接著來。而那些美好的，花和夢一般迷人的情景與事物，但願馭風飛行，羽翅掠過萬重山，掠過大西洋，掠過寂靜的原野與山峰……將祝福送去。而我總是會守候在東岸的書房，靜待明年返鄉時，期盼再相逢。朋友，請多珍重！

－2016.11.2 深夜寫於台東

　－刊美國《亞特蘭大新聞》亞城園地，2016.11.4，照片兩張。
　－臺灣《臺灣時報》，台灣文學版，〈迦路蘭東遊記〉，2016.11.10-2016.11.11 兩天，合照。

13. 旗津冬思

我永遠緬懷旗津海岸，在潮水與細碎的沙粒之間。

每個浪花，輕觸著腳踝，款款地抹去所有憂愁，足印也成泡沫拂走，但是，我不禁莞爾起來，不為那浪花來去自如，只為那撫平沙的曲線，一切復歸於自然。

每個人皆有喜歡的新奇事物，只要是接收到來自記憶中美好的部分，心也會跟著年輕。

記得二十多年前，曾在高雄海洋技術學院教書，印象深刻的是搭舢舨船上課的情景。當地居民和學生對它在習慣上早有認同，雖然設備簡陋，有時搖晃得令人頭暈，但船上可攜載機車、貨物，省卻物重的勞累。尤其在夏季靠岸後，汗略溼背，空氣中夾帶著些微腥鹹的海味；但返身瞭望灰青的大海，偶見遠方幾艘大型船隻，心胸為之一闊，實為難忘之快事。

我僅感到：心緒在波動，感官向萬物開啟。思維與潮聲合在一起，心中便鳴起了天樂般的妙音。是的，它是那樣讓我擎

起新的夢想。當船兒繞過蓊鬱的山嶺，邁向無垠的大海，眼界越來越宏闊……海岸的美，更像是我第一個願望與初戀，遊歷一次，便多一次相思。

仰頭看見紅霞半空，盤旋於天邊的幾點海鷗蹤影，襯在天幕上，我的聲音已預備頌讚。旗津，則是一個小小的宇宙。直到有些商販挑起了貨物準備下船時，我那飛翔的思緒，才降回到人世間來。

如今我卻明白，原來旗津島是高雄最早的發祥地。早期稱為「旗後半島」，是船舶往來津渡之地，因而稱為「旗津」。現在的海岸公園只是有了變化，並且增多了設施。內有海水浴場、生態區、觀景步道區及越野區，而渡輪站，依然是許多遊客走訪旗津老街、品嚐美食最深刻的記憶。航道上，可欣賞港都與海灣景色，時而有油輪、商船等大船盡收眼底。

風車公園內也有一排測風儀，寬敞的草坪上有馬賽克拼貼的海馬、魚類、螺等裝置藝術及雕塑，不僅園內可放風箏，也可在廣場看藝文活動表演。冬季，站在觀海平臺上，還可見識海浪的潮湧，微風萬頃，空曠幽靜。

純白的旗後燈塔是座類似文藝復興後期的巴洛克建築，百年來，它無間斷地發出光芒，守護著海上船隻，也見證了高雄港的變化。而我所喜歡的旗後天后宮，也是歷史悠久的寺廟，至今香火鼎盛，遠近馳名。

今夜繁星滿天，深厚濃重的黑暗包圍著東海岸的靜寂，但
我思潮起伏，交織在不停的回憶之中。對於旗津船隻、秋涼、
海天的情愫，也變成深淺不一的影像，在晚風中無聲搖晃。

霎時間，想起詩人紀伯倫（Kahlil Gibran）說：

記憶是一種相聚的方式。忘卻是一種自由的方式。

但我止不住想望，像是在滑翔，從銀河之窗俯瞰旗津……
黑暗中，我依然佇立，依然見到了那遠方的燈塔，透露著微茫
的光明，引領著我保持了更多充滿希望的精神。

－2016.11.21─刊臺灣《臺灣時報》，
　2016.12.8，圖文。
－刊中國大陸《羊城晚報》副刊，
　2016.12.06。

後　　記

　　本書承蒙山東大學文學院副院長吳開晉教授惠贈題字、美國詩人非馬（馬為義博士 Dr.William Marr）及 1985 年諾貝爾和平獎得主 prof.Ernesto Kahan 題詩，特此致謝。也謝謝曾為我英譯三本詩集的山東大學外語系吳鈞教授，因為有她的翻譯詩集而獲得許多殊榮。此外，也感謝海內外各刊物主編（亞特蘭大新聞）許月芳、柴松林、時雍、有敬法師、綠蒂、黃耀寬、莫云、朱學恕、彭正雄、彭瑞金、李昌憲、李魁賢、林佛兒、李若鶯、楊濤、王小攀、張智、張映勤、季宇、Dr.Elma.、義大利 Giovanni Campisi、羅繼仁、陳明、秀實等主編，及山東大學吳鈞教授、南京師範大學吳錦教授、集寧師範學院田智院長、甫田學院彭文宇教授、華中師範大學鄒建軍教授、鹽城師院薛家寶校長、郭錫健教授、陳義海教授、商丘師範學院高建立教授、郭德民教授、集寧師院田智院長，北京大學謝冕教授、吳思敬教授、古遠清教授、張智中教授、傅天虹教授、王珂教授、莊偉傑教授、譚五昌教授、王立世等教授的支持。特別感謝成功大學陳益源教授、、法國詩人翻譯家 Dr.Athanase Vantchev de Thracy、英格蘭詩人 Dr.**Norton Hodges**、楊允達博

士、Jacob Isaac 等詩友的鼓勵。也感謝文化部贊助民視新聞【飛閱文學地景】製作導演涂文權、助理導演莊晨鴻、余玉照教授、丁旭輝教授、莫渝、藍晶、琇月醫師等詩友的愛護。最後僅向尊敬的文史哲出版社發行人彭正雄先生及彭雅雲女士為本書所付出的辛勞致意。

林 明 理 寫於臺東市 2016.03

致出版家彭正雄

你用心編製我的書
書裡的每一行
都有你辛勤的影子
對我來說
你是出版界的奇才
如一首備受讚美的詩

－2017.3.13-（亞特蘭大新聞），
2017.3.17